SUPER BORN

Seduction of Being

by Keith Kornell

Published by:

Harper Landmark Books

New York / London

ISBN: 0982645201
ISBN-13: 9780982645208

INTRODUCTION

Batman wouldn't last a day in my world, thought the B.I.B., bitterly feeling the strain that newly manifested superpowers had brought to the life of the 33-year-old "normal" single mother. Gone was her known controllable existence, quietly raising her daughter and making ends meet. Gone were the simple days of drinking, dancing, and partying with her friends. Being "real" and being a superhero made for a unique combination. Sometimes it was a real bitch.

Her new powers were confusing, frustrating, yet wildly seductive, opening her mind to a new world. They surrounded her with questions and challenges but, worst of all, forced her to face them all alone. She could trust no one with her secret. To do so would endanger her daughter, her family.

How should she use the powers? How to deal with all those who now searched for her, wanting to share in, use, her strength? Who to trust? What really was "right" and what was "wrong" when the laws of man no longer applied to you? Then there was the "supersized" sexual fervor and compulsion that now made normal men seem like frustratingly fragile breakable toys.

Yet through the dangers and the challenges more doors opened than closed. Perhaps there was a route to a new level of being, perhaps even new level of romance. The ponderous weight of questions and possibilities she bore in isolation.

Alone and feeling sorry for herself on her birthday, she walked into O'Malley's Bar for a drink and started it all…

CHAPTER ONE

The Night My Life Changed Forever

This journal records events that have changed this man's life and, now and again, have been pretty damn amazing. I have given this a great deal of thought and feel I should forewarn you. If you are the "lucky" one who finds this journal, just sit back, get a drink and a snack, and prepare to enjoy a stimulating tale of romance, adventure, and wild unbridled sex. You can read about all those things after you finish my journal. It's not that long.

My tale begins on the cold cloudy evening last January 18. I had contacted a young, budding PhD professor and researcher in psychology from the University of Pennsylvania, Rashid Patel Jones. Dr. Jones is the son of learned Indian immigrants, his father a renowned environmental engineer, his mother a brilliant psychologist at Penn State often seen on Oprah and as a consultant to many noted soap operas.

Dr. Jones was hungry to eclipse the brilliance of his parents. I could sense that hunger in his energy and determination. After years of effort, he had created a startling theory that encompassed cutting-edge research from both his father and his mother's fields of learning and, now, he was trying—no, I should say was consumed by the need—to prove to the world the truth he felt so deeply.

Personally, I rated him a jack-off, but I thought there was a paycheck in his story. Boy, was that an underestimation. But as they say, "Hindsight is...looking up your ass," or maybe they don't.

I informed him that I was a syndicated columnist for the *Times*, and his hungers led him to grant me an immediate interview. Even after he found out I am only a freelance, rarely published writer and part-time bartender, he still honored the interview. *Damn, he must have been hungry*, I thought back then. I know now that he had other reasons for my selection, but back then I accepted the hungry theory backed by my magnetic personality, keen intellect, and six-foot-two cyclist's body, complete with firm butt.

Rather than spend hours on scientific mumbo jumbo that would probably shoot right over my aching head, Dr. Jones insisted that it would be much easier to demonstrate his theory in the field. He suggested that we meet at nine o'clock at a beat-up fifty-year-old house converted into a bar and grill called O'Malley's in the nearby city of Scranton, Pennsylvania. The decline of O'Malley's peeling white paint, blinking sign, and sagging gutters paralleled the decline of the city itself.

Scranton was the fourth-largest city in Pennsylvania, or at least it had been, but had been struggling through decades of economic and population declines. Jones had developed a radical theory to explain the downturn. Scranton was the center of Dr. Jones' research and had become his newly found home. He spoke of Scranton like one would speak of the woman he loved, or at least a good, inexpensive mistress.

When I finally arrived at run-down O'Malley's, I had to circle the block to find a parking space on the street. I slammed my car door, arms full of my laptop and case, the consummate professional writer. Is that what one looks like?

I started the short walk to the front door, determined to make the project with Dr. Jones work. I needed some money from somewhere. The tank was empty, if you know what I mean. I needed to completely focus on Jones' work. *Whoa, look at the major league yabbos on that chick*, I thought, as an attractive girl slithered by with her coat open, revealing a "Ravage Me" low-cut dress. Not that "Ravage Me" was a brand name or a designer or anything, but maybe it should be. I made a mental note to my "Get Rich Quick List" to start a line of women's clothing with that name. Now where was I? Oh, yeah, focus. Well maybe I wasn't completely focused on Jones' project, but I was in the neighborhood or county of focus the state for sure.

I pushed through the doors of O'Malley's promptly at 9:27 to be greeted by the stale smell of yesterday's spilled beer. I found Dr. Jones immediately, despite the dim lighting in the bar. There was only one man there that could be him. He was a short, dark man in his late twenties, wore dark glasses with thick frames, and had a gigantic endearing smile and a tornado of nervous energy. Compared to his short height, I seemed like a giant with my six-foot-two-inch, OK, six-foot…five-foot-ten-inch cyclist build…OK working on the cyclist part; hey, I did own a bike…once…OK, it had training wheels and it was awhile ago, but a bike nonetheless.

He greeted me with an endlessly pumping handshake that proved tough to break. After a minute, I pulled away and we sat at a table in the middle of the bar.

Jones gestured with open arms to the room around him, "There, do you see?" he asked.

I looked around, not wanting to feel stupid or intimidated right away…I'd save that for later, "Just what am I looking at, Professor?" I asked, opening up my laptop trying to look professional.

"Just look, look, my friend. Tell me what you see," he said as if all knowing.

I struggled to catch up. I began looking around the bar. "Well, over there I see two young men. One is trying to get through a closed door and the other is repeatedly opening the men's room door into his face…What assholes! Over there, I see a guy trying to get onto a bar stool and, every time he does, he slides off onto the floor! What a dick!"

"Good, good," said Jones excitedly. "And in the back room, can you see what is happening there, my friend?"

The lights were starting to come on in my head. "Yeah, yeah, I see five more guys back there. Some are wearing antlers on their heads and another has a rifle." There was a loud, repeated roar as the rifle fired several times. "And that guy is shooting at the guys with the antlers! Is this the hall of morons or what?"

Behind the bar, the grizzled old barkeep just shook his head and continued rinsing out glasses, unfazed as the gunshots rang out.

"Yes, yes, what else?" glowed Jones.

"Man, that guy is a lousy shot! He missed the guy with the antlers every time! He wasn't even close!" Just then the five men rotated antlers and rifle and began the process over again, filling the bar with explosions and smoke. "Holy shit! Somebody should call the cops! Why hasn't anyone called 911?"

"These men have been doing this a long time, now. It's tradition in this part of town. I doubt the police would even come. Would you say that is odd?" inquired Jones.

"Odd? It's freakin' unbelievable!"

"And, my friend, can you describe these men?"

I looked all over the bar. "Yeah, they're all young men, maybe late twenties early thirties."

"Good, good, and what would you say about the women?"

I didn't see any. I thought, *There are no freakin' women here. What kind of crappy dump is this?*

Jones could see my bewildered face as I panned my eyes across the bar, "No, no, look over here, my friend." His finger directed me to a booth next to the front door.

Kaboom! There sat a luscious, long-haired blonde, early thirties, head, blouse, and jeans full of goodies, with shining gray eyes. Then, as she took notice of my gaze, her eyes suddenly flashed right at me, blue then green, like the rotating light of a lighthouse. I had never seen anything like it. Then her eyes flashed at me again. Her eyes and her mouth gave me a quick smile of acknowledgement, both saying, *Hello, this way to heaven*. Instinctively, I turned toward her and stood up halfway, all the while feeling something growing and determinedly trying to escape from my pants. I looked over at Dr, Jones, who had surprisingly lost his cool, and he too was half standing looking at her with a tiny something trying to escape his pants as well.

"My God!" I was startled. "Where did she come from?"

Jones, ever the man of science, regained his composure, began to sit down, and with his hand on my shoulder gestured for me to sit as well. "Now, now, let's not forget that we are men of science here to promote a great discovery." He turned his head to the side, said, "Excuse me a moment," mumbled some things in an Indian dialect, and then proceeded to pound himself in the crotch two times and then once more. He turned back to me but might as well have been on the moon, as I couldn't take my eyes off of her.

"My friend! My friend!" he said loudly, shaking my arm. "You must be careful. A woman like that could fry you like an insect! Believe me, I know," said Jones, remembering and stroking his once-aching crotch.

I gave him a smirk of disbelief, then thought and began to wonder, *Do they really fry insects in India? Flour, a little salt… Just wondering…Oh, yeah, focus. You're a journalist, type something on the laptop, loser,* I thought to myself. Finally there was enough blood in my brain to rejoin him at the table." OK, what's the point, you horny little bastard?" I asked while typing, "I'm fucked…I'm fucked…" over and over on my laptop.

"Do you see that woman?"

I nodded slowly with my eyes glued to her.

"What is wrong with this picture?" Jones asked.

"Not a thing, Doc, not one stinking thing."

"Wrong! Look again. Do you not find this woman attractive?"

"Ohhh, yeah."

"I do as well, but there she sits alone. A room full of drunken young men and a desirable female with five empty lite beer bottles on her table, but there she sits alone. How can this be?"

"I can fix that," I said, still not getting the point and trying to get up and talk with her.

"No, no, this is a scientific experiment, and you cannot alter the controlled conditions we have here. Sit! Sit down, my friend, and I will tell you what it is that you're really seeing, the forces that are at work in this place."

Jones pulled a folded map out of his leather briefcase and unfolded it on our table, "Do you see all of these numbered locations on this map, a map of Scranton, Pennsylvania?"

I nodded.

"The small numbers here," Jones added, pointing to various locations on the map," are radiation readings for each of these sampling locations I have taken. This is the radiation level of the soil sample on the epsilon ray scale…I see you are puzzled, my friend."

Not really. The whole time he spoke, I was checking out the blonde, but I did get something about radiation, samples, and epsilon ray, whatever the heck that was. "Focus" was a distant memory. Had Jones said something? Whatever. Now I wish I had really been listening that night, but the view, oh the view.

"Epsilon rays are a rarely monitored type of radiation whose properties and frequencies are largely unknown. Do you see the radiation levels are highest in the center and slowly lower as you go outside the city? Just where do you think the highest recorded level is, here at the center of the circle?" He dropped his little finger dramatically on the center of the map. "Here, the highest levels are right here…And here is O'Malley's Bar where we sit at this very moment!"

It slowly started to make sense, believe it or not. As I looked around at the guy on the floor in front of the men's room, who had literally knocked himself out with the bathroom door, and another round of gunfire and idiotic laughing arose from the back room, I began to think that this funny little man had truly uncovered something. When two pairs of young men began a race around the bar with one on a chair and the other pushing the chair ending in a tragic crash, I was certain. Unfortunately, for both of us, this type of story required a real journalist, not a little-published freelancer. But, glancing over at the blonde as she downed a lite beer in one tilt of the bottle and then licked the bottle's rim, I was in love, L-U-V, and convinced myself I could fake it. "I'm fucked, I'm fucked," the laptop glowed.

"What exactly do you think is happening here?" I asked, trying to seem professional while also halfheartedly beginning to take notes on my laptop.

"Don't you see? Isn't it obvious, my friend?"

I began to smile and nod my head, then stopped and said, "Sort of," as I began stroking my goatee.

"Sort of? Sort of?" Jones was shocked and unsettled. He began digging through his case and pulled out page after page of calculations and graphs. "Here you go, you can see from these figures that I have calculated the half-life of the epsilon radiation and thereby pinpointed the exact year this environmental tragedy took place. It began," he said, nervously running his finger over a page, "in 1969 and continued through 1981, peeking in 1976. Do you see now?"

All I could do was rumple my face, embarrassed, and try to listen while I ran my fingers through my long, dark, disheveled crop of hair, as if trying to stroke my brain to life. Was it time to play my stupid intimidated card already?

"During that time, the area outlined on my map was exposed to massive amounts of epsilon radiation. This caused the soils to be contaminated for years. Obviously, all young men born in that time frame show reduced functionality disorder, RFD."

"RFD?"

"Yes, as you can see, they are morons!" he said, gesturing to the men around us in the bar. "Their judgment and ability to react to their environment is traumatically impaired. How else can you explain young, prime-of-their-lives men, incapable of even noticing a woman like that, let alone approaching her?"

"So, this radiation made all the men born in this town develop RFD?"

"Yes, yes. But there is more much more. The epsilon radiation has turned some of the women here into superwomen. It has had the opposite effect, based on the chemical makeup of estrogen. So you end up with a woman like that one over there at the other end of the scale with heightened senses and abilities."

I nodded with understanding, but my thoughts were on a different track. "So she's totally unsatisfied!"

"Yes, yes, that may very well be true. How can she be by such men as these?" said Jones, gesturing around the room as one man stuck between two bar stools moaned for help, as another round of shots went off, and the old barkeep ducked behind the bar before shaking his head.

Then the years of being a cynic crept into me. "Superwomen? Come on, is that really possible?"

"Proof is it you want? Well, try these shoes on for size, Mr. Doubting Thomas," Jones said, digging for more papers and pulling out a picture. "Try that puppy on for size, Mister!" he said excitedly, pointing at the picture.

"What's this?" I asked, expecting more than a photo of the 1972 Russian women's Olympic team.

"Do you see the year?"

I nodded.

"Do you see the medals around their necks? Those Russian women won 67.3 percent of all the medals that year. They are all gold!" When I failed to see the import, he frantically found a video file and played it on his laptop. "The woman in this video is the most famous woman celebrity of Russia from 1972-1976, Olga Settchuoff. She was their biggest model, their biggest movie star, their record-holding cosmonaut, and a damn fine cook too."

He played the video. It was a short film clip from one of her Russian movies. She said a few lines in her native Russian then turned her face to the camera for a close-up. When she did, her gray eyes suddenly flashed blue and then green like a lighthouse.

"Holy crap," I mumbled, remembering the look I had received from the blonde in the bar. "Did you see that?"

"See what?" asked Jones

"Her eyes, did you see what her eyes did?" I exclaimed.

"Oh, yes, my friend, her hazel eyes were her trademark. Lovely, don't you agree?"

"Hazel? Hazel eyes, my ass! She has gray eyes, and didn't you see them explode blue then green?"

Jones was puzzled. "There was no explosion, my friend. Perhaps it is because this is a very old film turned digital. Everyone knows about Olga's hazel eyes."

I looked at the laptop and started to realize how crazy I was sounding. *Hazel eyes, my ass,* I thought to myself.

I had become so involved by then that Jones knew he had me. He nodded. "Yes. I can see you are intrigued. This video came from my friend and colleague Demitri in Moscow. Demitri was my professor at Oxford. We are working on this project together. This movie is now restricted and stored in high security, but he managed to smuggle it into Germany and e-mailed me this footage."

I was still puzzled but fascinated. Damn, now I wish I had listened in school. I made a mental note: you should have listened in school, idiot; if you ever have a kid (fat chance) tell him to listen in school. Then I refocused on Jones. "But how does this stuff in Russia go with what happened here in Scranton?" (How's that for focus?)

Jones smiled because he knew he had the answer. "Guess what building is just behind this bar?"

"I drove by; it's a beer warehouse. What does that have to do with it?"

"Yes, my friend, it is a beer warehouse *today*, but what do you think it was between 1967 and 1989, the year the cold war ended?"

I shook my head. How could I know? Was it a trick question? I reminded myself, *listen in school.*

"It was the Miles Research Corporation, now known, through government Freedom of Information releases to be a front for the CIA, their Behavioral Sciences Section! How's that for your cold war mind-altering research shit?"

I struggled to keep up. "So you think this Miles Research, CIA, whatever, was trying to keep up with the Russians' research on epsilon radiation?"

"If they ever wanted to win another Olympic medal, they were...Just think of it as Russia's perfect weapon. They use epsilon radiation to make entire Western armies into morons who might just shoot themselves like these assholes, " he said, gesturing to the back room, "who can't reproduce because they can't even see the women let alone know what to do with them, the entire fortress of American soldiers morons, no longer able to defend Europe. Worst of all, their superwomen would then be the best in every field. America loses its biggest export, Hollywood movies. Russian superwomen would rule the box office, not to mention the complete loss of the American porn industry! It would be an economic disaster! They would just walk through our defenses, and our wrecked economy would be powerless to stop them for at least two half-lives of epsilon radiation, or about thirty years."

"Look, what has happened to Scranton since the epsilon release—years of a slowing economy, a population drop, birth rates drop, high alcoholism; the mafia has moved in and taken control. This is the model of the plans Russia had for the entire economy of the US. First, they would strike Europe and then the US mainland."

"But something went terribly wrong. Whereas the epsilon ray experimentation has only affected Scranton in the US, it seems to have had massive, wide-reaching effects in all of Russia. Look at what happened to Russia since their release of epsilon radiation—a bankrupt economy ends the cold war, population and birthrates drop, high alcoholism; the mafia takes control of the country. Can't you see the parallel connection? Do you still think a cowboy president Ronald Reagan bankrupted Russia and ended the cold war, or was it the result of their years of research in epsilon radiation gone out of control like Chernobyl?"

I remember looking at him puzzled, blinking, and then mumbling something stupid like, "What was the third choice?"

"I'm fucked…I'm fucked," glowed my laptop.

"I know this is a lot to absorb in a single sitting, but do you see the basis for my theory and the importance of it to us all?"

I remember looking at the blonde, looking at the RFD morons around me, and finally asking Jones to show me the Olga video again. I just wanted to be sure I wasn't imagining those eyes. But when I saw it again, she flashed me a blue/green eye flash that about melted my shorts. To my surprise, I could see Jones couldn't see the eye flashes as I did. Maybe I did have something unique to offer.

Thinking back now, I should have made it clear to Jones that I could see the same flashes in the eyes of the blonde at the bar as I did in the Olga's. I should have made certain he knew, but I didn't. Maybe because I wanted to feel I like deserved to be working with him. Maybe I liked being special in some way. Or maybe I was just a horny bastard. I should have told him. So if it turns out that it is you, Dr. Jones, who ends up reading this now, I just would like to say that I am sorry I didn't tell you then about the flashing eyes I could see and ha, na, na, na , na, na, in your face, homeboy!

I knew then that Jones was on to something, maybe something big. But what I didn't know was how it was going to take over my life from then on, "Yeah, I think you're onto something here, Doc...I can't write about just the theory."

"No, no, of course not, my friend. This is just the introduction, the wetting of your whistle so to speak. We have the RFDs as evidence," he said, gesturing as an RFD wearing antlers plowed full speed into a pillar beside us and fell backward on to the floor. "We need to find proof of the other half of the equation, the superwomen, before we go public with this puppy. I could use your help in this. In Russia, Demitri is already trying to locate Olga Settchuoff and the women on that Olympic team. He's also having a lot of luck with superwomen in the Russian personal ads, if you know what I mean. Just yesterday, he said he had found the small town where he believes Olga has hidden herself."

"You and I need to find the 'Olga Settchuoff' of Scranton. Once we find her and verify her powers, we go right to riches, to fame, the Nobel Prize, and maybe even TV talk shows."

That's when I gave in. "You got a deal, Doc," I said, reaching for his little hand to shake with images of a paycheck and a beautiful blonde as my rewards.

He took my hand and gave it a ferocious shake. "You won't be sorry; I am promising you this!"

We packed our cases, put on our coats, and started moving toward the door. I remember how excited Jones was to have converted someone to his theory. You could feel the energy oozing out of him, or maybe it was just the curry. I too felt the excitement of belonging to something that transcended the day to day. I just hoped there was a paycheck in it somewhere.

As we got near the door, we passed the blonde. As nobody else was noticing her, we became the immediate center of her attention. "How are you boys doing tonight?" she asked.

I felt like an ass, but all I could say, and all Jones could say in response were a few slurred senseless syllables, the SSS effect, as it later became known. I think Jones even drooled a little as well. I had wanted to approach her, but now, in her presence I was reduced to Jell-O.

We didn't stop at her table but continued in silence out the two sets of doors to the street, with stupid grins on our faces. Both doors pushed open but neither of us had to use our hands to do it. I'm not sure how. My memory of that instant remains a little foggy.

Outside, I followed Jones across the street until he stopped in front of another bar, The Banshee. By then, we had regained use of our brains. He shook my hand. "Thank you again, my friend. I will be in touch once I plan our next course of action in finding a Scranton super female. I am sure the answer is somewhere in here," he said, tapping his briefcase. "Now, if you will excuse me. In a town like this where men would not know a woman even if she was sitting right on their faces, even a guy like me can get lucky," he added, giving me a smile and a big thumbs-up. "Research, research, you know," he said, before turning to go into the bar. "Lots of research," I could hear him say as the door closed.

I remember I was glad for him, able to move on with the night. But for me, I felt disturbed, like I was suddenly aware of a different world than what I now lived in. I stood in front of The Banshee for a long moment as two RFDs walked by, one running head on into a lamppost that had suddenly jumped out in front of him; the other laughed, then tripped over the first's legs and slid down the icy sidewalk on his belly into the base of a trash can. "He's right, a city full of assholes!" I said to myself.

After watching a few of my cool deep breathes turn to clouds in the night air, I decided to follow the compass in my pants back across the street to O'Malley's. Luckily, I looked up in time to see a speeding beer truck appear around the corner and was able to stop before it flashed by and mashed me into the pavement…rough part of town. I was just about to reach for the door of O'Malley's, when it opened and a woman dressed all in black appeared quickly before me. I was taken aback. She paused a second as well. Her eyes were covered by a black Zorro mask, but I couldn't mistake the blue, then green, flash of her eyes that left me frozen. *Christ, does every woman's eyes do that now?* I wondered. She didn't hesitate any longer, and quickly disappeared into a fog that seemed to come out of nowhere and vanish with her.

When her image was gone, I was able to move again. I went into O'Malley's and soon found myself standing before the empty booth in which the blonde had been located. Stupid as it may seem now, I expected her to be there. I picked up one of her empty lite beer bottles and sniffed it like I was some sort of bloodhound or frickin' DNA machine. She had left nothing else except a twenty for a tip next to the empty bottles. I stood and looked at the twenty, knowing it would be good company for the empty wallet I had.

I was ready to reach for it when the old barkeep collected all of her bottles off the table into a plastic pail with one sweep of his forearm. He grabbed the twenty, gave the table a quick wipe, and then turned to me. "If you're looking for a drink, I recommend someplace other than here."

I turned and noticed that now he was wearing an army helmet.

"One of those guys back there is getting pretty good; might actually hit something, if you know what I mean."

"Thanks for the tip…" Then I couldn't resist asking, now that I had become a real investigative journalist, "The blonde that was sitting here, know who she is? Is she a regular?" I hoped.

"Not hardly, I might be an ol' fart but my heart is still ticking…I thinks I'd remember a bird like her."

"Did you happen to see her eyes?"

"Listen, "he said, getting upset, "I already told ya I was old! But I ain't dead…Least not that they told me! I done brought her a table full of beers; think I didn't notice them eyes?"

My heart began to pound in my chest. "You, you saw them?" I said, fearing I was not the only one.

"Oh yeah, I ain't seen hazel eyes sparkle like that since… since I was a young man."

I began to breathe again. *Hazel eyes, my ass*, I thought. "Thanks," I said, as I turned to leave.

The old man grabbed my arm. I was expecting fatherly advice. "I ever catch you tryin' to cop one of my tips again, you'll end up with a bottle up your ass."

I patted the old man on the shoulder, then tried to walk out of the bar as coolly as I could with my butt cheeks slammed shut.

CHAPTER TWO

How to Get an RFD Killed

When I woke up the next morning, I was convinced that I was being strangled and probed by aliens. To my relief, upon opening my eyes, I realized I had wrapped my mouth with a sheet and was being probed only by empty beer bottles; third time this week.

I found myself lying across the bed, sort of, with one leg dangling over the side. Looking around the messy bedroom and seeing the dim gray daylight of January. I felt everything was back to normal….yuk.

But then the morning glory that made a small tent in my boxers reminded me of the night before: Dr. Jones, Olga Settchuoff, and Ms. Blue/Green Eyes. Without any need for my usual caffeine IV, I was instantly alert. Today I had a purpose.

I turned on my computer, turned on the TV to the News Network, no less. Christ, I even took a shower and shaved. *Carpe diem*, I thought. *What an asshole.*

While I was trying to figure out what to use as a coffee filter, if one should not happen to have any more coffee filters, my attention was drawn to the TV by the words, "Now reporting on these mysterious events live from Scranton, Pennsylvania, is correspondent Janelle Roote..." I couldn't believe my ears... Janelle Roote? What kind of name is that?

"Good morning, Sarah," Janelle began, as I moved over in front of the TV, finally realizing the spot involved Scranton. "I'm reporting to you from the scene here on Penn Avenue where last night three bosses of the reputed Garbonzo crime family were found locked in the back of a beer truck that witnesses said, 'just dropped from the sky.' Each alleged crime figure was found hog-tied with black ropes, bows on their heads, and each was covered with incriminating documents taped to their bodies. Police officials with whom I have spoken indicate that this could be quite a blow to organized crime in the city. Not only were documents found with the alleged mobsters, but two of them have existing warrants outstanding."

"Witnesses claim it was quite a sight. As you can see behind me, workers are just now beginning to remove the truck, whose fall made quite an impression on Penn Ave., I'll tell you that!"

"Not the kind of impression you want to make, hey, Janelle?" asked Sarah the anchor.

"That's right, Sarah," said Janelle giving out a very fake laugh. "Let me show you the tape of an interview I had with an eyewitness earlier this morning..."

The tape ran of a young man introducing himself as Ed, wearing a leather helmet with half-broken antlers on it. He described the events from his vantage point, as he was leaving O'Malley's bar just across the street from The Banshee on Penn Avenue, where Jones and I had been the night before. For some reason, I didn't think the anchors were taking the young man very seriously as he described the events. "....The sound made me look up and that's when she dropped the truck and it fell; scared the shit out of me. We heard the people inside the truck, but none of us could figure out how to open the doors. Finally, I figured out that you had to lift the door up, and there they were all tied up."

"Well, Janelle, that sure sounds like an 'antler-raising' experience," said Sarah.

Janelle just nodded. "Lucky, it isn't deer season anymore. This is Janelle Roote, reporting live from Penn Avenue, keeping you informed on the unusual arrests that are sure to strike a major blow to organized crime in Scranton. Back to you, Sarah."

"Thank you, Janelle...After the break, we'll tell you what items in your kitchen cupboard could kill you or your loved ones at any moment. Then at the top of the hour, Noreen Dunn gives us the third installment of her ground-breaking series, 'The Dangers of Breathing.' You can't afford to miss it," Sarah said, leading into the commercial.

I couldn't believe they had missed it. They didn't believe a word Ed said, just because he was an RFD. But Ed had all the information I needed. Didn't anyone else hear him say "she"— "She dropped the truck"?

I pounded the Internet in search of any more information on the event. No one seemed to know how the truck came to be in the middle of the street. The only witnesses apparently being RFDs, no one bought the "fell from the sky" story. It looked like Ed and I had a date with destiny coming up; not that I believed in Ed so much as I believed in "she."

Wait a minute, breathing is dangerous? I gotta see that.

That night, I had to circle around disgruntled unionized city workers who toiled under work lamps to repair the damage from the previous night's beer truck landing on Penn Ave. It took two of them to do the work and another five to adequately convey their annoyance at being called in for double overtime work, forced to drink coffee, eat donuts, and scratch their butts for hours. Somehow they managed.

I returned to O'Malley's with a sense of anticipation, like anything could happen...what an asshole. Primarily, I was there to meet Ed, but I even prepared just in case "she" was there. This time, I vowed not to let the SSS effect keep me from speaking with her. The anticipation was like being six and coming downstairs Christmas morning hoping to find that toy you'd wanted all year.

I still had that excited anticipation when I burst through the door to see what O'Malley's held for me that night. I stopped just inside the door and looked for "her." But instead of finding that special toy, it was like the year I found only Uncle Ernie drunk under the tree; nothing, she wasn't there. So much for anything can happen when the one thing you want doesn't. Failing to find a beautiful blonde wearing only a bow under the tree (it could happen), I turned my attention to the same barkeep as the night before who stood at a table nearby. When he recognized me, I saw his eyes go wide, and he quickly reached over and gobbled up a tip that lay on a table beside him.

I walked confidently up to him. "How are things, tonight, my man?"

"I've been worse," he said, "...now you came." He began shaking his head.

"Have you seen Ed here tonight?" I asked.

The old man stroked his chin for a moment, "Well now, it seems to me that I ain't served you a drink yet, and this here is what you call a bar, not an information booth, ya see?"

"Got ya," I said feeling in my pocket for any signs of money. I pulled out a few rumpled bills and said, "Well, bartender,

I'd like two beers, one for me and one for my friend, Ed. Is he here?"

The barkeep took the money (not sure why two beers cost $20), returned with two bottles of beer, and pointed. "He's around back...But if you wants to talk with 'im, I suggest you do it quick like. He's next up wearing the antlers. That'll be 'im putting them antlers on right now," he said, pointing.

I slid into the back room with all the cool I could muster. I came up behind Ed and tapped him on the left shoulder. He looked back around over his right, but then eventually found me. "Hey, aren't you the guy from the news report this morning?"

Ed shyly nodded.

Beside us, Ed's friend, Ken, was fumbling, trying to load the rifle, trying to figure out which end of the bullet went which way.

"Wow, it's really cool to meet you, a TV star and all," I fluffed.

Ed smiled but didn't say a word. I guess an RFD can get SSS with anyone.

"It would blow my mind if you could sit down and tell me what you saw last night that was so amazing." We both sat. "Hey, can I buy ya a beer?" I said, handing him one.

"Thanks," he said, still with the slurred single syllables, but it was an intelligible word.

"So, Dude, what happened out there?"

It was slow and agonizing but, eventually, Ed told me the story of leaving the bar and hearing the whistling sound of wind. Then he heard a cell phone ring in the sky. That made him look up, and he saw this beer truck hanging in the sky with a woman all dressed in black holding it up with two fingers. With her other hand she answered a mobile phone, and he heard her say,

"Paige, is that you…No, Mommy's at work." That's when the truck slipped out of her fingers and it fell straight to the ground with a loud crash. The woman said, "Crap," and flew off. When I asked him for a description of the woman, he said she was dressed in all black with a black cape and a black mask over her eyes. When I confirmed his description, he said, "Yep, a flying beotch in black, B.I.B."

By then, the other RFDs were getting anxious to continue the antler game and I had enough of the info I needed. So I thanked Ed, told him to enjoy his beer, and he quickly began the game.

Beotch in black…B.I.B., I thought to myself. That name's better than Ms. Blue/Green Eyes, if you know what I mean. So RFDs could be creative, who knew?

I walked back into the front room to talk with the barkeep. I had to wait while he helped up an RFD that had somehow fallen over the bar, his feet dangling in the air.

"What can I do for ya now?" he asked, knowing I wasn't there for more drinks.

"If you should see the blonde that was here the other night come in again, can you give me a call?" I said, handing him a business card I'd printed on my computer.

He took it but didn't even look at it. "What's in it for me?" he asked sternly.

I dug through my pockets again, but came up dry. "A hundred bucks," I said boldly.

"A hundred bucks?"

I stammered a bit, "Yeah, a hundred bucks….you take a check?"

Just then a shot rang out from the back room. It was not the usual-sounding rifle, and it was not followed by many other shots as usual, nor was there the usual idiotic laughing. Instead, we could hear the RFDs buzzing and yelling at one another.

The barkeep knew there was something wrong as well, and we both moved quickly to the back room.

We found Ken and another RFD wrestling with the rifle, and on the floor across the bar from them lay Ed shot in the head, antlers broken again.

"My God," said the barkeep, "I never dreamed one of 'im would actually hit somebody."

Seeing that Ken's rifle was open and doubting he had ever loaded it, I wasn't so sure. *Somebody's killing witnesses*, I thought to myself. Followed by, *And maybe they're killing journalists who talk to witnesses!* My feet did their duty.

The next morning the papers were calling it a terrible bar room accidental shooting and the mayor was calling for the prohibition of the use of live ammo in the bars allowing the antler game. Duh.

That night, while I was licking my wounds with beer, lots of beer, and a little wine, Jones called and asked me to come to his place. He had a job for me. So I headed on over.

When I got to his apartment, I wanted to tell him everything I had learned. I wanted to come clean about the blonde's eyes. I wanted someone to tell Ed's story to, make some sense of it. But I couldn't bring myself to do it, and Jones was so excited that he wouldn't let me get a word in. So I kept the tale of Ed's beotch in black—or B.I.B., as I now referred to her—to myself and felt guilty.

"Yes, yes, I have for you a very important job. I told you the answer to finding the super female was in my briefcase and here it is," he said, pointing to a blackboard that covered the entire wall of his apartment. The blackboard was covered with mathematical formulas. The entire room was more a messy research lab than an apartment, with papers and books stacked everywhere. Incense filled the air.

"Before we start, mind if I get myself a drink?" I mumbled, stinking from guilt and alcohol.

"Help yourself, my friend, there in the refrigerator. Help yourself."

I slumped into the tiny kitchen and pulled open the fridge. Immediately, a gray cat meowed and jumped out. Inside, I could find only psychology textbooks and a small overripe container of Indian takeout. I realized it was useless, so I went back into the living room, unsatisfied as usual.

Jones was at the blackboard putting a big circle around the final computation. "Yes, there it is," he said and then turned to the desk full of papers. He gingerly plucked a pair of sheer purple thong panties off of a textbook, looked up at me with a self-conscious grin, and said, "Research, research, you know," and then proceeded to look something up in the textbook.

The drunken part of me felt sorry for the sap. Here he thought the answer was in those numbers, and I already knew so much more about the real-life B.I.B. I would humor him anyway, but I was the guy with all the answers, not him. Unfortunately, I was also the guy who had gotten Ed killed, or so I had convinced myself. Should I tell him about the danger? No, he was locked in his little world with his formulas. He was safe.

"Tomorrow, first thing, you must go to the Hall of Records. I have used the epsilon radiation readings, adjusted for half-lives and periodic conversion, of course, to tell me the most likely time that a super female would have been born and where. According to my calculations, she would have been born in Scranton at one of these two hospitals during the Super Bowl of 1976. That would make it…January 18, 1976. The closer to half time she was born, the more likely it is that she would develop into a super female."

I had a hard time keeping a straight face. Super Bowl? What does that have to do with anything? I began to doubt Jones, right then and there. Christ, I knew more than he did. This was true crap. But I hid my smile and nodded my head, what a pro.

"So you must check for women born in Scranton on January 18, 1976. Make a list of them all. We will prioritize them by how close to half time they were born. Then, all we have to do is find them all until we find, 'her.'" Jones smiled and handed me a paper with all the date and time information written down. "So, can you do this tomorrow, my friend?"

I saluted with a couple of fingers. "Can do."

There was a sound of rustling and a female voice from the other room. Jones looked at the bedroom door and then turned nervously back to me. "Well, research calls, my friend...Just checking to see if that's 'her,' you see."

"And how's that going for ya? Was she born January eighteenth?" I joked.

"No, no, no, my friend, I don't believe either of them were. So if you will excuse me..." He turned away and then turned back to me. "You will be needing some funding by now, I am guessing." He opened a drawer, pulled out a stack of bills with a wrapper saying "$5,000" on its middle, and tossed it to me.

I caught it and felt its comforting crunch in my hand. *Just what the doctor ordered*, I thought to myself, trying to contain the smile I felt inside as if this happened to me every day.

Again, I beat feet. It was beginning to become a habit.

The next day, I halfheartedly began work on the assignment Jones had given me. After all, there was nothing for me to do until "she" surfaced again, so I might as well keep busy with this. As it ended up, the information was mostly online, so assembling the list of births was easy. Of the nine thousand some births that year, only thirty-two were on January 18. Surprisingly, thirty-one of them were female, and twenty-seven of them were born during the Super Bowl. Those percentages defied all statistical logic; there should have been one or two more boys than girls born, and they should have been more spread out throughout the day. I started to rekindle my belief in Jones, so that gave my work some inspiration.

Where the work became difficult was following what happened to these thirty-one women after that. With name changes from marriage, divorce, remarriage, death, movement around the country, unlisted phones, phones in others' names, it became hard to follow, and I often lost the trail. With only pizza and beer as my assistants, I continued diligently all day and into the night (not really, but you get the idea).

Little did I know that, while I toiled that night over a hot laptop, events were already in motion elsewhere in Scranton.

CHAPTER THREE

Miracle of Flight 118 (my ass)

Across town, at that very instant, Flight 118 had just risen from the runway into the darkness above the Wilkes-Barre/Scranton International Airport, containing 137 souls. In the left engine of the two-engine jet, dozens of turbine blades approached two thousand degrees after eighty-seven seconds of full throttle flight, when one shattered from the strain. A domino effect broke blade after blade, until the engine exploded, sending thousands of daggers of two-thousand-degree alloy through the engine cowling into the wing and fuselage, cutting through flight controls and electrical circuits, shredding the tail. With the sudden drop of power on the left and the continuance of full power on the right, the plane twisted, and the right wing rose. The turbulence made the right engine stall and flame out, causing the plane to nose down to the left.

Inside the cockpit, the alarm bells sounded as the pilots feverishly tried to figure out what had happened. With no power and some of the flight surface controls not responding, they had little control over the plane. They contacted the tower declaring an emergency and fought to restart the right engine. There were routines they had trained on for loss of one engine, loss of two engines, or loss of flight controls, but with none working, they had few options. They needed to restart the right engine; the left was obviously gone.

Flight attendants clicked on their training and instructed the passengers to assume a "safe" crash position, while one tried to reach the captain for instructions.

In the back of the plane, a young mother sat between her seven-year-old daughter and six-year-old son. Her heart was full of terror as she pulled her children to her, unable to answer their repeated pleas, "What's going on, Mommy?"

A young college student and his girlfriend sat in the front right of the plane. The girl clutched the young man's arm and screamed, while his sense of the "immortality of youth" began to fall into disbelief.

A stewardess hung on to the overhead and angled her body against the tilt in the plane, while she tried to help a young mother strap her newborn into the car seat carrier beside her. "What's going on!" the mother cried, while the stewardess insisted that her baby needed to be in the carrier.

The entire passenger compartment was full of screams and disbelief. The captain fought the controls, while the copilot went through the restart sequence on the right engine. Ahead of them in the darkness, darker than the sky around it, loomed the peak of North Mountain.

The Pilot knew that if he had enough power, he could fly a milk crate through a water pipe. He was also confident they could start the right engine, if they had the time. "Jason! I need that engine, now!" he shouted to the copilot. But looking at the switches he had set and those that were yet to go before he could try the engine, the pilot began at realize that they didn't have the time. He looked at North Mountain's rapid approach and settled back in his seat, "Jason!"

"Just a minute, Skipper, I'm almost ready," answered the copilot, committed to his work.

The captain glanced up to see North Mountain's approach. Although his hands and feet never faltered or left the controls, his mind began to race. He had lost both his parents in rapid succession two years before so the only family he had left was his wife and their two sons, who were already young men. His thoughts turned to them in the best of times: his wife's smiling, laughing face, his sons as young boys, and their faces full of joy upon the arrival of a new puppy. As he took another look at the face of North Mountain, it filled his windshield only seconds away. He thought again of his wife and sons' faces, and then felt himself reaching for his parents' welcoming arms.

It was at that moment that the pilot felt the nose of the plane rise and the image of North Mountain disappeared beneath him. Then he felt the plane enter a gentle bank to the left, circling back to the airport, its airspeed increasing. The two pilots looked at each other in disbelief. They looked at the controls for an explanation. Both engines showed zero thrust, zero rpms. The alarms still rang. Their steering yokes turned by themselves. For those used to being in control of tons of metal and hundreds of lives, it was a baffling, disconcerting experience.

The copilot tried to turn the wheel, only to find it violently push back to the way it was going. He continued to try to restart the engine, even as the plane flew under control. Their training was based on science and control, and he knew of no other way to function.

The passengers cared not about the how or why. They cared not that they were flying without any engine noise. All they knew was that the jet was level and seemingly back in control. They cheered. They cried. They hugged one another.

The woman in the back with two children pulled them close and sobbed uncontrollably. Now her daughter asked, "Why are you crying, Mommy?"

The young college student's girlfriend buried her head in his chest and shivered with tears, while the young man sat upright, staring forward, with tears watering in his eyes.

The flight attendants tried to help calm the plane, while thanking their training and their pilots' training for their apparent deliverance. Yet their experience told them something was wrong and this was not over.

In the cockpit, the captain was the first to let go of the controls, becoming aware that something out of the flight manuals was at work. The radio crackled in his ear. The voice of the controller remained calm and professional, but in the background, the pilot could hear cheers, "Way to go 118, we copy you level and on return course vector. We have cleared everything below you for landing on runway one-niner west. Over."

"Copy that, one-niner, over," answered the pilot without knowing how he could comply. How could he tell them the truth of what was happening?

"Whole lotta people down here are waiting to shake your hand and buy you a beer, 118. Over."

"Take you up on that, control. Over."

By now, the copilot was unable to control himself. "Jim, what the hell is going on? How do we land this thing?"

The pilot just shook his head slowly. "You tell me. All I know is that we're not in pieces on that mountain; we're slowly losing altitude on a perfect approach to the airport. I'm not flying. You're not flying. We have no engines, yet we're still here.

What controls do we have that are working? If you try to take control it fights you back to do what it wants."

"It?" said the copilot perplexed.

"Look at our airspeed. In theory, this plane can't be still in the air at this slow speed, but we are!" continued the pilot.

It was then the radio crackled again. "One eighteen, we track you now off approach vector for one-niner. Are you able to make one-niner, over," asked the tower.

"One moment, control," was all the pilot could think to answer.

The plane continued its slow, controlled decent, but now was passing over the runway toward the terminal. As the pilots tried to make heads or tails of their situation, there came a knock outside the pilot's side screen, then a head appeared. It was the head of a woman with a rat's nest of blonde hair blowing and tangling in the winds outside the cabin. She wore a black mask over her eyes and was trying to mouth something. If the pilot had not been belted in, he would probably have jumped into the copilot's lap with surprise. The pilot could not understand what the apparition wanted. The copilot was still trying to cling to logic.

"Is that a passenger?" he asked before short circuiting. He was reduced to SSS, slurred single syllables, for the rest of the flight.

Then the head dropped down and the pilot could see the movement of arms and shoulders as if the woman was laboring to change her grip. Then her hand appeared in the window with her head much lower than before. She gestured with her fingers starting out horizontal and then tipping down slowly to vertical. She did it over and over again.

The pilot stared at the apparition for a long moment, and then a gigantic smile grew on his face. "She wants me to drop the landing gear! Christ, what kind of pilots are we? Drop the gear! Prepare for landing!" And then he gave her an OK gesture. She responded with thumbs up, and then appeared to labor to climb back down the fuselage.

The radio crackled frantically. "One eighteen, apply power and climb immediately! One eighteen, do you copy? Pull up! Pull up!"

The pilot had no reply to give them that made any sense, so he sat smiling, and then turned off all the alarms and began the checklist for landing. The copilot was still frantically trying to restart the engine, when the pilot reached over and pulled his hands away from the controls. "It's OK, Jason, just let go. Prepare for landing."

Jason gave the pilot a wary look from short-circuited eyes, then reduced his panic and began preparing to shut the plane down. Within thirty seconds, the plane had stopped its forward motion and began a short descent as if it were a helicopter. It set down gently just outside the gate from which it had departed. The captain unbuckled and leapt to the window where the woman had been. *The FAA is gonna love this one,* he said to himself. The copilot sat SSS-ing. Half of the passenger cabin leapt to their collective feet and began cheering. The other half remained in shock. An RFD with two flash wands stood for twenty minutes waving the plane into the gate before realizing that the plane wasn't moving or listening to him. Several other RFDs claimed to have seen a flash in black run out from under the plane after it landed, but who believes them?

I didn't go very far after the landing. I hid in the nearby shadows, all the while rubbing and stretching my sore arms and shoulders that

had been in an awkward position to keep the jet stable. It wasn't the 77,000 lb. weight of the aircraft that was the problem; it was the difficult shape that made it hard to control. And the idiots in the cockpit constantly trying to change course and start the second engine were no help either. It burned between my shoulder blades where the fuselage had rested.

I watched until all the passengers had left the plane with no one requiring assistance and no one injured. I smiled with satisfaction when, finally, the flight crew walked out looking good, except the copilot who didn't look like he was ready to party any time soon.

The airline and Federal Aviation Administration people began inspecting the mangled wing, engine, and tail section that was shredded with holes. I gave out a small laugh as I watched the airline and FAA people rush onto the plane to retrieve the "black box" recorders, because I could imagine the readings and cockpit voice recordings they would find.

With my job done, I got ready to leave. I caught the image of my reflection in a window and saw the tangled mess of my blonde hair. "Crap," I said, "I hate this high speed shit…ponytail next time," I vowed. Then I was gone.

When I got home to my apartment, I was pumped with excitement. The adrenalin from the high speed challenge of saving flight 118 coursed through my veins. The sheer joy of what I had done, saving all of those lives, seeing them walking, smiling, breathing, seeing children safe in their mother's arms, made me want to laugh and dance, spin mindlessly.

I remember approaching the plane not knowing if I could handle it. Not knowing if I would be helping the people inside or merely end up being a close-up useless witness to their death. But when the plane responded to my will…it was amazing.

What a high I was feeling. Maybe all that was just a day's work for a superhero, but I was new at this and for an average single mom this was a remarkable feeling. I just wanted to share it with the world, let everyone know there was hope, no one was alone anymore. They didn't need to fear the random acts of man. Then with a bit of surprise I realized that I could even help them defy fate itself.

I wanted to hug my daughter and look at the smiling pride in her face that she would feel for a mother that could do all I had done. Giving birth to Paige when I was just in high school had changed my life, changed our life. But now things would be different. I would get back everything I had invested, sacrificed, postponed, and more. Her belief in me and my belief in myself would make it all even more worthwhile. I felt like I was on the top of the world and I just wanted to share my ecstasy with someone.

I was still giddy and gleeful when I ditched my mask and cape in my car then headed through the front door. But there awaited my sixteen-year-old daughter, Paige, not smiling.

"Mom!" she yelled upon seeing her mother with ratty hair, torn clothes, and smelling of jet fuel. "I know you weren't at work!"

Immediately, glee was a faded memory. I crashed into reality like Flight 118 would have hit North Mountain. There was no way to share my triumph with her, and it hurt. I stopped and pointed my palm at Paige. "I don't wanna hear this right now!" I said sternly, and then began to walk down the hallway to my bedroom.

"I warned you not to go back to The Banshee! Those guys there are losers!"

I stopped in the hallway and quieted Paige with a frosty glare. Then I continued down the hall.

"And what's with the black clothes all the time? Makes you look like…"

I slammed the door making the hinges rattle, then leaned my back against it. Sometimes, being a single mom with superpowers could be a real bitch.

I stood against the door, while Paige, I knew, stood in the hall with her arms folded. Simultaneously, we both sighed and said to ourselves, "She'll never understand."

I tell you this story as it occurred chronologically, so that you can understand the sequence of events, even though I did not have all of this information until months later. It took being a real journalist to assemble it all, or me to assemble it, on a lucky day.

When I first heard about the incident, they were calling it the "miracle of flight 118," praising the captain's incredible skills. As I read and saw more, I smelled a rat, or beer bottles; anyway, it was something that didn't smell right. That was made much easier for me than most, because I knew about the superpowers at work in Scranton. I started with $500 put into the palm of a man who worked the airport tower that night. He didn't say too much, but it was enough to get me started. I gathered the rest of this article from interviews, research of records, TV interviews and reports, and the written words of others. Even though I wrote it, you can believe it's all true… really, no kidding.

When Dr. Jones heard my story, he danced around like a featherless chicken on a hot grill—not that I have ever seen such a thing, or that anyone else in the world has for that matter. Chickens don't routinely dance, to my knowledge. That's just how his image struck me at the time. He made random, quick arm and leg movements as he paraded around his apartment.

"My boy, I am telling you now, that we are so close! It's not a theory anymore! She is here, and we will be finding her soon, very soon, I'm telling you! What did I say! This will be the story of your lifetime!" Then he bent over for a second, tapped his butt, and said, "Mom and Dad, you will be kissing my professional ass!"

I had told him everything about Ed's story of the beer truck, just leaving out the minor detail of his death. I had told him about flight 118, how I had researched and interviewed my ass off to get the story, until I was certain the miracle of flight 118 was just a pretty myth that even the FAA was starting to doubt publicly. I embellished on how much it had cost me to do. I just could not bring myself to tell him about the blue/green eye flashes and that we had been within inches of our prey days before; we had just been unable to speak or function normally at the time. This information had started the chicken dance.

Then, when I told him that I had tracked down the first of the women born during the Super Bowl and I would be meeting with her that evening, the dance started again. It made him so happy that he literally showered me with money. Not stopping his dance, he grabbed a wrapped stack of bills, each time he passed his desk, and threw them up in an arc to me, mumbling and muttering joyfully to himself as he went. If he spoke English or an Indian dialect I could not tell, only to say that I just kept waiting for him to pass that desk again. $1,000...$500...$2,000.

Finally, he began to pant a little and slowed down. "You have done well, my friend. This is true progress. Are you prepared for your meeting with this woman? Was she born near half time?"

After I stuffed the stacks of bills in my coat pocket, I took out my notebook and fingered down the list, "Her name is Jennifer Lowe. She owns a flower shop. And she was born the first closest to half time of them all."

"She has lived here her whole life?" he asked, patting the sweat on his forehead with a black bra he lifted off of his desk.

"Yes, her whole life. That's what made her so easy to find, never been married."

"Can you blame her, in this town? Nothing more notable in her background than a florist?"

"No...but our B.I.B...that's what I call her..."

"B.I.B.? I think I like it. Kind of catchy and with no connotations like 'super female' has. Kind'a personal too, don't you think? What does it stand for?"

I told him the story of how Ed had come up with the name, beotch in black.

Jones shook his head. "Best we stay with just B.I.B., OK?"

"Sure...what I was saying was our B.I.B. is undercover. She's not like Olga Settchuoff—movie star, cosmonaut, and the whole nine yards. She doesn't want to be known, so she will have a cover. She could be a florist, an accountant, anyone."

"Maybe we should have this Jennifer Lowe followed, a private investigator, perhaps?"

Inside I thought, *Fat friggin chance! This girl's eyes glow and you'll never see me again!* Outside I said, "If she looks like a good candidate after our meeting, it would be a good idea."

"You have all the papers from the university about the research project and survey?"

"Yes," I said, as he referred to the "real" Penn State Psychology Department survey that would be my cover to meet Jennifer.

"Good," he said, then patted me on the shoulder and pushed me toward the door. "I'm certain you're right about the private eye. Good luck and good hunting, my friend. Now, if you will excuse me, it's ladies night at The Banshee."

CHAPTER FOUR

Jennifer Lowe (bitch): Not My Finest Hour

I now know what a bug feels like just before it gets to a bug zapper light. The exhilaration heightened by anticipation and hope totally overrides what should be an impending sense of risk and doom. As I approached the coffee shop where I was to meet Jennifer Lowe, the hope that she would be the blonde with flashing eyes made me ignore all else. Simple things like how I was going to communicate in more than single slurred syllables, SSS language, or how I could come anywhere close to controlling the meeting, or what in heaven I could offer someone like her, or if I would end up like Ed if I got too close and she felt exposed.

I concluded that the excitement I had felt since learning of her existence made the risk worth it. She had brought me back from a dull life to one of risky anticipation of what was around every corner. But in actuality, it wasn't a logical choice at all; I was emotionally compelled to be there, and that was that; just a bug drawn to a light.

I arrived way early to be certain I got there first and found a table near the window, so I could see the entrance and the whole parking lot. I would see her before she saw me—that was for sure. What possible good that would do was beyond the extent of my plan, but give me credit; it sounded good. Despite not needing the artificial energy, I sipped a coffee and waited.

For the next half hour, people came and went with their lattes and chai teas; some were groups, couples, and the occasional lone female. No one I saw fit the bill. I was just about ready to get a refill of my coffee, when a voice beckoned. "You must be Mr. Penn State," said Jennifer in a cheery tone, suddenly standing beside me.

I got through an instant of surprise and panic without showing much of it, then rose and put out my hand. "You must be Jennifer," I said to the woman, who was obviously not the blonde. "I'm Tom," I lied. "Have a seat. Can I get you a…."

"Latte, please, extra foam," she answered taking off her coat revealing a rack you wouldn't soon forget, unless you had a vagina or wanted one.

"And…"

"How about a cinnamon roll," she said, sitting down, crossing her legs, revealing skater's thighs.

I went to the counter, ordered my refill and her food, and then leaned back against it to look at her while I waited. She was not the blonde I had seen before. She had reddish-brown hair down to her shoulders and was built in the image of the new woman. These days, out was the hour-glass figure, and in was the woman with curves, they called it. That was short for a bit of a belly and proud of it. When I hear the word curves, I think nothing in nature can compete with the curves of wide hips and a thin waist, but, if you hadn't noticed yet, I don't make the rules. She wore jeans and a light-colored blouse, expensive but not flashy; but oh, the way she filled them.

I grabbed our cups when the order arrived and nestled back in my chair, studying her face as I did. She had a very average face and young skin. I could barely see her eyes that hid behind glasses; you know the type that lighten or darken in the light.

"You need those dark glasses in here? I can barely read my survey," I taunted.

She gave a little laugh and then pulled off her glasses, folded them, and put them in her pocket. "No need for them in here," she said.

Her eyes looked almost colorless gray to me, but the only thing that mattered was that they didn't flash blue then green at me.

When she saw me staring at her, she added, "Don't go staring at my common hazel eyes; you'll make me self-conscious."

I looked away thinking, *Hazel eyes, my ass*! Then my eyes dropped, or should I say were pulled down, to notice that somehow the top two buttons of her blouse had mysteriously become unbuttoned since I'd left her, revealing echoing cleavage.

But again, the consummate trooper, I recovered without too much embarrassment or drool, and began pulling out the authentic Penn State survey and a very professional, expensive chromed pen Dr. Jones had given me.

"Everything you said on the phone is true, right? You're not trying sell me a time share or something, are you?" she said, putting her head in her hands, her elbows spread on the table, leaning forward, inviting me back to Mammary Canyon.

I chuckled as if such a thought was absurd, then pulled out a business card and Penn State ID Jones had prepared for me. "There, you can see it's all legal. And we really appreciate your taking the time to participate in this program." Talking, trying to be cool, yet still getting an occasional look down the canyon was difficult but possible, I concluded.

I started to read the questions on the survey form, which seemed pretty stupid to me, but I wasn't the PhD. I wasn't having much trouble speaking, but my handwriting was a little slow, due to my anxiety level and unfamiliarity with the forms or the field of study for the survey.

She picked up on that and slid into the chair next to me, in the process being certain to brush her chest against my side. "Why don't I move over here? It'll make it easier for me to see the form."

"OK, sure," I answered and pointed a shaking pen point at question number 4.

She began running her hands through my messy dark hair and looked at me like I was a juicy steak—OK, hamburger at least, and not fast food…no pickles. Jennifer used her thumb and forefinger to run an outline along my goatee. "My answer would have to be my father, definitely my father," she said, not even looking at the form as her left hand began to roam my thigh.

I wrote down her answer. When I moved on to question 5, she moved up to my crotch. I couldn't have felt less in control if I were falling out of an airplane without a chute…again. I was surprised, yes, shocked, yes, but then totally dismayed. Never before had my little man failed to answer with a woman knocking on the door. But now it had failed to rise to the occasion; nothing. Her hand stayed there a good while, but didn't find anything firm.

Without giving it much thought, as was my method, I stood up, began packing my things, and stammering, "Sorry, I just forgot that I was supposed to meet my boss. I have to be going. I'll leave you the survey to fill out. There's a stamped envelope to mail it back at your convenience." (Bull shit, bull shit, bull shit.)

All was still in my pants, nothing. Just to be sure, I took a good long look at her chest as she rose…nothing, nothing but panic.

I remember heading out the door, thinking, *Twenty or thirty superwomen to meet and you choose now to do this!* I hovered outside the doorway facing right and then left, not moving, trying to convince myself that I had handled that well. (Not)

I didn't learn this till weeks later, but back at the table, Jennifer wasn't very happy at being rejected either, and my pen now lay in a molten puddle on the table. She blew out the small flames that ringed the puddle and the metal instantly cooled. *Either he's already marked, he's gay, or he's English*, she thought to herself. *Maybe gay and English,* she thought, shaking her head and buttoning her blouse.

It took me days to recover from my meeting with Jennifer. During that time, I didn't accomplish much of anything. I didn't even return Dr. Jones' phone calls. I suppose I had just been too overconfident, excited, or whatever. I thought she might be the B.I.B. I expected more from myself and my buddy in my pants, as far as managing the meeting. Many beers and long meaningful conversations with my buddy failed to resolve anything. Christ, I had a lot more of them to schedule, and I hoped they all wouldn't end like that. I needed the break to get it back together.

CHAPTER FIVE

She Reappears (thank God)

After a few days, these three articles in the local Scranton paper, to which I now subscribed, awoke me from the doldrums. They appeared in different sections of the paper a day apart, but I knew they were related:

Mysterious Woman Saves Cat...Twice

(Scranton) Scranton native Billy O'Leary credits a mysterious woman dressed all in black for saving the life of his pet and best friend Mr. Jingles, not once but twice. The first event happened at 10:00 a.m. Monday when Mr. Jingles accidentally got out of the O'Leary Monroe Street home. Mr. O'Leary tells the story:

"I blames meself. I brought in some groceries and didn't quite close the door. Right then, Mr. Jingles shot through the door, out in the yard. He's not what you would call an 'outdoor' cat, no claws, ya know. By the time I put down me bags and headed after 'im, he was out in the road. I looked down the road, and here comes this beer truck, not slowing down a bit. There was no way I could reach 'im in time, and he wouldn't come when I called to 'im—cat, ya know. I was sure he was a goner and I turns me head, ya see."

"When I looks back, afraid of what I might see, there she was. This woman dressed all in black from head to foot with a mask around her eyes, carrying Mr. Jingles like he was a baby. He was liking that, ya know. From the look of her, there's no way I can tell who she is; all black with blonde hair."

"I tries to thank 'er, but she don't say a word, just hands me Mr. Jingles. But he don'ts wanna leave her and tries staying in her arms, purring, as it were. I never wanted to be a cat so much in me whole life. Finally, she gets 'im out of 'er arms and then she's gone, just like that."

Apparently, Mr. Jingles again escaped Mr. O'Leary's home that afternoon. Luckily for him, the woman in black was there, again, to save him from yet another of the beer trucks that frequent Monroe Street.

But the story didn't end there. The next morning, Mr. Jingles apparently broke through a window; his feeding dish was found outside, and again he ran for the street in an attempt to be "saved" yet again by the mystery woman. Unfortunately for Mr. Jingles, this time she was not there to scoop him up, and he was hit by yet another beer truck. He is in stable condition at a local veterinarian hospital. The vets expect him to make a complete recovery, although they are unable to stop him from purring.

On a humorous note, on Wednesday, Mr. O'Leary ran out into Monroe Street, apparently in an attempt to also be "saved" by the woman in black. Unfortunately for Mr. O'Leary, she was not there to save him either, but a speeding beer truck was. He is listed in stable but guarded condition at Mercy Hospital. Doctors expect him to also make a full recovery, which is unfortunately being slowed in regard to his damaged ribs by the fact that Mr. O'Leary can be laid only on his side. If he is on his stomach he tips over and, if he is on his back, the hospital does not have a sheet large enough to cover him, due to "tent pole" effect.

Mystery Female Weds Twenty Couples

(Scranton) Twenty couples had planned that Saturday was to be the day they were married in a mass group wedding to benefit the Lackawanna Branch of the Pennsylvania Association for the Blind. The event was to take place at the Lackawanna Station Hotel with Reverend Thomas Price presiding. Just before the event was to begin at 1:00 p.m., all gathered were informed by an unidentified woman that Reverend Price had been arrested for child abuse and that she would be taking his place.

The woman was unknown to all present, wore a black formal dress, but also had on a black mask to cover her eyes, plastic bat wings on her back, and in her blonde hair she sported a brightly colored bow taken from one of the wedding gifts.

Reportedly, she then began to rearrange the couples, matching different brides and grooms before marrying them all in a short, but lovely ceremony.

On a humorous note, 85 percent of the couples find that they prefer their new spouse to the one they had originally planned to marry.

Enigmatic Woman Corrals Local Reverend

(Scranton) A lone woman, unknown to anyone, walked into Central Police Station in Scranton today pulling a duct-taped and embarrassed Reverend Thomas Price behind her on a dog leash. The young woman, described only as average, wearing dark clothing, did not stay to explain but, instead, merely handed the leash and a few assorted dog treats to the officer on duty. Taped to the reverend were several videotapes, the contents of which were not immediately released.

On a humorous note, at this hour, Reverend Price is still in custody.

I was beginning to love her sense of humor. Not only did she help people but she had a way of taking the seriousness out of the events with her humor.

Even to my Jennifer-stupefied brain, it was clear that the B.I.B. had surfaced again…and again. Luckily for me, writers on different beats handling what seemed to be minor stories had not put it all together that the same woman was the subject of each story. They weren't looking for her as I was. I remember being struck by the new way she was appearing. Before, she had remained hidden and mostly unseen at night. Now, here she was in open daylight, unconcerned about being noticed. She didn't seem like someone who would end poor Ed's days just because he saw her; but you know women, she could have just changed her mind. The more I thought about the articles, the more I imagined being there in the crowd and seeing her. The more I thought about that, the more I wanted to be that damn cat.

CHAPTER SIX

Spinderella (because it deserves its own chapter)

Certain another brain would do me a great deal of good about now, I gathered everything up on the B.I.B. and headed for Dr. Jones' apartment. Now I had some good news to counteract the bad news about Jennifer Lowe.

When I reached Jones' place, I soon found out why he hadn't been concerned about my meeting with Lowe. He was a wreck, obviously not having cleaned up or changed clothes in days.

"Dr. Jones, what's wrong? Something happened?"

He stared at the ground and took a few deep breaths. It was an obvious chore for him to tell the tale, "My friend," he started with his voice breaking, "Demitri...I received an e-mail relayed through my colleagues in Oxford that Demitri is dead..." He paused and shook a bit. "He wrote me four days ago saying that he had found Olga Settchuoff and that he hoped to meet with her any day. He was very excited that all his work had paid off, the proof was so close...The next thing I know, I received a second e-mail saying that he was found dead by Russian authorities...Accidental causes, they said. But I...I know better. His body was sent to his relatives in Moscow, but now they have to delay the burial. It seems three teams of morticians have been working for days trying to get rid of the smile on his face. A dead man with a huge grin just seems too ghoulish. So, then, they decided on a closed-casket funeral. Now, they can't close the lid…" Now Jones was really pushing himself to speak. "It seems that his penis is frozen erect, twisted into a corkscrew shape…The morticians have never seen anything like it. They can't get pants on him. They tried turning him sideways to no avail. No one has the nerve to use a saw."

"Wait! Does this mean…"

"Exactly, my astute friend. Woe to us all, Olga has perfected the mythical spinderella move, and it turns out to be deadly."

"How can that be? I thought it was just a story…" Then I thought for a moment. "Wait. Doesn't that chick have to be in her sixties by now?"

"Exactly, I see you understand the import of this event. We have various birth dates for her, but they all put her in either her late or early sixties."

"An old broad tears him up like that?"

"No, no, my friend, do not underestimate her as Demitri did. That old broad is lethal…obviously. If so, what is a younger version capable of? No, it is too dangerous to continue. We have opened Pandora's box, or at least Olga's. You must stop searching for your B.I.B. To find her would be certain death… maybe a happy one, but still a certain one."

It all was crashing in my head like waves going in opposite directions. I had gone there excited at the new sightings to tell Jones about and now back at me came this deadly news of Demitri. Jones was obviously resigned to the end of his research, but I could not bring myself to believe that a woman who saved cats and married people could also be a cold-hearted killer, accidental or not. I had almost convinced myself that she could not have killed Ed, but now this news reopened that can of worms.

"Sorry, Doc, I can't stop now. We're too close."

"That is what Demitri said."

"But we now have this information. We can be more careful."

Jones shook his head and dropped his arm in disgust. "I don't know…"

Sensing the tiniest of openings, I pushed ahead. I told him about Jennifer Lowe glossing over everything just to say I didn't think she was the one. I then got a lot more excited, talking about the newspaper articles and showing them to him. "How can a woman who does these things be a killer? And look, she's starting to do it in daylight, like she's not afraid to be seen and known anymore."

"Or maybe she just has to be home at night to feed a sick mother or something."

I ignored him. "If she's not afraid to be known, then she'll have no reason to kill anyone who finds her out. Maybe she even wants to be recognized now. And if I know what she can do, I can stay away from those situations," I lied.

"You are both persuasive and brave," he said. Boy, did I have him fooled.

"It's my job…We can't stop now."

"You, you, can't stop now. I can stop anytime. Look, its two-for-Tuesday at The Banshee and I ain't goin'," he said proudly, pounding his chest. "You go on, but if I must, I will be telling you over your grave that it's your doing, not mine."

I considered it a victory and decided Jones would jump back on board at the first sign of progress. On the way home, I thought about Ed, I thought about Demitri, but most of all, I thought about the B.I.B.…and the spinderella move. She wouldn't kill me would she? My brain said that light up ahead's a bug zapper; my heart said, so what…Just a bug drawn to the light.

CHAPTER SEVEN

My Web Site Is Born: But No Seconds on Meat Loaf

Looking back now, had I known that the B.I.B. had started showing herself during the day only because she needed to be home at night to keep peace with her daughter, I might have acted differently. But under the bold assumption of a shift in the B.I.B.'s attitude, I took a radical approach.

I contacted all the fledgling beat writers who had each written a separate piece on the B.I.B. and offered them mounds of Jones' cash to turn over any item to me that they might come across on a woman dressed in black doing any kind of unusual deed. I greased palms at any bar of consequence for any sighting of a woman in black, offering further grease if they notified me in time to get there to check if it was her. I created a Web site, *thebib.org*. On the site, I placed copies of the articles about her, a blog, a bulletin board, a hot e-mail for sightings, and propaganda I had written about "Scranton's True Superhero." As time went by, this became a job within itself, trying to keep the site updated with the latest events and respond to the e-mails.

The beat writers remained unaware of the connection among themselves, and they fed me like Jabba the Hutt. By the time I had posted a beat writer's article about the arrest of Tony Turtulio, "the Tool," on Valentine's Day, the site was starting to get a lot of hits. A local news channel, whose broadcast I also linked, then picked up the article from the web site...

"Scranton police received a Valentine's Day gift today as Tony Turtulio, also known as "the Tool," was delivered by a delivery woman to Third Precinct headquarters. To the amazement and delight of the officers, in keeping with the holiday, the Tool was delivered, as seen in this brief amateur video, unconscious, dressed as a strawberry, and wearing a floppy, leafy-green hat, and red clothes, with his torso dipped in chocolate," read the female anchor.

"Not just any chocolate, Maria. It was Gertrude Hall milk chocolate, made right here at their Scranton plant," added the male anchor; apparently Gertrude Hall Candies was an advertiser.

"Thanks, Tom. The Tool has several outstanding warrants for his arrest and is reputed to be the number four man in the Scranton mob. With some of the federal warrants carrying twenty-year sentences if convicted, it looks like the Tool will be spending a number of Valentine's Days to come behind bars, where chocolate-covered strawberries will be hard to find..."

"Gertrude Hall chocolate strawberries, that is," added Tom.

The video was priceless and, along with my commentary attributing the capture to the B.I.B. and speculating on how she had done it—the chocolate dipping I mean—the site began to flourish. Sure, most of the people contacting the site were whackos, but the sheer volume of interest was building.

By now, I was in love with her sense of humor; the giant strawberry on Valentine's Day cracked me up. She was just doing it for fun and to embarrass the crime boys. Blending her two lives had to be amazingly difficult. Everything she did was so remarkable and significant, yet humble. By now I had to confess I was in love with her, all of her…Crap. Did I just say all that? What's wrong with me? Doesn't even sound like me… it's OK, I can edit it out later.

No way I'd let her read that, risk her saying something crushingly female like, "I never thought of you that way," OUCH! or "You're just not my type ." Crap, how could I be a superhero's type? Apparently, I was risking a whack from rejection by foolishly hanging out my feelings like that. If revenge is a dish best served cold, then rejection is a dish I just wasn't prepared to even order. In fact, I make a point of leaving any restaurant that has "rejection" on the menu….even as a side dish…even if I have a discount coupon. No way, Jose, I'll edit out that mushy part. That will be a big edit, delete, delete.

The next showing of the B.I.B. really put my little site on the map as "the" source for B.I.B. information. This time she was on tape and we had it.

My daughter, Paige, ran right into the kitchen after bursting through the front door of our apartment. She scanned the counter of the kitchen, then began opening and checking all the cabinets. She scanned the small kitchen table and then went out into the living room and searched the entire room, before shouting to me, "Mom? Have you seen the big box of chocolates Billy gave me?"

I stood fifth in line at my bank like a regular, everyday woman dressed in black, having to deposit checks from my regular job and a part-time job I held to make ends meet for me and my daughter. It

was a complicated deposit, as I had to transfer some of the funds and get out some cash, so I decided to do it in person. As the line moved slowly, I looked at my watch, not wanting to be late for work. One of the tellers was busy counting rolls of pennies and dimes for an old man, while the other was arguing with a man over bounced check charges. I sighed. **No lunch again today***.*

That was when three men ran into the bank with ski masks, shouting, ordering everyone to the ground. One thug stood by the door and the other two moved toward the tellers. "Tellers, hands in the air where I can see them. Anyone touching a silent alarm is the first shot. Everyone else, get on the floor. Anyone who doesn't get down right now is dead!" said the leader nearest the tellers.

People screamed and dove to the ground. The tellers nervously held up their arms and looked at one another for a clue on what to do with the alarm buttons so close.

The leader was on an adrenalin high, watching all those he commanded. When he saw one lone woman standing with her back to him in front of a fake potted palm tree, he was first surprised then pissed off.

I dropped my bag and my deposits. When I turned to face the leader, I had the black mask over my face and said, "You're gonna make me late for work. Do you really have to do this today?"

The leader's eyes turned to fire. "You don't wanna listen, do ya, bitch?" he said, determined to make an example of me.

I moved slowly toward him. "Oh! This must be what they meant by 'stupid is as stupid does.'"

He aimed his gun at the center of my body. With his veins full of adrenalin and a sadistic grin on his face, he pulled the trigger of his 9 mm four times. His shots totally wasted the plastic palm tree and pot that had been behind me. As he felt his wrist break and watched his gun drop to the floor, his expression changed to shock and amazement.

After he felt the blow to the back of his head everything went mercifully gray and then black.

The thug by the door watched in horror. He tore off his mask, pulled open the bank door, and was gone in a flash.

The third thug looked at the limp body of the leader with his badly mangled wrist as he lay unmoving on the floor. He dropped his gun and put his hands out in front of him. "Hey, I don't want no trouble!"

"Then I guess you picked the wrong career, the wrong bank, and the wrong woman," I said moving in on him.

He raised his arms up to protect his face, and then also fell limply to the ground.

I stood behind him, looked around for any more of the gang, and then walked over to recover my bag and deposits.

With the shots having been fired, no one else moved. They just whimpered or listened to the course of events.

I grabbed my things and started toward the side door as the police stormed through the front door. A commander saw me walking away and gestured to a patrolman beside him. "Go stop her and bring her back," he said as he pointed at the side door.

The patrolman nodded, then turned and halted. "Stop who, sir?" he asked.

The commander pointed before he looked at the empty hall and closed door.

The security camera tapes were gold. I won't tell you how much it cost or what laws I bent to have them anonymously e-mailed to the site, but it was worth it. Suddenly, the site was taking thousands of hits. Webmasters and advertisers were contacting the site for links and ad space. B.I.B. sightings were pouring in, most of them trash. The video turned the Web site into a real job.

When the security tape first arrived, I was disappointed and almost deleted it in disgust. The beginning part that immediately preceded the robbery was full of digital static. I could barely make out the fact that it was a bank and the people were all foggy. But then, as the gunmen entered the bank and began the robbery, it all went suddenly clear. The image of the B.I.B. moving from the palm tree to the first gunman appeared just like a straight line going from the tree to the gunman in a frame or two. The same when she moved toward the last gunman. But that wasn't what I loved most about the video. When I replayed it again and again, frame by frame, I discovered that there was one frame at the beginning, just before the static started, that showed a young woman dressed in black entering the bank from the street. When I froze that frame, I saw a grainy image that I felt certain was the blonde I had seen at O'Malley's that night. I wouldn't want to make a portrait from it, but I had a strong "feeling" from the image. It made me feel that I was on the right track. Delusion can be fun.

There was a growing sentiment from the people e-mailing into the Web site that the city authorities should be embracing the B.I.B. and encouraging her efforts. Many said the mayor should invite her out of the shadows to work directly with police.

A day later, as I was digging through the e-mail leads people had sent in, in response to my "reward" program, I knew I was on the right track. A young man, on temporary assignment in Scranton from Texas, sent in a picture of a woman dressed in black with blonde hair, a black mask over her eyes, a gigantic bling on her finger, smiling and proudly displaying a bottle of Miner's Lite beer in her outstretched hand. Again, it was a very grainy picture taken in a dark bar using a cell phone, but her image leaped out at me the second I saw it. The young man claimed to have taken the picture at a pub called Skelly's several nights before. He said he had partied with the woman and her friends there. After a few beers, she had brought out the mask and worn it for a few minutes, saying she was the B.I.B. He then took the picture, sure she was joking. He said he also had some pictures of her later that night making a really good "fish face," if I wanted those. He thought nothing of it until someone had introduced him to our Web site and told him to send the picture in for the reward.

I immediately contacted the young man, sent him a reward, and offered more for the fish-face pictures. I asked him if he had her number or address or had seen her again, and he replied that they had gone to his place afterward and he had no way of getting in touch with her again.

Next, I put the picture front and center on the Web site home page with the title, "This is the BIB!" Then I used my contacts at the *Times Tribune* to get me a meeting with the editor. It was a hard sell, back then, but I got him to agree to let me create a B.I.B. column in the paper. I explained to him the interest people had in my site and was certain his readers would likewise be interested. I gave him the picture and my first feature, which I had taken from various things I had already written for the Web site. He buried it on page 8 the next day.

Many times each week, Paige and I have dinner at my sister Lori's house, which is located near our apartment. It was convenient, saved on the expense of cooking for only two, and allowed some time with the family. On this night, I had worked late. By the time we arrived

at Lori's, her husband and kids had finished their dinners, so it was only Paige, Lori, and me at the table.

We sat at the dining room table, digging into our reheated dinners, while Lori paged through the newspaper. "Can you believe these stories about this B.I.B. woman?" asked Lori, as she reached page 8. "She's amazing…Now they have a picture of her in the paper."

I stopped, a forkful of mashed potatoes just before my lips. "Picture?"

"Yeah, look, there she is," said Lori showing the paper to me. "But with that costume, what good is the picture? She could be anyone."

My fork continued to my mouth, relieved that even my own sister was unable to put the picture together with me. "Boy, she looks great," I added, remembering the night the picture was taken. I smiled briefly, thinking about the bar and Mr. Texas that night. Then the smile drained. I've got to be more careful, I thought, remembering the number of beers I had that night.

"Let me see, let me see," Paige demanded eagerly. She studied the picture and skimmed through the article as Lori held it before her. "I think Mom's the B.I.B.!" said Paige proudly, after Lori pulled back the paper.

My mashed potatoes came to a sudden halt halfway down my throat.

"You should have seen her the other night when she came home after going to The Banshee!" said Paige to Lori, laughing.

"The Banshee?" asked Lori like a mother to a child. "I thought you said you weren't going there."

I was relieved that Paige was only joking and my mashed potatoes continued on their way. "Don't worry; I'm not going there anymore."

"Promise?"

"Yes, I promise."

"You should have seen her...RAT WOMAN! Her hair was a mess! And the smell!" Paige continued, joking.

"Now, that's enough," Lori said, coming to my defense. "She said she promised and that's good enough for me...I gotta look at this Web site in the article, THEBIB.org."

"Catchy," I said.

"Yep, hard to forget a Web address like that, THEBIB.org," said Lori.

"I think it sucks!" Paige added.

Lori studied the picture in the paper more closely, "Didn't you have a ring like this? I remember you wore it at Christmas," she said holding the paper toward me so that I could see the picture. Women remember everything.

"Nope, never had one like that...The cut is totally different on the one I wore at Christmas...Imagine me...having a ring like the B.I.B." I laughed, knowing Lori was totally correct.

"Let me see," demanded Paige, pulling at the paper. "No, Mom. Yours looks..."

I knew I had to stop her before she could finish. I had the pepper shaker in my hand. With the super speed of which I was now capable, I released a cloud of pepper with a few dozen shakes that only took a millisecond and then sent the cloud to Paige's nose at the other end of the table with one powerful high velocity breath. It worked; a violent sneeze interrupted her words, then another, then another.

"Ouuu, what was that?" Paige exclaimed between sneezes, bringing her hand to cover her nose. The frequent sneezes began making it hard for Paige to catch her breath.

Lori looked at Paige, puzzled, and then at me in shocked concern, wondering what had happened. I shrugged and we both rose, the epitome of female nurturing. I needed to play my part knowing that Paige would be fine, but needing to show my concern. Lori, on the other hand, lost it, as was the way of her people.

By now, Paige was out of her chair, hunched over, sneezing, wheezing a little, and beginning to have beads of sweat form on her forehead. Lori hovered over her trying to evaluate and console, but Paige was barely able to talk.

Lori looked at me with a face that had changed from adult concern to total freak out. "It was my fucking meat loaf, wasn't it!"

Now I had two to calm down. I turned from Paige to grab Lori around the shoulders, "It wasn't the meat loaf!"

"She's having an allergic reaction to the Goddamn meatloaf! I'm killing your daughter!"

"No one's dying. She'll be fine…Get her a cup of water. Do you have any nasal saline spray?" I tried to ask calmly to get her mind off of panic.

"Her throat's closing! We have to get her to the hospital! Can't you see she's having an allergic reaction? Don't you ever watch the fucking news? I saw this on the 'Dangers of Breathing' report they had!"

Now I had two who needed to get to the hospital. Lori was a bright shade of panicked red and her breathing was worse than Paige's. Consoling Lori was no use, so I turned my attention to Paige as Lori ran out of the room and I heard the eruption of voices and the spread of panic in the next room as she tried to enlist her husband in the "save Paige" effort.

I found some nasal saline in the cupboard of the little half bath next to the kitchen and began the job of corralling Paige and rinsing out her nasal passages as best I could, while Lori flashed by, slipping her coat over one arm and rattling her keys, heading for the car in the garage. "Never reheat meatloaf…" she muttered in passing.

Even before the nasal spray, Paige was better. But now, with the added help of a few sips of water, her symptoms were subsiding. I sat her back down and she took a few deep, healing breaths. "You OK?" She nodded. It was now my turn to feel badly for putting her through the pain, but it had worked, and the cut of my Goddamn ring was the furthest thing from anyone's mind.

Lori came back into the kitchen prepared to be a paramedic (is one medic a medic and two medics a paramedic, always wondered) as her husband, pulled miraculously from his recliner, stepped into the doorway at the other side of the kitchen and rubbed his belly with a Miner's Lite in his other hand. I assured them that everything was fine, and Paige even tried to smile to reassure them. That prompted Lori's husband to disappear, and Lori to grab the meatloaf platter and toss it into the trash on top of the folded picture-of-the-ring newspaper I had already sent there. So ended the "Bling-Ring-Pepper" debate… and any chance for seconds on meatloaf…(That ring was toast as soon as I got home.)

CHAPTER EIGHT

"We are No Longer Afraid"

It was the next adventure of the B.I.B. that made me a true public figure. It was just a few days after the picture taken at Skelly's was published. I sat on the couch and watched the evening news, while Paige worked on her MySpace page on her computer, texted on her phone, and listened to music in the earphones of her personal music player. We were both dressed for comfort only and planned on being in for the night.

I lay on my side on the sofa, slowly munching and savoring a Gertrude Hall milk chocolate, while beginning to unwrap another. The news article on the TV showed a brokenhearted, crying woman, Alisa Gonzalez, whose daughter Emilia had been abducted from their Scranton home. Alisa wailed for her daughter's return in front of her low-income home.

In my mind, I started to put together the story of Francisco Gonzalez, a midlevel mob member who had disappeared a month earlier. On the streets, I had heard rumors that he swam with the fishes. Others said he was in witness protection. Either way, I was sure it connected to the little girl's abduction. Something about the mother's pleas clicked in my head.

I walked over to Paige, pulled out an earphone, and said, "I have to go out for a minute, you be OK by yourself?"

Paige nodded.

"OK, don't go out or let anyone in."

Paige said nothing but nodded her head vigorously, put the earphone back in place, and returned to her multitasking.

It wasn't that hard to get a location on young Emilia's whereabouts. A couple of midranking thugs, left smiling unconscious in alleys later, and I was outside the rundown mob safe house, where they were holding Emilia. I doubted that Scranton's finest had looked very hard for Emilia, since she was the daughter of a mobster.

The windows were all covered, but through a crack, I could see two thugs, and I saw the little girl bound on a long leash in the corner. I guessed there were probably more mobsters somewhere; I heard something on the second floor. *I'll start with the two down here. Maybe I'll get lucky*, I thought. Slipping in the dilapidated back door was easy. Merging into the shadows of the darkly lit living room was fun.

The two thugs sat across from one another, one watching an old movie on TV, with a gun on the arm of his chair beneath his hand, while the other had placed his mobile phone and pistol on the small table beside his chair to begin cleaning the gun; wrong time for that.

The thug watching TV was relaxed, a song playing in his head, zoned out to the point where he barely saw the program he was watching. As he wasn't expecting any trouble on this cake job, it took him a few shocked seconds to realize that his gun hand had risen up. He watched in surprise as his hand pointed the gun at the thug across from him and fired; first a hit to the knee and then a second shot to the shoulder.

The wounded thug screamed out, "Manny, what the hell are you doing?" before he fell over and went into shock.

The little girl tried to scream through her gagged mouth and struggled with the ropes that bound her.

The TV thug then became horrified when he saw his own gun pointing at his face, finally revealing my black-clothed hand that was guiding it toward him. At that point, the thug lost all bladder and bowel control, letting out a long fart and beginning to wet his pants. My voice saying, "Manny, you stink," was the last thing he heard before a hammer fist to the back of his neck made everything go black.

After that, I slipped into the shadows of the room when I heard the footsteps on the stairway. The footsteps stopped, and all was quiet for some time. Finally, a figure of a man slipped into the darkness along the wall. I listened for more thugs coming but heard none.

I appeared out of a shadow a few feet away from the third thug, an Asian man standing in a self-defense position. He nervously looked around the room for a weapon, his eyes pausing on the gun that lay at the feet of one of the thugs. So I knew he was unarmed. When he saw that his attacker was a woman in a costume, he disregarded the evidence around him and tried to act cocky. "What's all this about? You're a little late for Halloween."

"Maybe I'm just early," I said, circling him as he circled away.

"What the hell you supposed to be, some kind of witch?" he said with the fear on his face betraying his false bravado.

I stopped. "Let's get it right. It's not witch...It's bitch," I said, unleashing a front kick that easily powered through his attempt at a forearm block.

The Asian thug thought the kick hurt immensely, until he felt the pain of being sent through the two-by-fours and siding of the old house. By the time he landed with traumatic injuries in the snowy yard, he was unconscious.

I looked at the hole in the wall through which cold air and flakes of snow now swirled into the room and then to the window two feet away, wondering how I could have missed sending him through the *window as planned. Then I dropped to the shadows again and listened intently. All I could hear, besides the girl's whimpers, were the buzzing of lights, a muffled TV, the mumble of a set of earphones for a personal music player on the second floor—probably the Asian's—and the sound of a mouse in the basement behind the furnace with a bad case of indigestion. All was clear.*

I turned my attention to Emilia. As I untied her and took off her gag, the girl was full of fear and tried to escape. I held on to her, tried to make her know that she was safe, and that she would be taken home to her mother, but that she would have to be quiet. Eventually, the girl calmed down but still couldn't stop whimpering.

"You OK?" I asked.

Emilia nodded.

I took the thug's mobile phone off of the table, placed a "911 shots fired" call, gave the address, closed the phone, and dropped it at the thug's feet. Making the call that would lead to his arrest from his own phone gave me a little satisfaction. I cradled the little girl under her arm and we were gone.

It was late when we reached Emilia's house. Alisa was reluctant to open the door until she heard her daughter's voice, then the door flew open. They combined in a tearful hug that went on for a long time. Finally, Alisa became aware of me while her daughter still clung to her legs.

"Santa Maria!" she cried, "It is you! I saw you in the papers. I prayed for you to save my daughter and now you are here!"

Emilia joined in, "She brought me home, Mama. She kicked those men that took me away."

Alisa took my hand and kissed it. "You are an angel from heaven. I can never repay you."

I waited, tried to be gracious, but needed to express my concern. "Mrs. Gonzalez, perhaps you should leave. The men that did this may come back again. You're not safe here."

Alisa's eyes pooled with tears, but shined with joy and confidence. "We are safe as long as you are here…These men think that I know where Francisco has gone. They are afraid he will tell people what he knows about them. I told them I don't know where he has gone, so they think if they take Emilia that I will tell them or that he will come back to save her…With you here, they will not come back. You are a gift from God and I will tell everyone this."

I knew there was no use debating the subject with her. At any rate, it was a joy to see them back together, and I was happy for that moment. Still, that was the first time I began to feel the descent of a yoke of responsibility that I hadn't asked for or wanted.

When I slipped back home that evening, I found Paige exactly where I had left her, multitasking past her bedtime. I got back into my comfy clothes and moved over behind Paige, enveloping her in a tight hug as Paige sat at the computer.

Paige pulled her earphones out, turned, and protested, "Mom!"

I just hugged her tighter, not wanting to let go.

The next morning media people crowded Alisa's tiny front yard and porch. They stuck microphones in her face and brightly lit her and her daughter with camera lights. She spoke happily of her daughter's return thanks to the B.I.B. She spoke in glowing terms of the angel that had saved her daughter and was here to save the city from evildoers and devils. Like someone in a single-minded trance, she told the audience that the mayor and police needed to set up communication with the B.I.B. and work with her for the good of the city. She ended by saying that, with the B.I.B. to protect her, she was no longer afraid.

When I put that TV footage on the Web site, the response was a groundswell to bring the B.I.B. out into the open, to embrace her as a hero. "We are no longer afraid!" became the new slogan of everyone on the Web site. So when I wrote my latest article for the *Times Tribune*, I continued with that theme and used Alisa Gonzalez's words to make an outcry to open communications between the B.I.B. and public authorities. In actuality, I thought making her more public would help me find her. I couldn't have guessed back then where that would ultimately lead. As long as there was a paycheck in it and it brought me closer to her, *what the hell*, I thought.

CHAPTER NINE

The Mob Takes Note of "My" Girl

The mayor leaned back in his chair with his shiny Italian shoes on the desk, admiring the view outside his large window. He was a stately, well-dressed, mature man with neatly cut silver hair. When the "special" mobile phone rang in his pocket, his feet slipped off the desk, and he almost fell out of his chair in surprise and apprehension. "Yes?" he said in a blank tone, not knowing what to expect from the other end.

"Usual place, 2:00 p.m." The phone clicked off.

The mayor nervously rung his hands and paced a few steps around the room. *What do they want now?* he thought.

The mayor walked into Giovanni's restaurant precisely at 2:00 p.m. and was escorted back to a private booth in the corner, where Gregorio Gambrelli, a major Mafia boss in Scranton awaited, eating a plate of pasta. Encircling the booth were obviously old-framed black-and-white photos of Gambrelli's ancestors. Two muscular men stood beside Gregorio in suits with their arms folded. Another large man, Vito, with fingers the size of saplings sat across from Gregorio. When the mayor arrived, Gregorio gestured to Vito, and he left the booth and stood with the others.

The mayor sat down anxiously and turned his attention to Gambrelli.

"You know about this…this…B.I.B. woman in the papers?" Gregorio asked.

The mayor nodded.

"She's not good for business. She's cost me some good men. She sent a busload of our girls one way to Vegas…Ever hear of anyone winning at the numbers? It happened last week…Now, in the paper I read today, they want you to 'communicate, coordinate,' with her," he said, picking up the paper and dropping it on the table.

"Don't worry," began the mayor nervously, "I won't let that happen."

Gregorio was upset and raised his hands in the air. "You see? This is why I have to do all the thinking for you politicians," he said, looking at the three thugs beside him. "You don't think," he said pounding his head. "You don't get it… Get this straight," he said, looking the mayor deeply in the eye. "I want you to communicate with her. I want you to bring her out. I can't kill what I can't find, capisce?"

The mayor stared, blanking in surprise and then nodded.

"You and your boys downtown come up with some way to make her show up when you call her, and my boys will take care of the rest."

"I can do that," the mayor said.

"Good, I'd hate to think I got you elected for nothing."

"You can trust me."

"I hope so. For your sake, I hope so. Now, if you will excuse me, I have other business," Gambrelli concluded, as two men pulled an unwilling man toward the table.

In the mayor's conference room that night, he bit into a sandwich from the local deli, while he paced and spoke with his advisers. "Somebody's got to have some idea how we can contact this woman!"

The room was full of blank stares and yawns from the six people surrounding the big table at the center of the room.

As he chewed, the mayor asked, "Edwards, what did you find out about the B.I.B. Web site? There has to be some contact info there."

Edwards, a young Ivy League type with glasses, shook his head. "We had no trouble getting into the server, but it looks like there is nothing more there than what you see on the site. We tracked the e-mail of that picture they printed in the paper back to some guy's laptop. We leaned on him pretty heavy, but all he could tell us was where he was that night. He didn't know who she was or where to find her again…The site's a mess; it's like somebody's attic."

The mayor threw up his hands, sending lettuce from the sandwich into the air. "Anybody, anybody got an idea?"

Edwards added, "The site is already offering rewards. I don't think that will work."

"How about a full-page ad in the paper?" offered Elizabeth, a young woman who worked with Edwards.

The mayor thought about it. "Yeah, but if she's under cover, why would she respond? Any other ideas…Anybody?"

There was quiet in the room, until a young hippie/geeky guy sitting away from the others against the back wall chimed in. "She's like a superhero, dudes. You have to treat her with honor and respect. You have to acknowledge her, man."

"So, so?" asked the mayor circling the finger of his hand for the geek to speed up and get to the point.

"You gotta do somethin' like Batman. Ya know? They had this searchlight thing that they turned on whenever he was needed. It was a special thing. You know, like we need you, man. We need you right now. How could a superhero dude ignore that?"

The mayor thought about it. "Dramatic, yes, but it might work."

Then Edwards chimed in. "You know, Mr. Mayor, the new Batman movie…Batman twenty-five or whatever it is, is opening next week. If we could time it with the release of the movie, I bet my contacts at the movie distributor could get us some free air play and maybe even get us the searchlight prop we could use. With the free publicity, we could make a big event out of it. How could she ignore Hollywood?"

The mayor thought about it as he paced. "OK, full media blitz! Take out the ads in the paper, use the radio, and get the TV guys to cover it. We have to make sure she knows about it and what kind of event it's going to be. We'll offer her overnight celebrity status…Get the art department to turn that picture in the paper into a silhouette that we can put on the searchlight. What woman can refuse that?"

Edwards immediately thought that the mayor's three divorces didn't qualify him as an expert on women, but he said nothing and went about as ordered.

I remember thinking what a douche the mayor was when I heard his plan. But I contained myself and my comments on the Web site and in the paper. I wasn't doing much better with my project of meeting the woman born during the Super Bowl. I had met two more of them with no green/blue eye flashes, no indication of super female status, meaning no SSS episodes or wiener-that-wouldn't-work.

CHAPTER TEN

Rebecca Dupes the Simple Fellow

That night I had just met the next one on the list, Rebecca Sans, at the same coffee shop where I had met Jennifer Lowe. After some initial discomfort, I finally got used to being there, sitting at exactly the same table as I had with Jennifer, in fact.

Rebecca was a lively, bright girl, but no superwoman. She was a graphic designer who wore up-to-date clothes, short brown hair, and a pair of rose-colored glasses. We did the survey shtick, drank some coffee, and chatted awhile. After a while , she talked about the Web site she was working on, and it dawned on me what a graphic designer does for a living. With my site becoming a cluttered mess as I tried to maintain and grow it, I spontaneously offered her the job of redoing my B.I.B. site. She said that sounded "cool" working with the B.I.B. and agreed, just that quickly. She said she could start in a couple of days. We agreed to talk again, soon, and she was gone. Amazing how my policy of not thinking things through often comes back to bite me in the ass.

As I packed my Penn State materials in my bag, I revealed a little hole gouged into the table top. I ran my finger over it, thinking it was an odd shape.

A guy who was cleaning tables next to me saw what I was doing, "Yeah, that's weird, huh? I had to dig that out. Somebody melted a pen and it left that hole. It was a bitch getting it out."

"Melted a pen? How do you do that?"

"Beats me, all I know is, if you look down in the center you can see part of the clip of the pen with the brand name on it. I couldn't get it all out."

I looked in the center and saw what he was talking about. It was the same expensive brand chrome pen I had left with Jennifer Lowe.

That was the first time I even began to wonder, could there be more than one? Along with that came wondering what Rebecca Sans would be like in bed, or Jennifer Lowe, for that matter, or Rebecca and Jennifer. I was being very thoughtful and philosophical that night but not totally focused.

Rebecca Sans reached for her mobile phone as she bounced toward her car with a big smile on her face. She dialed a speed dial and waited beside her car door for it to answer. "Hi. I just got done. We talked for an hour or so. We did the stupid survey. I tried to act interested…No, I don't think he's gay…Well, he's probably just marked…Sure, it went just as you thought it would. He offered me the job, and I start in a couple of days… Of course, I think it's a good idea. How else are we gonna find her? Believe me, I've tried everything else…You're right, she could have been the one who marked him…No, he's not English either…OK, I'll see ya later." She hung up, took a look back at the coffee shop, smiled knowingly, then got into the driver's seat and set off on her way home.

On the other end of the line, Jennifer Lowe was more serious, her face blank, her mind calculating, as she closed her mobile phone and finished tying a young man's hand to her bed frame.

CHAPTER ELEVEN

The Searchlight Event: Another Magical Night

The buildup for the B.I.B. searchlight event was everything the mayor had promised and proved to be a boon for Dr. Jones and myself, being the only two bona fide B.I.B. experts available. He and I bounced from radio program to TV program, offering our opinions and knowledge of the B.I.B, sometimes even passing each other in the hall en route to one show or another. Everyone eventually asked, "So do you think she will show up after the searchlight goes on?" Thinking the mayor was an ass and the B.I.B. was calling the shots, it was tough for me to answer diplomatically. So I finally developed a spiel about how well the mayor was going about the preparations for the event, and who would be there, and how much I hoped she would turn up, but, "You know women." At any rate, it proved a boon for my ability to plug the Web site. Hits on the site grew. Advertisers came a running; my income grew. Best of all, chicks began to notice me, big time (for the first time).

Rebecca Sans had reworked the site just in time for the searchlight event. *She proved to be a graphic genius, what a "lucky" find for me,* I thought. She turned my hodgepodge of windows, buttons, and text into a sleek, mysterious, and feminine tribute to the B.I.B. The colors of the backgrounds and headers were dark and secretive but never black. She used purples and violets and some neon tones. From somewhere, she got B.I.B. silhouettes in various positions that appeared and disappeared around the screen.

My favorite part of the site were the three video games visitors (and Web site owners) could play for free. With them, Rebecca definitely outdid herself. I didn't even ask her to make them—that I can remember anyway.

The first game was B.I.B. Rescue. In that one, your custom tuned character walked through the realistic high-definition streets of Scranton, avoiding speeding beer trucks, mob drive-bys, road construction, bill collectors, bullies, and did I mention speeding beer trucks, in the hope of being "saved" by the B.I.B. Around the next corner could be a twenty-ton diesel or the rescuing arms of a digital B.I.B. flying you off to add fifty thousand points to your score.

The second game was B.I.B. Pub Crawler. In that one, you go from Scranton pub to Scranton pub searching for the B.I.B. It was also done in fabulously detailed graphics. The graphics were so good, we were able to customize each bar to its real appearance and sell ads on the game to the bars. The concept was simple; you only have so much money to spend buying drinks. The more drinks you buy friends, the more clues you get as to her whereabouts. Unfortunately, the more drinks you buy, the more are bought for you to drink in return. If you find her drinking a Miner Lite before you get drunk or run out of money, you win. The game was adjusted for body weight and constantly showed a meter of your blood alcohol level. You could lower your alcohol level with costly coffee stops and earn or lose points by picking up the right or wrong person in the bar, adjusted for sexual preference naturally. A drop-down menu of pickup lines was available. Funny faces and playing drinking games could also earn you points and clues.

The third was a real shoot 'em up version of the antler game. The user controlled the rifle and tried to shoot bar patrons wearing antlers. You got fifty points for each antler wearer you hit but lost five hundred points for each person you hit without antlers. Hit the flying B.I.B. and you lost, for sure. It even had a challenging RFD vision level, in which your ability to aim and fire was limited to the capabilities of an RFD. We ended up offering a prize for anyone hitting an antler wearer on that level.

With Rebecca's success and my lazy grasshopper nature, I turned more and more of the site over to her. Now she was the first to receive any e-mail leads, sightings, or documents sent in for the reward program. I let her view just about everything and decide for me if it was something she should handle or if I needed to deal with it. I gave her access and authority to the entire site. This she did completely remotely. She texted, e-mailed, called me by phone, but never really needed to meet with me. Like an RFD with an antler helmet on backward, I had given her the keys to the candy store, and she was eating all my candy.

Advertisers loved the site, and the local Miner's Lite beer distributor not only advertised and linked the site, but co-created a B.I.B. Miner's Lite T-shirt that we sold on the site, based on the photo with her holding the Miner's Lite bottle at Skelly's. Owning the copyrights for the terms "B.I.B." and "We're not Afraid Anymore," we had a piece of all the T-shirt action as the Miner's Lite and "Not Afraid" T-shirts became the unofficial official attire for the Searchlight Event.

That led Rebecca to create the B.I.B. Online Store for all the B.I.B. products people were coming up with. An Ohio company came up with masks and capes. There were coffee cups, beer mugs, glasses, letter openers, stickers, but most of all were the T-shirts. Rebecca's system directly referred all the orders to a subcontracted T-shirt manufacturer, but I knew they had a hard time keeping the orders filled. Street vendors planned to sell them the night of the event, but supplies that could be made in time were limited. I hadn't been able to meet the B.I.B. for the second time, and she was already making me into a surprising financial success. Nevertheless, more than the money and the notoriety, I hoped she would show up or, better yet, that I would somehow find her again. The money and the celebrity were turning my head, but my heart and below were locked on finding her.

The preparations at the event site were elaborate, in more ways than one. The event was timed with the release of the latest Batman movie. The mayor had received the movie prop searchlight he had requested, and it was placed on a high balcony outside of the mayor's conference room using a helicopter. I covered the copter lift for the local news. The conference room was turned into a media room complete with refreshments. Only invited media members and dignitaries were allowed in the area around the searchlight. The mayor made certain everyone knew that he was the one promoting the event. With the public demand for the B.I.B. growing, he hoped to skyrocket his popularity.

Gregorio also had made elaborate preparations for the event. On the buildings across from the searchlight location, which were to be kept with no illumination on the night of the event, he had placed four teams of snipers and a central spotter at various angles and elevations from the searchlight and the podium next to it. This way, they would have a clear shot of the entire balcony. The placement of the searchlight and the small podium were, in fact, made by Gregorio's spotter to ensure his men would have the best possible shot.

The spotter would control all four teams of snipers via a radio link, not only to keep one team from going "maverick " but also to provide the power of multiple shots ensuring a hit. Also, any authority with the nerve to raise his head after the shots were fired would be confused as to the number and direction of the shots, as they echoed off the downtown skyline. Gregorio imported a team of snipers from Providence and Newark that were supposed to be the best available to supplement his two local teams. The B.I.B. would be walking into the searchlight event, but they would be carrying her out in pieces.

Of course, the mayor was not made aware of the presence of the snipers. He was led to believe that this first meeting would be to make contact with the B.I.B., and taking her out would happen more discretely, later, when he was not around. They did this out of fear that, if the mayor knew of the snipers, something about his nervousness or body language would betray the plan. Anyone knowing that bullets would soon be hitting the person next to them would be a nervous wreck. Gregorio reasoned that if a stray bullet, fragment, or ricochet were to also hit the mayor that he could be easily replaced.

Thirty seconds after the shots were fired, the spotter would cue technicians to cut the power to the entire building, creating panic and chaos that would cover everyone's escape.

There I was the night of the searchlight event, standing among the crowd on the balcony with my media badge on and a glass of champagne in my hand. I had even worn an all-black outfit as a personal joke to the B.I.B. should she arrive and see me. I hoped she'd get the joke. We all stood in the cold night air, but no one was bothered by it. As I mingled, I could hear the greatest speculation was about how the B.I.B. would choose to arrive. Would she fly in, walk in, just appear? Was she going to be a disguised member of the crowd and then suddenly remove her street clothes to reveal her costume and reveal herself? Was she you? Was she me? Or being that it was Batman premiere night, would she drive up in some high-tech car or motorcycle? Would one of those bat ropes suddenly raise her up to the balcony from the sidewalk below?

My money was on what I had seen outside O'Malley's the first time I had seen her. A fog would appear and then she would appear from out of it. That was my guess.

With all I had been through in recent days, and even though I thought the mayor's plan was lame, I could not help but feel a pounding in my chest and feel vibrantly alive with expectation. I had no clue what was going to happen and, for the first time in my life, I was quite happy for things to be that way. I was not controlling this, but it was completely exhilarating. Right there I should have known the rug was about to be pulled.

Finally, the mayor emerged from the Media Room to an enthusiastic round of applause. The mayor had every right to feel that this was one of his moments. He walked over to the podium, accepted the applause, opened his coat and jacket to expose a Miner's Lite/B.I.B. T-shirt, and after milking the renewed applause, began, "Tonight is an historic time. It is a proud moment for me as your mayor as, with the lighting of this searchlight, we invite the woman known fondly to us all as the B.I.B. to become our partner in moving our city forward to better and safer times."

The applause spiked again. I stood and thought to myself, *That T-shirt is mine. The B.I.B. name, that's mine.* It blew my mind, could this be happening?

"So without further ado, let me here and now say to the B.I.B., the City of Scranton needs you, wants to be your partner, and is asking for your help. Please join us, whenever you see this light."

With that, the mayor nodded to a technician who started the generator that ran the searchlight. When the generator had reached full power, the technician nodded back to the mayor, who dramatically raised a large lever on the electrical box that controlled the light. A huge beam burst forth several hundred feet into the sky until the beam found enough cloud cover to support a gigantic sexy silhouette of the B.I.B. surrounded in a white circle. Everyone in the crowd screamed joyously, but you could barely hear them over the sound of the diesel generator. With the sound and the fact that we all stared up at the light, we were not aware of the response to the beacon, but it was immediate.

On the streets below came the sounds of car horns and then the sound of crashing metal as drivers, whose attention had been drawn to the sky, plowed headlong into other cars and lampposts, ran up over curbs onto mailboxes, or into the windows of retail stores. There were shouts. There were screams. Virtually every dog in the city began to bark nonstop. Small fires erupted. City workers stepped straight into open manholes. The engineers of a freight train could not help themselves from staring at the silhouette and ran a stop signal, derailing the engine and three cars.

Gregorio's spotter lost track of his snipers. He called to them on the radio with no response. Then the spotter looked up at the silhouette and dropped his radio to the ground.

At the air traffic control center that covered Scranton, controllers put down their coffee cups and spread the alarm as dozens of small aircraft and a few larger aircraft inbound to the Wilkes-Barre/Scranton International Airport suddenly left their flight plans and began converging on the air space above the city. They became frantic, watching the blips on their screens leave their nicely spaced order and begin a beeline for one another. A squadron of fighter jets was scrambled in fear that a mass highjacking was underway.

On the balcony, the mayor stared hopefully at the silhouette. After a few minutes, he noticed small orange and red explosions around it. He smiled and turned to his assistant, Edwards, and had to literally shout in his ear, "Good Job. I think the fireworks are a great effect!"

After a second, Edwards shouted back in the mayor's ear, "Sir, I did not contract for any fireworks."

The mayor thought for a long moment; then his jaw dropped as he realized the "fireworks" were aircraft colliding after being drawn like moths to the B.I.B.'s image on the silhouette. He ran to the railing of the balcony to look down into the street. The totally stopped zigzag pattern of the cars below on the street and the sidewalk made him cringe. The image of a city bus, driven halfway into a coffee shop confirmed his worst fears. As slowly and stately as an asshole can walk, he moved to the searchlight and pulled down the handle. He extinguished the generator and its beam, put his head against the searchlight, and pounded it with open palm.

A mobile phone rang; Edwards answered it and handed it to the mayor. "Sir, it's the Federal Aviation Administration for you."

The mayor pounded his palm again and again.

Edwards stammered, trying to make sense of events then said to the mayor, "I…I guess we hyped this a little too much."

The mayor turned to Edwards while he boiled inside, then came at him like an attacking wolf, "Ya think!"

While the Searchlight fiasco was happening, Paige, her friend, and I were attending the Batman movie premiere; none of us were crazy about superhero action movies, least of all me, but the latest movie was supposed to be filled with "hunks." We sat watching the movie, wearing the B.I.B. T-shirts we had purchased from street vendors just before the searchlight was turned on. I wore the Miner's Lite beer/ B.I.B. shirt while the girls wore girly colored versions of the "We're not afraid anymore" shirt. It was hilarious to me to be the B.I.B. and wear a B.I.B. T-shirt with no one the wiser. How they had expected their lame event would motivate me into the public eye was beyond me. Anyway, the T-shirts were hot; well, I think so anyway.

Periodically throughout the entire movie, Paige glared at me, embarrassed in front of her friend, for her mother's laughter during the serious parts, including the fight scenes. Every time Batman would take a punch from a henchman or he would pull out some gadget from his belt, I would sputter, shake my head, and mumble "wimp" or "pansy." Eventually, Paige gave up and just tried to distance herself with a tilted body lean. I mean, seriously, Batman wouldn't last a day in my world.

On the way out after the movie, Paige's friend asked me if I liked the movie. "It was OK," I said before sneezing. "I didn't know it was a comedy," I added and then chuckled, remembering some scene in the movie. Paige's friend looked at Paige, who just shook her head and shrugged her shoulders.

When we got to the lobby, it was as if we had entered a different world. The first set of doors to the theatre was just so much broken glass, and a car with flat tires was in the lobby. The second set of doors was blocked on the outside by a car that had struck one of the outside supports to the building and turned broadside against the doors. Everyone was filing slowly, uncertainly out the third undamaged set of doors.

"What happened?" I asked a theater worker who had begun sweeping broken glass.

"When the mayor's searchlight went on downtown tonight, everybody was looking up, I guess. They say it was hypnotizing. Nobody was watching where they were going. I heard it's like this all over town."

"Looking up at what? Did the B.I.B. show up?" asked Paige, excited.

"I was behind the counter and didn't see anything. I heard everybody was looking at the searchlight and couldn't take their eyes off it." He shrugged and kept sweeping.

*I led the girls out into the street as a half-naked, panic-stricken man ran by through the cold night air and was gone. Out in the street, the RFDs (a term I learned from the B.I.B. Web site) had moved their antler game out of a local bar into the street, running and ducking behind cars that were on the sidewalk or had hit one another. Drivers stood around arguing and trying to reach 911 or a tow truck on jammed mobile phone lines. Other drivers whose cars were not that badly damaged tried to maneuver with crumpled fenders, dangling bumpers, or rubbing tires. **What a bunch of assholes**, I thought to myself.*

"It may take awhile, but we'll get home, girls. Don't worry," I said, sneezing, feeling a cold take over my head, and leading the girls to the parking lot.

Paige's friend asked, "Did the B.I.B. show up or not?"

"No, she didn't," I answered definitively, without any apparent way of knowing.

At the searchlight event, it took a long while for the crowd to understand that they were being told to leave, most having no idea what had happened until they got to the streets. What had happened wasn't wasted on the hippie/geeky mayor's assistant known in the papers as the one who came up with the searchlight idea. He crept along the wall until he had passed the mayor, found the door, and then he was gone in a flash.

I had dropped so quickly from a high to a low that I took it very hard. I hung my head and just stood as the crowd flowed by me. The mayor had escaped early on with all of his advisers. The news crews and their cameramen ran to cover the real story in the streets below. I remember at the time taking no special notice of it, but I saw Jennifer Lowe packed into the crowd as they filed by me. She wore a long, dark coat and a beret, but there was no mistaking her face, those glasses, and the familiar mound of the twins under her coat. She looked over at me, paused her gaze, and then looked ahead without the slightest sign of recognition on her face. Had my mind been working then, I would have questioned her appearance and saved myself a lot of grief later. But oh those knockers.

Finally, it was just me and a few workers in the cleanup crew. I stared up at the night sky that had been so alive with anticipation but now just felt cold and dark as the wind blew discarded cocktail napkins around my head.

On the neighboring buildings, the sniper teams tried to piece together what had happened. They all felt a blank period of time in their heads starting at when they had taken aim, till now, with their equipment on the ground and their targets leaving the scene.

The spotter hadn't thought it through but instinctively knew the mission was over, "Abort, all teams, abort. Let's get the hell out of here."

CHAPTER 12

The Mob Gets Even—or Odd…Whatever

Even though Gregorio Gambrelli had known of the search-light event disaster immediately after it had happened, the reminder of it in the next morning's paper stirred the embers of his anger. He sat in his booth at Giovanni's scowling at the front page.

"B.I.B. A NO SHOW," read the headline.

"EMERGENCY SERVICES OVERWHLEMED BY HUNDREDS OF ACCIDENTS," read a smaller heading, accompanied by:

"FAA SEARCHING WRECKAGE OF EIGHT AIRCRAFT FOR CAUSE OF CRASHES"

"INSURANCE INSTITUTE SAYS IT MAY TAKE WEEKS TO TOTAL LAST NIGHT'S DAMAGE"

"MAYOR DECLINES COMMENT ON NIGHT'S EVENTS"

"10% OFF SALE AT MACY'S"

Gregorio slammed down the paper and it slid across the table, falling to the floor in an unfolded mess. "…Just 10 percent? Such bullshit," he muttered. He looked up at the pictures of his ancestors ringing the booth, and they all appeared to be laughing at him, especially his paternal grandmother, who had never liked him. He imagined her sticking out her tongue and giving him the raspberries. He lowered his head, a man defeated by his trust for a politician. He reflected for a long moment, smiled, and then raised his head back up as a mob leader who was in charge. He fumbled through the pockets of his suit and pulled out the "special" mobile phone, but then pulled out another and another, until five of them were on the table before him. The sixth and last proved to be the one to call the mayor. As much as he disdained the mayor, he could still be useful. But this time, the plan would be his; this time, the mayor's role would be limited to what he could handle. With that he made the call.

Vito escorted the mayor to Gregorio's booth and then stood beside the table. The sheepish, neutered mayor slid into the booth like a child caught with his hand in the liquor cabinet.

"I have a job for you, and this time don't cock it up, putz," Gregorio said and began shaking a forkful of pasta at the mayor.

With his head down, the mayor answered, "What do you want me to do?"

"You talk to the DA and get the jurisdiction changed on Tony Turtulio's indictment. Get him moved from city jail to county. Let all the details of the transfer leak to the media, and be sure all the right cops are driving escort for the transfer."

The mayor was quiet for a moment, trying to measure his response to avoid sounding combative. "You've already made it clear that Tony will never serve a day of prison time. She'll know you're gonna spring him. She'll be waiting for you," he said, already defeated.

Gregorio got instantly angry, could not reach the mayor over the long table, and gestured to Vito, who then smacked the mayor on the side of the head. "I don't pay you to think anymore, understand? You just do it! Understand? Comprenda? Capisce?"

The mayor nodded. Gregorio nodded. Vito pulled the mayor out of the booth and sent him on his way.

After finishing the forkful in his hand, Gregorio wiped his mouth with his napkin and began making phone calls. He knew the B.I.B. would not let the Tool escape; he counted on it. While she stopped the crew, he would send to break the Tool out of the transfer truck, he would have every available thug, henchmen, and gun he could muster waiting for her to fall into the trap. He smiled as he dialed the first call and then flipped off a finger gesture at his grandmother's picture. He imagined her responding in kind.

The sneezes of a few days before had turned into a full-blown cold for me. I lay on my couch with a sore red nose and tissue in hand, watching the evening news. I had been to work that day but now realized I shouldn't have. I sipped a Miner's Lite beer, for purely medicinal purposes, feeling that it would do wonders for the aches and pains.

From the TV came the name Tony the Tool Turtulio, which caught my attention.

"…Sources, not wishing to be identified, have already stated that the Tool will never serve a day of his sentence. The transfer will take place tomorrow morning, accompanied by a heavily armed escort. Parts of several city streets will be closed during the transfer…"

I sniffled, then sipped my beer. I reflected for a long moment, then said to myself in a very nasal tone, "If you boys wanna play, we'll play," then blew my nose.

Just then, Paige came into the room, "Are we eating dinner or are we gonna starve?"

Jimmy, the cop, driving the prison transfer van, was a veteran of several of the mob's "arranged" events. They had gotten him promotions, money to blow in Vegas, and paid for his kid's schooling. On the morning of the Tool's transfer, he had lobbied for his nephew to ride shotgun in the van: his first exposure to duty that wouldn't go like he had learned at the police academy.

Understandably, his nephew, the rookie, was nervous, as the truck carrying them and the Tool approached the abandoned parking lot, where they were to change escort cars. "Jimmy, I don't like the looks of this. Why are we stopping here? We're sitting ducks."

"Don't worry. Just follow orders," said Jimmy, as he stopped the van and his escort cars drove away, "In a few minutes it will be all over."

After a couple of minutes, the rookie flinched and started to get up out of his seat, when he heard the back door to the van open. Jimmy put his hand on his shoulder and pushed him back down in his seat, "Relax. Just relax."

"Yeah, Officer Thompson's back there with that scumbag. We'll be OK," said the rookie, trying to convince himself.

The rookie remained nervous but Jimmy sat back in his chair and sipped some coffee. "Just relax. We're cool."

When the truck rocked back and forth or up and down, Jimmy again reassured his nephew with, "No problem," "Don't worry," or "Easy peasy."

Several minutes later, they heard the back door slam closed and someone slapped the side of the van to indicate they were ready. Jimmy sat up and got ready to drive. When the second set of police cars arrived as escorts, Jimmy said, "OK, here we go. Home free." As he put the truck in gear, he pulled in line behind the escorts, "Easy as pie." None of these folksy phrases helped the rookie feel any better.

But when they arrived at the county jail without incident, the rookie had chilled—a little. He was up and out of the van while Jimmy took his time. The rookie unlocked the rear door, began to open it, when the weight of something pushed the door open without effort. The unconscious body of a man dressed in a suit fell at his feet. The rookie instinctively unstrapped and raised his 9 mm. When the man didn't move, he turned to look into the van to find it littered with unconscious men. He was bending to handcuff the body on the ground, when Jimmy rounded the back of the truck and stopped in stark amazement.

"Jimmy, look," began the rookie, excited beyond belief. "This is 'No Neck' Nicky, and that's Franky the 'Fish,'" he said, pointing into the van. "There are outstanding warrants on all of these guys! Give me your cuffs," he said, taking them and putting them on the Fish. "We're gonna need a lot more cuffs."

Jimmy paused, knowing that this was not going down as planned, but knowing that he needed to flow with it. He also knew what good a couple of dozen collars of known criminals could do for his career and chances of early retirement. After an instant, he ran to the front of the van and returned with a box of plastic-wrap restraints that would have to do for now. He and the rookie were busy cuffing, searching, and stacking the henchmen like logs on the garage floor when other officers arrived, marveled at the sight, and began to dig in and help. When they reached the front of the van, under the pile, they found the Tool with a major league black eye, unconscious but well. Officer Thompson was there too with a jaw that just didn't look right. They called the medics.

After the "catch" had been revived and carted off to jail, the rookie stood tall and accepted handshakes and congratulations from anyone and everyone on a job well done, for a rookie. When everyone had moved on, he stood behind the van for a long while admiring the scene. He bent down when he noticed some plastic-wrap cuffs that hadn't been used lying where the pile of mobsters had been minutes before. He proudly picked up the unused cuffs, but then he noticed a used tissue that had been under the stack. He picked it up with ends of two fingers, "Someone's got a bad cold," he said to himself.

Gregorio Gambrelli's morning had been going well, full of confidence and anticipation. Even when he failed to hear reports of their success, he did not falter; after all, there were also no reports of failure. Little did he know that there was no one left from the hit squad to report anything.

The first hint of trouble, in fact disaster, came from a snitch at the police headquarters who regularly called when any of Gregorio's boys found their way there.

"Who's it this time?" barked Gregorio when he knew who was on the line.

The man stammered, "Well, it's everyone…Franky, Nicky, Topo…there must be twenty or thirty guys here!"

Gregorio felt the cannoli go bad in his stomach. Without any further information, he knew exactly what had happened. "…And Tony?"

"Yeah, yeah Tony's here too…He don't look good…What do you want me to do, boss… Boss?"

Gregorio sent the mobile phone flying. It missed Vito by inches, then flew through the kitchen door that had just swung open, landing with a splat in a freshly prepared pot of pasta. He took a bowl of linguine with marinara sauce that Vito had been working on and sent it flying into the side of an unlucky waiter's head.

Vito had seen this before and knew to get clear and stay clear until Gambrelli's anger had claimed enough victims to cool its wrath.

Gambrelli's head fell into his hands and he tried to calm himself, but that didn't work. He looked out the corner of his eye at the family pictures around the booth and imagined that they all had turned their backs on him, except his grandmother, who laughed at him with her thumbs in her ears.

The mayor had on the large TV in his office and listened to the special report.

"Today, police agents have captured twenty-seven alleged members of organized crime in the city. In what has been described as a massive sting operation, police used the transfer of Tony Turtulio to draw out the alleged gang members who allegedly tried to free him from a prison van. Never in the history of the city has there been such a massive apprehension of known criminals. Police predict that today's sting will deal a major blow to criminal operations that will be felt for months or even years to come," said the female reporter live from the police headquarters.

"Thank you, Sally. Great news…And finally, some good news for our beleaguered mayor," concluded the male newsroom anchor.

As the anchor spoke, the mayor stood behind his desk and repeatedly pounded his head into the wall.

Across town, I walked up to my supervisor with a doctor's note that explained why I had been late to work that morning. My supervisor, an old prune of a lady, gave me a good look over. The puffy watery eyes, the red runny nose, the mouth-breathing, all seemed to confirm that I was truly sick. The old prune thought about which she wanted more, for me to get back to work or for me to get away and not infect her with my cold. Finally, she decided to send me back to work and would just stay away from me for a few days, before rubbing her hands with hand sanitizer.

What she didn't see were the abrasions on my arms and legs and the knife wound on my side, that I had stitched closed myself. Being a single mom with superpowers, working for an asshole could really be a bitch.

The paper, the next day, ran a big picture of Jimmy and the Rookie smiling. Above it was the headline, "Local Boys Take a Bite Out of Crime." Amazingly, the department's attempt to spin the van event as a planned sting seemed to hold up. I thought they wouldn't even have the nerve to try it, but it worked.

On the other hand, I ran my Web site with the certitude that the B.I.B. had foiled the mob's attempt at freeing the Tool. The logic and logistics behind this assertion were strong. Common sense—no, even less than common sense—no, even an RFD could see that two officers could not take down the Gambrelli family in a morning. Had the B.I.B. come out and taken credit for the collars, everyone would have believed it in a second. When she didn't take credit for the Tool and did not show up at the searchlight event, her window of opportunity to fame and fortune passed. Worst of all, my T-shirt sales dipped…a lot. I had no desire to go back to actually working for a living.

I was so concerned about my business, that I played only one round of B.I.B. Rescue and three rounds of B.I.B. Pub Crawler before lunch and only twice that many in the afternoon. In Pub Crawler, I thought I had located the B.I.B. at Skelly's bar, but I ran into the Nelson twins, and you could guess what happened…again. Those two (four) can drink.

I remember those two events, the searchlight, and the twenty-seven collars, as being a temporary climax for the B.I.B., at least from my point of view. I began to call that period, the Two Days, because the tumultuous events were so close together. It just seemed like everything slowed down a bit, reorganized, and consolidated after that.

I didn't see Dr. Jones for a while. The mayor had added him to his staff after realizing he needed something to rebuild his Swiss-cheesed image. His pollsters told him that the public would approve of further connection with him to the B.I.B. So he took on Jones.

For Organized Crime, it was a consolidation. For Gregorio Gambrelli it was the end of a crime family. There is a military adage that, if you cut an army off from its leadership and reduce the fighting force by half, that even with the large number of the remaining half, the army will, in effect, cease to function. That is what occurred. With all of Gambrelli's middle managers in jail, he became separated from his foot soldiers. Other members of his organization fled, fearing that those in prison would be cutting deals. The other crime families became like sharks smelling blood in the water. It was only a matter of time until one of Gambrelli's corporals, a young man with the ambition of ten, cut a deal with the Providence mob to fund him. Quickly, the old mob had to fall in line with him or be run over. After Gambrelli's second-in-command ended up swimming upside down in the river, the Gambrelli foot soldiers, including Vito, jumped to get in line. In a morning's work, the B.I.B. had used Gambrelli's overconfidence to bring him to his knees.

CHAPTER THIRTEEN

Frustration, Road Trip, Beer—Did I Mention Frustration?

For the B.I.B., it seemed to be a slow time as well, a time to reevaluate. There were far fewer sightings reported on my Web site. After the two days, I think she took a rest and began to evaluate what she was really doing.

In the days that followed, I even took occasion to visit the old barkeep at O'Malley's. Whether I wanted to get connected with the place where I had last seen her, or I really expected her to be there, or I hoped the old barkeep had seen her, I don't know. But it felt comfortable to be there and feel how far I had come.

The barkeep wasn't sure how to take me. "Hey, how have you been?" I asked.

"Respectable, I guess," he said, wiping dry some glasses.

"She been in lately?"

"She...? Oh, you mean the blonde bird...Ms. Twenty Dollars, I call her. Always remember a good tipper. No, I ain't had the pleasure since that night...Shame."

I handed him $100 and my new fancy business card. "My offer is still good. She shows up, call me right away, and there's another $100 for your trouble."

"Like I said, always remember a good tip…But you ain't always been a good tipper now, have ya? Must be doin' all right for yourself."

"Respectable," I said, looking around and noting that the bar looked just as it did in the B.I.B. Pub Crawler game, right down to the tablecloths with stains.

Little did he know that while he and the barkeep reminisced, no more than two blocks away, I sat drinking with friends at Flanagan's. Paige would be at her friend's house for the weekend, so I felt I was due some fun, a break from the intensity of recent days. My friends from work were entirely clueless about my activities as the B.I.B. On the occasions when I was available, my friends welcomed the opportunity to "put the antlers on" with me. I would transform from a shy, quiet type into a wild "fish face" making showboat. Even if the only men we met were RFDs, we still had a good time.

On this night, I was feeling hemmed in with frustration. I knew I had helped, in fact, saved the lives of hundreds of people in recent weeks. I had kept an airliner from crashing, brought a kidnapped little girl home to her mother, brought down a crime family, and exposed an inept and corrupt mayor, all within a matter of weeks. I had learned to use and focus my power without being corrupted by it. I had inspired the coolest Internet video games, my fav being the Pub Crawler. Yet, through it all, I felt empty. Strange as it sounded, there it was. I had to admit that I did not feel joyous but, instead, was frustrated and empty. A part of it all was missing. If I couldn't even find myself on Pub Crawler, how could I ever find my purpose in reality?

Unable to put my finger on it, I concluded that it was my time to blow off some steam, not over analyze, and just "be" for the next few days. I was going to have some fun, but making fish faces can only take you so far. By now, certain types of fun had become difficult for me.

*In recent months, it had begun to take more and more to get me off…I mean sexually. Recently, whenever I had just begun to be in the general neighborhood of satisfaction, I would end up breaking one thing or another on my partner's anatomy. My last two boyfriends had ended up in the hospital, neither wanting a repeat performance. I sat feeling the weight of that reality for a moment, then thought, **Just screw it**, and downed the remaining half of my Miner's Lite in one long drag. "I deserve some fun," I said to myself and struck a perfect fish face, complete with moving mouth for my friends, who roared their approval.*

That night, reports started coming in of Miner's Lite beer trucks falling from the sky, minus their drivers and their cargo. The first couple of news reports were in time for the late night news and were covered like one would cover a joke or an event like a charity domino fall. But when they continued all weekend, the coverage gained concern and became criminal. As the B.I.B. had used beer trucks before and was forever bonded to Miner's Lite by the picture from Skelly's featured on the B.I.B. T-shirts, it became a foregone conclusion that the B.I.B. was responsible. In fact, there was no other suspect possible to carry and drop a large truck. As the media loves to tarnish and bring down the image of actors caught with DUIs or in affairs with nannies, they loved to rip at the image of the B.I.B. When a truck fell in the playground of a then closed day care center, smashing the swings and teeter-totter, the media was in an uproar over what could have happened had the center been open.

In a weekend, there were suddenly calls that the B.I.B. was not above the law and needed to be brought to justice. Another call was made for the mayor to communicate with her. It was the random unsuspecting appearance of the trucks that made their menace frightening, like walking in a minefield, where any step a person took could be the last, without warning; even while just sitting in their houses no one felt safe.

Rebecca added falling beer trucks to the hazards on the B.I.B. Rescue game.

Sunday night's news reported that the mayor would hold a news conference the next morning.

I awoke uncertainly. My eyes were fogged and my head pounded. I felt my stomach tumbling. I knew I was lying in a dark cluttered bedroom, but that was about the extent of my knowledge. Where it was, when it was, or how it had become so, I had no idea. Next, I put together that I was naked, lying on my stomach, the room reeked of sex, and the heavy drapes had been drawn. Beyond them, I could see sunshine through the cracks. With effort, I righted myself and sat on the edge of the bed, resting my head in my hands, then pushing back a mop of hair. I sighed and then went through the considerable effort to rise. I staggered a few feet to the window, fingered back the drape, and saw a midday street in Las Vegas below. The row of theme hotels and casinos made it unmistakable. "Holy shit," I mumbled to myself, sobering up some from the discovery. I moved around the hotel room finding my clothes, yet somehow missed finding my panties. After they didn't turn up, I decided to get dressed anyway and venture out to find what enlightening discoveries awaited me outside the door.

I paused at the door and then pulled it open to reveal the living room of a hotel suite with another bedroom and small kitchen. Ten feet to my left stood a young, thin, college-aged man in his boxer shorts. When he looked over and saw me, panic ran over his face. He groaned, cupped his hands around his swollen, red genitals, and slowly backed away from me, as if I were an enraged bear. He backed into the bathroom and closed and locked the door. To my right, another young man dropped from the sofa like a fish dropping to the deck of a boat. He grunted while dragging himself and a nonfunctioning leg behind the protection of the sofa. I stood in startled amazement trying to figure out the scene. Then, from the kitchen, a third spindly, young, college boy wearing only sweat pants slid toward me and spoke. "Good Afternoon," was all he said.

"Good Afternoon," I said, walking toward him slowly. "This may sound a bit silly, but I've figured out that this is Las Vegas, but I have no idea when it is or who you are."

The young man took a couple of steps toward me, hunched over and crippled, like an eighty-five-year-old. "I'm Kevin. The dude in the bathroom is Josh. Cory's behind the sofa. And Matt was the guy we dropped off at the hospital."

"Hospital?"

"Oh, right, dude, you probably don't remember him. That's cool… Anyway, they say he should be able to walk again with some good old therapy."

I pointed at him and his hunched back. "Did I do this to you?"

Kevin smiled, "Oh yeah, dude. You drained a year's worth out of me, I'll bet…just got raisins down there now. But, it's cool."

"Sorry, I'm really sorry…Rough night, I guess."

"Rough? Oh yeah, rough…" He smiled again, nodding. "You know rough doesn't really cover it.…Awesome, It was awesome.… Dude, I never saw a chick move like that." Then he said upon reflection, staring at the floor, "They'll probably make us pay for those holes in the ceiling. My dad's really gonna be pissed…How am I gonna explain that one, man?"

"What day is this?" I asked beginning to get upset and frustrated, mopping my hair back again.

"It's a righteous Sunday afternoon in Vegas, man…" He took a drink from a beer. "Can I get you one? You were downing them like a pro last night. Never seen a chick drink like that before," he said, indicating the table covered with filled and empty Miner's Lite bottles.

"No, no thanks…Have you seen…" I said gesturing to my waist and crotch.

"Your underwear?"

I nodded.

He smiled again and pointed to the living room ceiling, and the panties that were up there. "Don't worry, it's all good…They say you can tell if you had a good time by whether they stick to the ceiling… Those have been up there a long time…a really long time…Can I get them down for ya?"

I looked down totally embarrassed by now. "Don't bother…My treat."

"Cool."

"Have you seen my coat, my bag?"

"Over by the door."

"Well, thank you…Kevin. I best be going," I said, backing away red faced and awkward.

When I reached the door, Kevin took a couple of steps forward and asked, "Hey, if in a month my back is up to it, can I call you?"

"Sweet…but I don't think that's ever gonna happen."

"It's cool."

With that, I left the college boys and headed down the hotel hallway trying to figure out what the hell had happened. I quickly put together that my drunken logic had picked Las Vegas, because no one knew me there; what happens in Vegas…you know. Not being known as a slut, figuring out the college kids took a little longer. Finally, I decided, because of my recent problems in breaking men before I could get satisfied, I had reasoned that maybe four men might equal one good one. By the looks of the college kids afterward and by the feeling between my legs, you could cross that theory off the list.

When I reached the window and the elevators at the end of the hall, it was decision time. Paige would be home at 7:00 p.m. Should I fly home or should I "FLY" home?

CHAPTER 14

Hazel Eyes, My Ass!

I was front and center at the mayor's news conference the next morning wearing my press credentials. I had even worn a suit jacket and a new expensive dress shirt; but I wasn't to the tie stage just yet. I was armed with my briefcase, a laptop, my mobile phone, and a new combative reporter's attitude. Christ, I was even forty minutes early. That gave me time for a record score on B.I.B. rescue and another attempt at Pub Crawler, damn those half-price margaritas at Flanagan's. I've never been early for anything in my life, but there I was with my choice of front row seats. Part of me was proud of my newfound skills. The rest of me was just waiting for the crash.

Over time, the room filled, the camera lights went on, and the room bustled with noise and activity. Then exactly at ten o'clock with no warning or fanfare, the mayor and his team filed in and sat behind a long table with a podium and microphone at its center. Among the team was Dr. Jones. Apparently the mayor preferred his scientific mumbo jumbo to my streetwise expertise. When the mayor started to speak, hell, I even had a digital recorder to turn on; scary.

"I would like to start by saying good morning to all the members of the media and to the people of Scranton. Thank you all for coming.

"At nine o'clock last night, in a closed secret session of the City Council, using the emergency powers granted me, I signed an executive order that prohibits the manufacture, transportation, distribution, sale, and consumption of all Miner's Lite beer products within city limits. I further ordered the confiscation of these same products, an endeavor that was carried out by members of law enforcement personnel throughout the evening. We have done this in the name of public safety in response to the series of accidents involving Miner's Beer trucks that have fallen from the sky onto the property of the city's land owners and threatened to harm residents who may be in the random path of these vehicles. I have further impounded all trucks in the Miner's Delivery fleet. This ordinance is temporary and will expire when conditions of public safety have been ensured. Penalties for not complying with the new ordinance are outlined in the copy of the ordinance that will be made available to you all. I will now take your questions."

Hands went up all over the room.

"Yes, here in the second row."

"Has your administration determined that the B.I.B is behind these falling beer trucks, and are there any plans to issue a warrant for her arrest?" asked a young reporter behind me.

"Sorry, Bill, as you know, I cannot comment on an ongoing investigation. I can say, however, that she is a person of interest in the case," BS'ed the mayor.

Voices rang out from all over. "Have you made contact with her?"

"Sorry, let's do this one at a time...How about you, Colin?" he said, pointing across the room.

"Is it safe to say that your administration is beginning to change its attitude toward the benevolence of the B.I.B.? And as a follow-up, what plans do you have to deal with her?"

The mayor smiled and gave a short laugh. "Colin, let me start by saying that there have been a number of incidents that have shown the B.I.B. to have allegedly helped law enforcement. However, her refusal to communicate and these recent, highly dangerous events may force us to rethink our interpretation of past events."

"Are you saying that she is a danger to the community?" the reporter continued.

The mayor smiled again. "I can only let you decide that for yourself once justice has taken its course." Then the mayor pointed to me.

"Mr. Mayor, haven't you really instituted this Miner's Beer embargo as an attempt to 'starve out' the B.I.B., knowing her fondness for Miner's Lite?"

He smiled, ignored me, and pointed to the chubby guy with glasses beside me.

"Have you made any attempts to communicate with the B.I.B. over her possible involvement in the beer truck incidents?" he drawled out slowly.

"There has been no attempt to contact her at this point. At any rate, how do you contact someone who does not want to communicate?" he answered as if a sensitive nerve had been hit.

There was an uproar from all over the room. "What have you done to communicate with her? Why don't you just ask her? Why don't you try to establish communication with her? Couldn't this be resolved easily by talking?" I have to admit I was one of them. It became obvious that the reporter revolt had caused the mayor to lose his control. Beads of sweat formed on his forehead, and he appeared nervous as he held up his arms. "OK, OK, you all know the lengths I have gone through to communicate with that woman, the B.I.B.," he said, looking squarely at the audience but pointing his finger to the side. "I don't have to remind you of the newspaper ads and the plans we made for the searchlight event. Heaven knows how I have tried to bring that woman to the table, and every time, she's just screwed me over…Whenever I've tried, do I get to speak with her? No. I'll tell you what I get, crashing cars and train wrecks, and let's not forget the planes…the God damned planes. They're crashing and crashing. And I'm just waiting like an asshole for someone who never shows…They just kept crashing….Then the FAA's got my ass!" At that point, Edwards, the mayor's assistant, gestured to two large men in the wings who came out and escorted the mayor off the stage, still babbling about the night of the searchlight event.

Edwards went to the podium and introduced Dr. Jones. "Perhaps questions about the B.I.B. could be better answered by the mayor's expert on the subject." Jones rose and took over the podium. He pointed to a woman in the back of the hall.

"Dr. Jones, can you answer the question about communications with the B.I.B.?"

"Certainly, I can try. We have, for some time now, been attempting to locate and communicate with the B.I.B. I began this process even before I joined the mayor's staff. We feel that, with time, we can accomplish this."

"Do you have any idea who she is?" yelled out a voice tired of waiting to be called upon.

"We have little to go on beside the Skelly's photo, which we believe is genuine. From this she appears to be a female, early thirties in age, about five-foot-five to five-foot-seven inches in height, blonde hair, and very piercing hazel eyes that kind of glow when she smiles." You could tell he was drifting away, describing his love and not just the B.I.B. "But with the extensive costume it has been impossible to determine precisely who she is."

"You have no leads, then?" shouted a man in the front.

"Oh, no, I did not say that. We have been working on a very scientific formula to determine her identity. We expect to find her...I certainly expect to find her," he said, becoming more animated. "And when I do, I am confident that all will be just fine and that she will help our city."

A sarcastic middle-aged reporter held up a blown-up picture of the day care center with a beer truck flattening the swing set. "Is this what you mean by 'just fine,' letting this animal run above the law, endangering our children?"

Jones stammered.

"We don't need to 'communicate'; we need to arrest her, and now, before someone gets hurt! Do you want your child under that truck, Dr. Jones?" the middle-aged reporter continued. "Do you?"

Dr. Jones started mumbling in an Indian dialect, then seemed to get enraged by the idea of the B.I.B. being anything but his perfect discovery. He ripped open his jacket and shirt to reveal a Miner's Lite/B.I.B. T-shirt and began shouting in the same dialect. Again, Edwards gestured to the two men who escorted Dr. Jones off the stage. I felt sorry for the sap.

From the other side of the stage came a very large man wearing an expensive suit. He introduced himself as Vito and declared that the news conference was now over. I noticed that he had his little finger in the mouth of a half empty Miner's Lite bottle and that he had two Miner's Lite bottles in the side pocket of his jacket.

"With the embargo on, where'd you get the Miner's Lite?" I shouted as the crowd around me buzzed with the chaos surrounding the end of the meeting.

"Hey, where'd you get the Miner's Lite?" I screamed again.

Vito pointed his sapling-sized finger at me. "Hey, Buddy, you just made the list."

Another voice yelled, "Where'd you get the Miner's?" And then another and another.

Vito just turned and walked off the stage toward a set of doors, ignoring us all.

I raised my fist, shook it defiantly, and yelled at the top of my lungs, "Hazel eyes, my ass!"

CHAPTER 15

We Consider New Possibilities

For me, the news conference was a frustration and a disappointment. It caused me to reconsider and take inventory of the things going on in my life. I realized I'd been spoiled by the rapid changes in the last few months. I thought everything had to just keep going up and up from here. Listening to myself say that now, I can see how deluded I'd been by a little taste of success. Being saved by the B.I.B. on B.I.B. rescue wasn't the same as in reality.

When I got home, I started to take inventory just by noticing what was there. In the apartment where once were strewn dirty T-shirts and jeans, now were strewn fitted silk shirts, expensive shoes, and underwear that had been worn only once. A new large screen TV stood where old reliable had once been. When I checked the Web site, I now had a new site; I was in for another surprise. When I took the time to check the online store sales, the advertising revenue, and the hit counts, I had no idea how successful the site had become. So there was a reason I was writing all those big checks to Rebecca Sans. I had allowed myself to become separated from the site, trusting in Rebecca, and being lazy. It was like seeing it for the first time. It was a great-looking and popular site. I hadn't taken the time to read the e-mails and postings on the reward line. They were still there. Some of the same idiots were still posting trash, but ordinary people were adding their supportive comments. Everyone wanted to believe, so today, most of the comments were those refusing to believe the B.I.B. could have dropped beer trucks on us or, if she had, it was her sense of humor. No one had been hurt was the catch phrase.

I took off my silk shirt, put on a B.I.B. T-shirt and jeans, popped the cap off of a Miner's Lite, the last one in the fridge, and began to write a blog I had not updated for days. The theme was that the B.I.B. was innocent of the truck drops and someone wanted her discredited. It started out mostly as intuition based on the behaviors I had seen at the news conference and the presence of Vito, but then inspiration hit and the blog became quite convincing. Hell, even I believed my own BS.

When I was done, my thoughts turned to where I had come from, what the mission was that had brought me the diversions of success. I needed to get back to my research of the women born during the Super Bowl. It was the only way I could think to look for her. None of the glitz, none of the glamour, none of the fame had lured the B.I.B. to show herself. It would require work and effort to pull her out for a one-on-one meeting. The spotlight could have been hers but she didn't take it. I was sure that Dr. Jones had not shared his Super Bowl theory with anyone else. It was the one connection he and I had left. The appearance of Jennifer Lowe at the searchlight event and her melted pen at the coffee shop made me feel certain Dr. Jones' theory was correct. But at that time, I still didn't know if Jennifer was there to help me or stop me.

Jennifer Lowe and Rebecca Sans sat across from each other on leather sofas before a small gas fireplace in Jennifer's penthouse condominium. Jennifer had her legs tucked up under her while she played with and sipped on a long-stemmed wine glass. She seemed the image of relaxation and comfort.

Rebecca sat hunched over a small coffee table between the sofas, not sure what to do with her glass of wine.

"I'm sorry about the wine. I know you like that Miner's Lite beer, but you just can't get it anymore. I even tried to black market a few for you. No one's got any," Jennifer apologized, trying to be the gracious host and calm Rebecca who seemed nervous.

Rebecca spun the wine glass in her hands and looked around the condo with its large windowed view of the city. Nothing in Scranton was really tall but this was about as high as it gets. "Your place is amazing," she said, getting up and walking to the windows. "How do you afford a place like this being a florist?" she asked, then she turned and walked back to the sofa. "Your family have money?"

Jennifer laughed out loud. "Me? My family had nothing. You wouldn't want to know where I came from."

"So, how'd a florist get all this?" Rebecca asked, sitting back down and drinking some of her wine.

"Rebecca, I'm about as much 'just' a florist as you are 'just' a graphics designer." Then when Jennifer saw Rebecca's blank face and eyes blink she put down her wine. "Oh dear, you *are* just a graphics designer…"

Rebecca's face became upset. "Yes, I am and a damn good one!"

"I'm sorry," Jennifer said, coming off her sofa to console and apologize. She put her hand on Rebecca's shoulder. "I know you are. I know what you did on that B.I.B. Web site. It's terrific."

"It is! Everyone likes it! I started from nothing and now look at it. That was the first time in my career someone just let me take the ball and run with it. He's really given me the freedom to be creative and not look over my shoulder all the time! He gives me a cut of all the money the site takes in, and I'm doing very well, thank you very much…I just wish I didn't have to hide things and lie to him," Rebecca said. She began to run a full circle of emotions and insecurity. "I told you I wasn't a wine drinker," she said as an excuse and put down her glass, tears appearing in the corners of her eyes.

Jennifer could feel a connection flowing between them like an electrical circuit running from Rebecca's shoulder through Jennifer's arm and into her body. "Rebecca," she began, sitting down on the sofa with her," do you mind if we don't talk shop tonight? Let's forget about finding the B.I.B. and Web sites and everything for a while. Would that be OK?"

Rebecca nodded. "Sure."

"This may sound a little out of nowhere, but do you find it hard to have sex now that you're finding your powers?"

"Oh yeah, do I. The men I've met lately are like toys—five or six quick ones and they can barely move afterward, and there I am without even getting my motor running…I can't even tell you how many batteries I buy a month."

Jennifer picked up Rebecca's wine glass, put it to her lips, and tilted it. "Here, you're gonna need this."

"What?" Rebecca tried to say as the wine started down her throat.

Jennifer didn't stop until the glass was empty. It was a new concept to her, but Jennifer reasoned that, if even a bunch of men over and over could not satisfy a superwoman, then maybe a superwoman could. She began to move slowly toward Rebecca until they were nose to nose.

"What are you doing?" Rebecca asked. Then Rebecca began to feel the power in Jennifer's hands as they roamed her shoulders, neck, and hair. She pulled off Rebecca's glasses and removed her own. She slowly ran her hands down Rebecca's chest, took hold of her sweater at the waist and lifted it over Rebecca's head. A stunned Rebecca sat motionless, while Jennifer tossed the sweater and her bra to the ground. Jennifer began a show of slowly unbuttoning her own silk shirt, all the while smiling and staring into Rebecca's hypnotized eyes. When she released the last button with flair, Rebecca looked down to see Jennifer's ultra feminine form bare to the navel. She trembled, waiting in anticipation and uncertainty. In a second, the slow dance was over and they were a combined mass of lips, arms, thighs, and hands.

One minute twenty-nine seconds later, Rebecca and Jennifer emerged from her now messy bedroom and walked back topless toward the living room, searching for clothes and straightening hair. As they reached the living room, Rebecca was in the lead and said, without turning, "Well that sucked!"

Jennifer followed and shook her head. "Yeah, what the hell was I thinking? You wanna talk shop?"

"Definitely," Rebecca answered, bending for her sweater and glasses.

"Good...I'll get the ice cream."

Sometimes the sex life of a woman with superpowers can be a real bitch.

CHAPTER 16

Proud to Be Appreciated but Not to Be Hunted

When I got home from work, I called for Paige without results. She wasn't at the computer cultivating her Internet page. I went down the hall to Paige's bedroom and could not see her there either. On the bed I noticed an opened box and a large envelope. I found a poster in the box and unrolled it. To my amazement, I stared at a six-foot poster of myself taken from the Skelly's picture. I was on a poster and my daughter had purchased one. It seemed bizarre. I went through the other items to see various B.I.B. trinkets: coffee cup, beer mug, another T-shirt, all with some sort of B.I.B. picture or silhouette on them. I looked around the room at Paige's clothes on the floor and saw three or four B.I.B. shirts next to black jeans making a complete B.I.B. outfit. How had I missed my daughter becoming a B.I.B. groupie, and how did I feel about it—proud or concerned?

From behind me Paige appeared. "Mom!" she yelled, as she grabbed the beer mug out of my hand, "that was supposed to be a surprise gift for you. Now, you've ruined it."

"What is all this stuff, honey?"

"I bought it off that Web site Aunt Lori found. Isn't it cool?" she said, unfolding the poster and trying it against various locations on the wall, then finally taping it to the back of the door. Then she came back to her speechless mother by the bed. "The two mugs are *for you. The rest is for me. Hope you like it. Lori ordered a cape and mask. I can't wait to try them on! I'll bet you'd look good in them. You already wear black all the time."*

"When did you get into the whole B.I.B. thing?"

"Oh, I love her," Paige said, excited. "Ever since I saw that article in the paper, I've been reading up on her. She's my hero. Did you know about all the things she did before they knew her by name? There were dozens of articles in the paper about a mysterious woman before anyone tied it all together."

"Oh, really?"

"Yep."

"And you know this because…"

"I'm doing my English paper about her. That Web site, THEBIB. org, that Lori told me about is dedicated to her. It's all about her history and has a whole file of newspaper links telling her story as it happened. They have the coolest games ever. On one, the B.I.B. saves you and this other one is a drinking game you'd probably like. Then there are people who report sightings, all the latest news, and the Webmaster writes a column about how he interprets what's happening. Like he says, the B.I.B. is getting set up for the dropping beer trucks, that she couldn't have done it."

"How would he know?" I asked, amazed at her steadfast belief.

"You have to read it for yourself. All I know is that my English paper is gonna write itself thanks to that site. I know some other girls that are writing about her too."

I felt an uncontrollable pride building within me. I was very happy that my daughter was so connected with what I was doing. I wanted to confess right then and there and admit that I was the B.I.B. But I knew there was a reason I couldn't and a reason I didn't. If anyone ever discovered who I really was, my whole family, but most of all Paige, would not be safe.

"You know the weirdest thing?" Paige asked, while holding up her latest T-shirt purchase against her chest and checking it out in the mirror. "The guy who runs that site says he actually met the B.I.B."

"Really?" I said jokingly but, in reality, seriously.

"In one article he says he saw her once in a bar downtown and was standing right next to her. Man, I'd love to meet her. She is so awesome. I understand now why you were laughing at the Batman movie. He's a movie, but she's real… You like how this looks?"

"It looks great," I said, relieved and happy. "I'll go start dinner," I added, turning to leave.

"Ohhh, I thought we were going to Lori's. I wanna see if she got her mask and stuff."

"Maybe tomorrow," I said, as I left Paige's room.

"OK, but you really should check out that Web site. It is so awesome," Paige yelled down the hall.

In the kitchen I pulled a bottle of Miner's Lite out of the fridge. As I knew where they were impounding the Miner's Lite, I had an almost endless supply at my disposal. I prepared some dinner, and while it was cooking, drifted over to the computer. I typed in the Web address and then sat back, astonished when the site came up. In one night, I had discovered that my daughter "got it" and now there was a whole group of people that "got it." The whole site honored me and made me seem so much more than the single mom from Scranton. I started reading the comments on the site's bulletin board. It was surprisingly easy to ignore the occasional garbage comments of some idiot or another for all the positive ones. I got a good laugh out of pictures that people had submitted, allegedly of the B.I.B. in action somewhere. None were real, except the Skelly's photo, so the others made me feel like "Big Foot"; so many anxious to prove that I existed.

I did manage to get through four bars in Pub Crawler, got up to twelve hundred points in the Antler Game, and saved myself twice in B.I.B. Rescue. The video games rocked.

I smiled and put the cursor over the "Add A Comment" button. I clicked it and a window appeared for me to enter my comments. My fingers hovered over the keys, and then I closed the window.

Just then, Paige came in and, seeing the Miner's Lite bottle on the desk, said, "You know those are illegal, don't you? Criminal..."

"Just be quiet," I joked, standing up and heading for the kitchen.

Carmine Camino was the Gambrelli corporal that had ousted his former boss. Unlike Gambrelli, Carmine ran his mob business out of the offices for a unionized and legitimate waste-removal company. The building looked run down, like you would imagine a company that handled the slime of trash might look. But on the second floor, Carmine's isolated office was more like a palace.

Carmine was a midthirties, dark-haired man. Unlike Gambrelli, he was fit, vibrant, and mentally sharp. He sat behind his glossy black desk just staring off into space, thinking. On his mind was the rebuilding and expansion of his mob business. He would not let himself fall into the same trap as Gambrelli. He knew his organization was fragile, vulnerable, like a newborn. He was aware that Gambrelli's plan to eliminate the B.I.B. with power of force had caused his downfall. He had to keep her at arm's length while his organization gained strength, or his tenure as boss would be over before it started.

The mayor's feeble beer embargo was having no effect and was now just pissing people off. His searchlight event had been a disaster. It was obvious to Carmine that the B.I.B. did not want to join hands with the city or make herself known to the public.

He settled on the idea of trying to turn the public against her, disgrace her in some way, so that she would be occupied defending herself or hiding, instead of standing in his way. Carmine knew Gambrelli had started working along those lines by shooting the first witness to have actually seen her, Ed, and trying to blame the murder on the B.I.B., but it had never taken off. The police were content to deal with the death as an accident.

Carmine's first attempt had been to drop beer trucks, as the B.I.B. had done. They had trucks moved by helicopter, moving at high altitudes to areas of town or at times of day when there would be no witnesses, and then dropped the trucks, all along having a team on the ground to serve as witnesses to the event. Carmine had thought the drop on the day care center would really get the sentiment going against the B.I.B., but it only moved a little.

This time, he would have to come up with a better idea and execute the plan more precisely. He had found his answer earlier in the day when he had checked out that B.I.B. Web site. The site was to become a battleground. The thoughts gelled; Carmine smiled, and entered thebib.org on his Web browser, then clicked on Pub Crawler. He smiled at the detailed game and, before long, was drawn into a two-hour search for the B.I.B. He was certain he had her cornered in the Banshee but, instead, ran into the Nelson Twins. "Crap!" he said, pounding his fist on the desk as his blood alcohol level spiked over the legal limit and his avatar crumbled to the floor with a smile on its face.

Lori and I had found some time together to go shopping at the mall downtown on Saturday afternoon. We walked, talked, and picked,

finding a few bargains but not much. On the way out I noticed a small T-shirt boutique near the exit that had large window signs advertising "new" B.I.B. T-shirts. Well, I had to look and pulled Lori in reluctantly by the arm.

Inside the store we found chaos. More crowds were leaving the tiny store disappointed than were entering. We soon found out why. The tables of B.I.B. shirts were all but empty with only odd sizes or colors left sparsely covering the racks.

Lori studied one of the new shirts, inspecting its price tag before anything else. "Do you see how much they want for these! Who can afford this?"

"You and I. Paige will want these new designs, look," I said holding up a couple of shirts. The first new design said, "I'm the B.I.B.," with an arrow pointing up in various cool colors; the second said, "I'm with the B.I.B.," with an arrow pointing sideways; the third had a picture of the B.I.B. silhouette on a round searchlight with a red line slanting through it with letters saying, "I Survived Searchlight Night"; and the last one was a takeoff of the Miner's Lite/B.I.B. picture saying, "B.I.B. Pub Crawler High Scorer." Unfortunately all that was left were x-smalls or XXXX. "Come on," I said, "You know you want one, everybody will."

Lori continued her frustration. "I like the 'I'm the B.I.B.' one but there are no mediums or blue ones," she said, digging through the sparse stock and ending up battling with other customers who were also searching for sizes. You could hear them all saying, "There's no larges" or "Wish they had this in pink."

Above and behind Lori was a young stock clerk on a metal four-wheeled ladder struggling with a large box of shirts to bring down and replenish the display tables. I looked up to watch him sway and struggle with the heavy box, ending with him and the box falling off the ladder. For certain, Lori was going to cushion his landing. So I acted. It was taking him forever to fall, so I spent the time in super speed intercepting the box, placing the colors and sizes everyone needed in their hands, stocking the tables by shirt and size, and when the clerk finally was about to land on Lori, I diverted him, turned him vertical, and softened his landing on his feet. To anyone watching he appeared to be quite an acrobat, drawing their attention while their shirts and sizes suddenly appeared in their hands. Lori, with her back to the clerk, didn't even see that.

I came up behind her, "What do you mean? There's a blue medium in your hand."

Lori looked at the shirt in her hands in surprise, "Oh, God, it's terrible to turn thirty. My mind is just gone."

I quickly piled shirts in her hands, rattling off who they were for as I went. "And this one's for you," I said putting my favorite, the original Miner's Lite/B.I.B. shirt, on the stack. "I know you don't have one and the B.I.B. just looks so gorgeous in that picture."

"You don't have to," Lori protested.

"My treat. Come on, Paige told me that you had a cape and mask ordered off the Internet, so I know you're a fan."

Lori smiled and nodded, "Yeah, I guess I am a closet B.I.B. fan, thanks."

As we prepared to check out we found a long and slow-moving line, only one cashier, a teenage girl who didn't really want to be there, you could tell.

After a long wait we were next in line when the middle-aged woman in front of us started giving the lazy cashier a rough time. When she didn't get what she wanted, she loudly demanded to see the manager, prompting everyone behind her in line to sigh heavily and roll their eyes. The old woman was just being selfish and rude. As I watched her mouth forming her nasty words, she reminded me of my supervisor at work, old Mrs. Prune Face. The cashier struggled to find the number to page the manager, convincing me that something needed to be done. It may not have been a nice thing to do or something the B.I.B. would do, but it was something "I" would.

Moving quickly in super speed, I dropped the middle-aged woman to the floor for being so inconsiderate of all of the rest of us, put a T-shirt in her mouth, and a paper shopping bag over her head. Then as an added touch, 'cause I was feeling a bit goofy that day, I moved Lori and put her hand on the woman's head. To the cashier it looked like the woman had suddenly just dropped straight down below the counter. To everyone in line it looked like a flash with Lori pulling the woman down and bagging her. Everyone in line cheered and applauded Lori as she stood uncomfortably with her hand on the woman's head as the woman struggled to remove the bag and get up. I took the opportunity to put our shirts on the counter and get the cashier to check us out, which she was glad to do with a smile.

"Boy, you're feeling a little assertive today, aren't you?" I said to a confused Lori who finally lifted her hand off the struggling woman and smiled a little smile to her cheering supporters, still not sure what had happened.

"What's wrong with you? My son's a lawyer!" the middle-aged woman screamed after she had righted herself and removed the tee from her mouth.

I took Lori's arm and led her out of the store quickly with our bag of shirts, "What got into you, Tiger?" I said continuing to confuse Lori, "She piss you off that much?"

Lori stammered, "I don't know…I just…"

"I know, it's terrible to turn thirty…The old mind starts goin' on ya."

"I just…."

We left the mall with our bags of treasure while the store clerks consoled the middle-aged woman. I made Lori put on her new blue "I'm the B.I.B." tee shirt over her top. It looked great. Out onto the sidewalk of a busy downtown street on our way to the parking lot, I could see a car about to hurry through a yellow caution light.

At the same time a young boy had broken away from his mother's grip and began chasing some little thing he had dropped in the street. The wide-eyed driver slammed on his brakes, but I doubted the car would ever stop in time to avoid hurting the little boy. There was a life at risk right in the street beside us, so I took action. Without my costume I chose a more amusing way to protect my identity.

Taking hold of Lori's hand, I super-speeded into the street, stopped the car with my outstretched hands inches from the little boy, put Lori's hands where mine had been, and then retreated innocently to the sidewalk. It felt like I was getting faster every day. To all who saw it, Lori had stopped the car with her hands, saving the boy, and causing a major murmuring in the crowd. Some just spoke of their amazement at what had happened while you could hear others mumbling the words, "B.I.B." Lori just stood in the street with her hands on the car, wearing her "I'm the B.I.B." tee shirt, and a stunned look on her face for a long moment, before she meekly walked over to me on the sidewalk and the crowd applauded her again. The driver of the car and the mother with her little boy, now clamped to her side, came and thanked Lori.

"What did you eat this morning?" I teased her. "What's gotten into you today? Over thirty, my ass."

Lori just stood with her head down in total confusion, "Did I just…"

"You did! Is there something you want to tell me?" I taunted. "That's like B.I.B. stuff. Maybe it's that new T-shirt, you know, 'I am the B.I.B.'"

"Maybe we should go home, now…I don't even remember doing it…" she mumbled as if to herself as we walked to the car.

"Paige is going to love this!" I teased. "Her aunt doing B.I.B. shit."

"I should just go home…" Lori repeated.

After a minute I looked at her seriously, but was laughing my ass off inside. "Sis, If you were the B.I.B., you'd tell me…right?"

Lori looked at me with a blank look on her face, "I should just go home now."

Then a smile crawled up her face thinking about what she had done, or thought she had done, before it slowly drained away. "I'm a fucking hero," she said in a low tone of disbelief.

"Yeah, but don't let it go to your head, "I said, putting my arm around her. "It's not all it's cracked up to be."

We turned a corner almost to our car, when a man rounded the corner in a hurry and bumped into both of us without apology. Little Lori instantly pushed him into a storefront with both hands, "Back off, loser!" she said in a guttural low tone that I had never heard before.

"Hey, sorry, lady. No need to get physical."

She kept him frozen with her stare for a long time then picked up her bags and we continued on to the car while the man muttered, "Fuckin' psycho bitch," a language I understood.

I looked over at Lori's stern face, wondering if I had created a monster.

CHAPTER 17

Frustration and Hell Night for Scranton

I was almost there. I could feel the warm surge of blood in my abdomen, my muscles starting to convulse. My breaths became short, interrupted by short moans. I closed my eyes to concentrate on the feeling. I felt a tidal wave forming between my legs and a scream forming in my throat. My ass began to roll and my legs widened apart and lifted off the bed. I was right there, and I could feel the surging waves coming at long last. I had waited so many months but was now finally ready to explode.

Then the comforting buzzing between my legs began to hesitate, stutter, then stalled and went suddenly silent. "No! No! Not now!" I shouted in my head, "Not now! Crap!" Without the buzzing of my toy, all the feelings and sensations began to drop off. When the frustration kicked in and the mental component disappeared, the feelings dropped off the charts.

I rocketed up to sit on the edge of the bed and threw my powerless toy on the floor, where it landed, crashing into a large pile of equally powerless batteries that I had gone through that evening. With my head down, I slammed my fist into the mattress with frustration over and over. "Son of a fucking Goddamn bitch," I yelled bitterly through gritted teeth. Then I took some breaths and pushed my blonde hair *back over my forehead. I sighed and stared blindly for a moment then lifted my eyes to look at myself in the large nearby dressing mirror.*

I didn't seem to know myself anymore. It was a very difficult time for me. To anyone else, the naked woman in the mirror would seem quite attractive, a well-formed woman near her prime. There may have been something rounded here or there that should have been angled, but all in all, I was built like a classic beauty; I just didn't feel that way. For years, I had battled being a teenage mother and then a single mother. I had allowed it to pigeonhole me, to value me by my circumstances rather than my character or my talents. Eventually, I took on the labels and restrictions and didn't question it. The woman in the mirror became, not a classic beauty, but just a single mom. I had accepted that for years.

Now, as my powers had manifested themselves, I didn't know what was true anymore. The powers were intriguing, enticing, yet new and foreign. The new powerful me couldn't see the woman in the mirror either. All I saw were the limits and restrictions that the powers had brought: the need for secrecy, the fear of being found out, and the frustration of using up forty batteries and still not being able to get off. Which "her" was I? Could I make them all live together inside me?

I brushed back my hair again, took a long look in the mirror, uncertain what I saw, looked down at the pile of batteries and then sighed. The "mom" in me bent down, put the toy in the nightstand, and piled the batteries in a bag for the trash. The "B.I.B." in me was frustrated and angry. I threw the bag of dead batteries on the bed and marched to my closet, digging in a hidden box behind a box behind a box, pulling out my B.I.B. clothes and mask. My frustration needed to be satisfied one way or another and someone would pay. Tonight, I would go a hunting.

Before, I had always had a target, a plan, in mind, before donning the outfit; but not tonight. Tonight, I would be on the prowl for a new way to use my powers. I didn't feel like hiding or being cautious. With Paige at a friend's house for the night, the opportunity was there. I wanted some action and a chance to show how strong I could be. After I dressed, I looked at myself in the mirror, proud of the way my tight slacks clung to my hips and thighs, and slowly smiled. Then the smile faded as "single mom" saw a bulging thigh instead. I turned to begin the hunt, but then, the "mom" reemerged to be certain to take the bag of batteries out to the trash.

When I awoke the next morning, my eyes slowly opened and began to focus. I had slept like a log, and it took a minute to become aware of my surroundings. When my eyes did focus, a shot of adrenaline made me leap to my feet. My hands—there was dried blood on my knuckles, on the side of my hand below the little finger. In horror, I flipped my hands around over and over searching for the wound from which the blood had come. There was nothing. I inspected my bare arms and torso, but found no source for the blood. I ran to the dressing mirror to check my entire body. Then came another shot of adrenaline at the sight of lines of blood on my cheek and even in my hair. On the floor beside the mirror was the pile of my black B.I.B. clothes ripped and stained with crimson that varied from specks to small pools.

My thoughts grew to panic, because I had no idea where the blood had come from and no recollection of what had happened last night. I remembered leaving the house; I remembered standing on a rooftop downtown with a strong breeze filling my hair and cape, then nothing else until waking up.

In alarm and frustration, I pounded the frame of the mirror with my fists, rattling the glass, until it almost broke. I slid down the mirror, until I was a ball on the floor. I sobbed, and tears began to run down my cheek, drifting through the blood and ending up pink as they dropped to the floor. After a moment, I gained control and opened my eyes to look into the mirror. I didn't know who this was either.

All of that changed in an instant, when I heard Paige's voice calling from down the hall. "Mom? You better get up or you'll be late for work…I'm leaving for school. Are you up?" she said, knocking on the door.

In an instant I was composed. "Mom" took immediate control. "Yeah, I'm up, honey. Have a good day," I said, quickly donning a robe.

"OK, see you at Lori's after work. I hope she's not having meat loaf again," said Paige as she turned to leave.

I quickly got to the door, one-eyed my face beyond the door jamb, and waved. "Love you."

When I heard the door slam, I leapt to the bathroom and started the shower. How much water would it take to rid me of the blood?

All day at work, my mind was an unfocused maze of thoughts and fears. Occasionally, I would hear co-workers talking about the news, something that had happened the night before. Now and then, I would hear someone use the word "B.I.B." I wanted to ask them what had happened or check for the news on my computer but was afraid of what I might find. Finally, just before lunch my friend Jan came by.

"Some crazy night, huh?"

"What?" I asked, sheepishly, afraid to hear.

"Haven't you heard?" said Jan, excited to find someone who hadn't heard the news, "The B.I.B., nobody sees her for a while and then, bam, sounds like she was in five places at once last night. Of course, nobody will confirm it was her, but who else could it be? There were a lot of witnesses. They're talkin' about the police going after her this time."

"Anybody hurt?" I finally had the courage to ask.

"Shit yeah, lots of people. Hospitals and jail are full of 'em. Mostly lowlifes. I would think twice before committing a crime after that. She didn't arrest 'em; she pummeled their asses first this time. It's all good as far as I'm concerned though. I heard she broke bones on two wife beaters and nearly castrated some guy while he was having sex with his ten-year-old stepdaughter, sick shit. All in one night! She was like everywhere, man. Just goes to show you the amount of crap happening every day. It's scary, "Jan said, munching on a cookie.

When Jan saw that I was not talking, she asked, "You OK?"

"Didn't sleep well. I'll be fine."

"Can I buy you lunch?"

I shook my head. "I've got to pick up something for Paige. I'll take a rain check."

"OK, she ya later."

"Maybe we can go tomorrow."

Jan waved and nodded as she left.

I took a deep breath, sighed, and then looked at my reflection in the window for a long moment. Who was I?

CHAPTER 18

Who Was I?

When my lunch break came, I walked out of the building into a sunny windswept afternoon that was warm for this time of April. I buttoned my light coat and hurried off down the sidewalk.

With only a short lunch break, I had to rush to pick up the clothes I had ordered for Paige from a store near the office. Ahead, I could see the streetlight about to change, so I broke into a jog to cross the street in time. At the same time, a young man with a large bag draped over his shoulder emerged from an alleyway with his head down. Neither of us expected the other to be there, but, in an instant, we had collided and almost knocked each other over. The collision had sent the man's bag to the ground with a metallic clang and made me lean on the man to keep from falling.

At first, with no damage being done, I laughed, apologized, and tried to make light of the incident. But the scrawny, dark-haired man seemed panicked. His dark eyes grew wide and he flailed his arms to get away from me. That was just rude. Quickly, I knew something was wrong.

He pounced on his bag but not before I could see that it was filled with five or six pipes, capped at both ends. He clutched it to his chest, gave me a threatening look, and then ran back down the alley from where he had come.

I had a quick choice to make. Should I let him go, knowing a bag full of pipe bombs might go with him, or grab him now, right now. But, I didn't want to be the B.I.B. right now. The events of the previous night had made me frightened and uncertain of the course I was on. Who did I want to be? In that instant, I would have to decide. With my costume lying bloody in the closet, I had no cover for my actions.

Before he had traveled twenty feet, I was on him and his collar jerked back in my hand. His body snapped back and his feet left the ground. I swung my arm to the left, and he flew like a shot into the wall of a building and the dumpster that was beside it. He didn't move, and his arm twisted unnaturally beneath him. I lifted the bag from the ground and held it at arm's length, while I heard the sounds of voices coming down the alley. A burly biker dude, a middle-aged woman clutching her purse, and a young man and woman were coming my way.

The biker came up behind me and stopped. "You OK, lady? What'd this loser try to pull? I saw him hit you."

I didn't know what to do as I stood with my back to him. Was I the B.I.B., a single mom from Scranton, or something else?

"Hey, lady?" he said, touching my shoulder.

I hesitated for a long moment, turned, and handed the biker the bag, saying, "Call 911," then assumed the best disguise I could muster, a deep profoundly puckered fish face. The biker looked at the bag, saw the pipes, but before he could look up, I moved down the alley away from the crowd as quickly as I dared, turned a corner, and was gone.

"Hey, lady!" called the biker as the others gathered around the bag of pipes and began a shocked chatter.

The events of the previous night were a gold mine for my Web site. I was like a friggin' six-year-old on Christmas morning again. There were dozens and dozens of sightings, reports, comments, and even some pictures. It sounded like the B.I.B. had been everywhere that night—in so many places I had to think most of them were fake reports. There was so much content on my Web site that I had to call Rebecca Sans and ask her to reorganize and expand it. Despite the fact that the B.I.B. had dished out her own sense of justice this time, the opinion on the site was overwhelmingly positive.

The newspaper had the same problem, as I did, with volume of content. Eventually, they chose to run all of the news reports in the same section of the paper under the banner, "The B.I.B.?" When I looked at the paper and saw four pages of short articles of alleged this and possible that, it brought a large smile to my face. I was no closer to finding the B.I.B., but I had to marvel at what she had done…again.

For the first time since the searchlight event, the network news made mention of the B.I.B., calling her the "Scranton vigilante." The network entertainment shows picked up on her for the first time, running spots that were somewhat tongue-in-cheek, disbelieving the news they were reporting. It was pretty much like, "Those nuts in Scranton, here they go again…" but with somewhat more serious tones. I could tell many of the photos used were pimped from my site. I really needed to find an attorney. There was a short cell phone video of her messing with some big guy in the streets that ended rather abruptly when the big guy didn't take the B.I.B. seriously and she dropped him like she was brushing her hair. Then it ended with a blowup of the Skelly's photo; still my favorite and still my copyright, thank you very much.

When I saw the paper and I began to read the articles, my jaw dropped, then my hand went up over my mouth as I dropped the paper, "Oh, my God," I said softly, trying to come to grips with the fact that I had done all those things. The second the paper hit the floor, Paige had it in her hands and was laughing and smiling as she read, "Whoa, this is cool!"

Carmine Camino read through the articles in the paper and then scrolled through the B.I.B. Web site in astonishment. He had no idea that the B.I.B. was capable of all this. He felt glad that he had not moved against her, knowing, now, that he would have underestimated her. He sat at his office desk with his shirt unbuttoned, shoes off, and grasping a can of beer. Carmine sat back, took a large hit from the can, thought for a moment, clicked the cancel button on his B.I.B. Rescue game, and then clicked on the "Give us your comments" button on the Web site and began to type.

As Jennifer Lowe and Rebecca Sans read the paper together and compared it to the reports on the Web site, their mutual reaction was a calm acceptance. Jennifer looked at Rebecca. "I think she's about ready."

Rebecca nodded. "More than ready."

CHAPTER 19

Jones and I Regroup at O'Malley's

That entire day, I could not lose a nervous little feeling. I felt antsy and foreboding about who knew what. After all, the media attention was making my Web site ring like a cash register. While I sat, advertisers were paying for hit after hit. What did I have to worry about? Yet I paced in my apartment like a caged cat; actually, it was more like a kinda slow meandering cat; OK, a large lap cat, a real nasty one after a full meal, but you get the picture.

I decided that my little voyage of discovery had gotten side-tracked by the publicity, the money, and the sense of what's-gonna-happen-next. Somewhere along the line, I had forgotten those blue/green flashing eyes, the way she could drain a full beer bottle, and the fact that she left twenties as tips. Just the remembrance of which had suddenly created a feeling in my pants that hadn't been there for what…weeks now. Holy shit! Weeks? What have I become, a friggin' nun? No, nuns were women, so I took solace in that. At least I wasn't becoming a nun, just somebody that wasn't getting any very often. But no one needs to know that, OK?

There was only one thing to do and that was to get back to where I had been, where I had started, keeping the money and celebrity of course. I wasn't crazy. So I called Dr. Jones and quickly got the feeling that he felt the same. So we decided to meet that night at eight—where else—at O'Malley's, where the whole thing had begun.

I arrived promptly at 8:17, and Dr. Jones arrived promptly at 8:32. Depressed cat pacing guys who aren't getting much tend to be late. We sat in the same booth. Everything around us seemed the same as it had in January. The RFDs were pulling the restroom door in the wrong direction, repeatedly, sliding off bar stools, and of course, there was the occasional sound of laughter and rifle shots from the back room, blank rifle shots these days. The only thing missing was the luscious blonde in the corner.

The same old barkeep was there. He came toward us to take our order, but then, upon recognizing us, he hesitated and began to turn around. I called to him and assured him that we would order something this time and he came reluctantly.

"What's it to be this time, gents? A wee bit of soda water? Cup of ice?" he asked.

"No, my man, we will each have a Miner's Lite beer, shaken not stirred."

The barkeep was not amused. "Will this be a cash transaction?" he asked sarcastically.

I pulled out a wad of bills and laid them on the table. "Yes, my dear man, it will be cash and there's more where that came from," I said, gesturing toward a reluctant Dr. Jones. "Does this fine establishment serve any varieties of food to go with your outstanding liquors?"

The barkeep reached in his pocket and pulled out a crumpled black and white photo copy, straightened it a little, and then presented it over his forearm as if it were a menu from a five-star restaurant. "We do, me lord, can I get you anything?"

I quickly looked at the four or five selections. "Do you recommend the chili fries?"

"With me whole bleedin' heart."

"I believe we will try some," I said, looking at Jones for his agreement.

"Will that be one order, two plates, and a doggie bag, or are we blowin' the wad on two orders?"

I looked at Jones and confidently said, "That will be two orders, my good man."

The old man turned his eyes to the ceiling for a second as if in thought, then unexpectedly grabbed at my pile of bills until he had extracted full payment, plus some extra. Then he stopped, recalculated, and grabbed the tip in advance as well. "Now then, we're square." That done he turned to leave.

"I see, my friend, that you come here often," said Jones, noticing the warmth the barkeep and I had for each other.

A minute later, the barkeep delivered our beers and the promise, "You're fries are on their way; I wanta make sure they're good an fresh for ya." It made me wonder what fresh ingredients we might find in the fries. The scary thought hit me that he had too little hair to spare, so maybe he would be using a hard-to-see bodily fluid.

I took a long pull on my beer and fell back in the booth. Dr. Jones uncharacteristically was quiet and devoid of his usual energy. "I feel like we're messin' this up. I thought we were so close to her and now…now it's just a mess."

Jones nodded without looking at me. "Yes, my friend, I am feeling this way too. It used to be so fun, so exciting. I was scoring like a pinball machine. But now, I think she does not want to be found, and I haven't hit a Ladies Night at The Banshee for a month. We were so close. We were fools to get drawn into an alliance with the mayor. We were fools to have drifted so far from our plan...poor Demitri."

That was when a thought hit me hard, just like the chili fries would probably do to my stomach. The plan, the friggin' plan! "You are so right!"

Dr. Jones looked up at me startled. "I am?"

"The plan was working. We just got diverted. Your crazy... sorry...plan about the Super Bowl birth dates was right."

"And how are you knowing this?" Jones said, a bit affronted.

"OK, I haven't told you everything. The first woman I interviewed with the Super Bowl birthday seemed like an ordinary chick when I meet her. I didn't lie to you...not then at least." Jones turned his body toward me surprised, angry, and interested. "But later, I learned that she melted my pen, and then I saw her at the searchlight event. Why would she be there?"

"Melting your pen? She melts your pen and you don't think it's important enough to tell good ol' Dr. Jones? The same Dr. Jones that got you going in the first place? How do you melt a friggin' pen?"

"All I know is that I left her with the pen and, when I came back a few days later, the busboy tells me about her melting a pen, and I find it embedded in the table. How's that for your garden-variety weird?" I said, spinning my bottle of beer.

Jones thought for a long moment. "So I was right! The Super Bowl calculations are right! Let's go meet this woman!"

"Hold on, Sherlock," I said, pushing him back down in his seat. "That's not all of it. I think there's more than one. This woman melts pens and was the first-closest born to Super Bowl half time, but she's not the B.I.B."

Now Jones was acting like a little kid who wasn't told the secret everyone else knew. "And what is telling you this?"

I had to think a long time before answering that one. "I just know, OK. Let's just say there is more than one of them for sure and that your Super Bowl theory is also correct."

Jones was too busy thinking about how wonderful and what a genius he was to be mad at me or question me further. He smiled and gave out a little laugh. "I am, you know, right about this, about everything."

"OK, you are a genius. OK, I said it. You are...I've got to find the rest of those Super Bowl babies, get back to the plan, right? Is there anything else your calculations say that can help us?"

"Yes," he said folding his arms, "they say if you don't share with me all the information again, you will be finding a black loafer deep up your ass!"

"Fair...fair enough. I think I've told you everything," I lied. "Are there any other questions you'd like me to answer?"

"Yes, what is a chili fry? Do I get curry with that?"

On cue, the barkeep brought our chili fries in paper baskets and dropped them harshly on the table. "Bon appetite," he said, while I covered my money so he wouldn't take any more.

"That there, my friend, is what they call a chili fry."

"How are you supposed to eat it? Why is it looking at me like that?" asked Jones, suspiciously examining the food.

I explained to him the art of the chili fry and soon he had developed his own techniques based on licking off the chili or scraping it off by pulling one through a trough he made with his tongue. We stayed for a while, downing a few more beers, finishing our fries, and regathering our friendship. The whole while we remained unnoticing of the musical song of thuds, clangs, bangs, and gunfire of the RFDs.

Before long, Dr. Jones seemed his old self again. He smiled. His energy was back. "I think I shall be going now," he said, rising. "It is two-for-Tuesday at The Banshee across that very street," he added, pointing out the door.

I slapped him on the back as he left. "That's what I like to hear, the old Dr. Jones getting back in the saddle. By the look of your new chili fry techniques, I can tell some girl is in for the time of her life."

"Girls, my friend, we are talking 'girls' in the plural, as in many of them."

"Go get 'em, Tiger."

With that, he quickly shuffled out of the bar and the barkeep closed in. "Another beer for you? No, aye? How'd you like them fries?"

"My compliments to the chef…those were potatoes, right? No…extras?"

"Nothing but the finest for our best customers."

I lifted my finger with a quizzical look on my face and hesitated, about to ask the barkeep a question. He looked at me like he was two chapters ahead and shook his head sadly. "The blonde bird? No, she ain't been here since we last spoke. Heaven knows me empty wallet could sure use her visit…Good tipper that one."

"Yeah," was all I said, dejected, thinking how far down the list of her assets and values good tipping was.

The barkeep could sense how much it mattered to me. He put his hand on my shoulder. "Don't worry, friend, she'll show up one day." I thought I could feel him being truly sincere as he squeezed my shoulder. "But you'll hav' ta get to 'ur after me!" he said, ruining the moment.

CHAPTER TWENTY

I Start the Wheels to Cataclysm

The next morning, I was up at the crack of ten, maybe elevenish, feeling renewed and full of purpose. I even ignored a phone-pole of a morning glory that would normally have commanded immediate attention. I hit the computer with a steaming mocha latte in hand, minus the mocha and the milk, and checked out the Scranton news before logging onto my B.I.B. Web site. Other than the "buy one get one" sale on Miner's beer, only one item caught my eye.

There was an article about the "City Hall Pipe Bomber." Some stiff was caught intending to bomb the mayor's office. In the article, it mentioned that he was apprehended by a group of citizens after he attacked a woman in an alleyway. There was an interview with each of the citizens, except the woman who had been attacked. Witnesses described her as having blonde hair, thirty or so, but then spoke of how she had left the scene with her face hard to describe because it was a "fish face." Thirty and blonde immediately made my morning glory remind me of its presence. But the fish face struck my memory. I hit the keyboard and found the picture files I had bought when I purchased the "Skelly's" picture of the B.I.B. The guy sent me pictures of the same woman doing a "fish face." I pulled them up, and there she was, the B.I.B. doing a "fish face." My morning glory decided to take a nap.

There she was, blonde, thirty, and fish faced. The B.I.B. had stopped the bomber, not the citizen group, and she had used the fish face to escape without being ID'd. Sometimes she seemed like such an ordinary sweet chick and, at other times, so unapproachably powerful. I thought about her that night at O'Malley's, the flashing eyes, and tried to put that together with an ordinary woman. I tried to imagine what she would be like, what it would be like to stand beside her. The very thought made my morning glory wake up and try to escape down the leg of my boxers.

But I was the only one who knew. I was the only one who knew she had stopped the bomber. That would be the subject of my blog on the Web site. I broke the story on the site and published the fish-face picture for the first time. Now that's journalism…right?

I hurried through it because my real goal for the morning, after sobriety, was to research the only leads I had—Jennifer Lowe and the other Super Bowl born women. There had to be a connection. I needed to find the other women and learn more about Lowe.

The advantage of having a living room for your office is mostly comfort. I sat there for several hours in only my boxers and could bring the entire world to me. I had started with the crudest of searches. I did an Internet search for Jennifer Lowe and found some artists and dog trainers, but nothing about "my" Jennifer Lowe other than her little florist shop. I researched her name for real estate holdings and found nothing, not even a little bungalow somewhere. I was thinking about my next clever move, or at least a clever move, when I saw "Lowe LLC" on the real estate tax listings. The first listing matched the address of her florist shop. *Hello, hello*, I thought. But that was just the first of a dozen in the city. I cross-checked the listings to condos, office buildings, and restaurants. This bitch had it going on. Then I checked other cities and found listings for Lowe LLC in New York City, Chicago, Orlando, Dallas, and on Maui. If I had known how to do it, I'd have checked Europe and Asia and probably found more. Lowe was not a mere florist but a friggin' conglomerate—who melts pens, by the way.

So there were more than one and they all weren't doing like "my" sweetie and fighting crime and injustice. Now the question was, should I close in on Lowe or keep looking for the others. The image of the pen clip melted into the tabletop made me think I should look for the others.

CHAPTER TWENTY-ONE

First Contact; Getting What You Want…Getting Sick

When I saw my fish-faced picture on thebib.org home page, my hand flew up to cover my mouth, and my chair flew back a couple of inches, scratching across the tile floor. Then I moved in closer and covered the picture with my hand, as if that could block it from the world. I'm no IT wiz, but even I knew that wasn't going to help. I think you'd have to do that on every computer in the world to have any effect. I looked around to see if Paige was near, turning my mind into a full-blown panic. So far, I had gotten lucky, but that fish-face trick was well known to my friends and my family, anyone who really knew me. What would I tell Paige? What could I tell my family? All kinds of thoughts swirled in my head. Can I get the picture pulled from the site? Maybe I should admit it's me but say I'm not the B.I.B.? If I sue to get it off, I'll draw all kinds of attention. What to do? **Damn that guy from Texas**, I thought, after realizing the source of the photo. I put the cursor over the "Add Your Comments" button and clicked it. I sent this message to the site: "Hey, Asshole, that fish-face picture isn't the B.I.B., it's me. Some guy from Texas took it a few months ago. How'd you get it? I'm gonna sue your ass if you don't take that picture down immediately. No one should believe this site. That picture is not the B.I.B. just a single mom from Scranton."

About that time, I still hadn't dressed or left the house. Between scratching my butt and thinking of ordering some takeout, I saw her comments blink onto the site. I had been checking on hits for the day and planning to polish my blog when it happened. Don't ask me how, 'cause I'll deny it in court, but I knew it was her. Not only her but it was the sweetie side of her, fearful and vulnerable, the asshole comment not-withstanding. Suddenly, a shiver came over me. It wasn't an "I ate too many damn tacos" shiver, it was like my whole body became empty and frozen in place. I was just a pair of eyes and a brain trapped with a joyous, frightening, exhilarating, foreboding feeling that within my grasp was something that would change my life forever or be my biggest blunder, next to the Nelson Twins. I stared at the page, read her words, and thought until the pixels of the screen were burnt into my brain. Without direction or plan, as was usual for me, my hands began to move the cursor. I went to the hypertext version of the Web site's home page, found the picture, clicked on it, clicked "delete," and then republished the site. In an instant there was a gigantic hole on the page, but I had something far more valuable. Through the hit history, I could track back and see her computer address. I fell back in my chair and felt the shivers come over me again in waves like the surf on the north shore of Maui. Hey, I was there…once…OK, I read about it. I watched my hands shaking, even worse than St. Paddy's Day last year. I couldn't move, just sat in the glory of knowing I had just communicated with her…Well, it was a start.

Little did I know that she was going through the same thing on her end, minus the shivers, joy, fear, exhilaration, or foreboding, and probably not the shakes or the profound sense of glory or communication. Let's just say she was friggin' surprised.

I stared at the empty space on the screen in shock, my mind still racing in fear. I refreshed the page. I exited my browser and started it again to be sure the picture was gone. I looked down at the hand that had covered the screen and laughed to myself, half wondering if my powers could account for something like this. **Good work!** *I thought and then tried to make other parts of the site disappear with my hand to no avail. After a moment, I was confident that my words and not my powers were the cause, and I smiled and dropped my heart rate by twenty beats per minute. I sighed and enjoyed the moment for a while, but was then hit with the reality of how close I had come to being found and shook my head.*

While I was feeling better, I was getting hit by the north shore of Maui again. When the true impact of being this close to finding her hit me, it was a Maui wipeout. How would I talk with her, for starters? The last time I was near her I babbled "SSSs" and Dr. Jones drooled. How would I keep from screwing up? I wasn't always this cool, you know. I had almost exposed her by posting her picture. That could have gotten her in trouble or hurt. The mob surely would love to know who she was and where her family lived. The mayor had been nearly ruined by her. And Jennifer Lowe, what was she doing at the searchlight event? Did she have plans for her too? The reality and the responsibility crashed over me. The room suddenly got hot. Perspiration beaded on my forehead. Either my thoughts were making me terribly ill, or I was in the middle of an alien movie with something about to burst from my chest. I ran to the bathroom and got violently ill.

After I began to feel better, I stood up and put one hand on each side of the doorjamb. I reflected for a moment and sighed. Sometimes getting what you go after can be a bitch. "Damn tacos," I mumbled, even though I hadn't eaten any. I needed something to make myself believe something other than my fears about the thing I wanted most had caused my own body to attack.

CHAPTER TWENTY-TWO

Jennifer and Carmine Get Lucky

While the journalist was merrily making himself ill, Jennifer Lowe was bringing her evening to an end, or so she thought. Jennifer sat the bar alone as she was often forced to do. She had gotten used to being the only one in her league. Company was rare. She finished her drink and stood up to leave, gathering her purse and coat, while nearby eyes were stuck staring at her cleavage as it tried to escape her black low-cut blouse. A tall, muscularly built oilman from out of the state took her leaving as his cue to move. He brushed back his dark hair then hurried to her side. "You can't leave just yet," he started.

"Why the hell not?" answered Lowe with disdain.

He brushed his drunken erection against her thigh and whispered in her ear, "'Cause I ain't fucked ya yet, darlin'."

"Oh, please. What kind of line is that?" she said while thinking, *Great, another drunken Texan. Why'd they have to discover that gas reserve here anyway?* She started to leave then turned back to stare at him with a large confident grin, much like a lioness might have upon seeing an injured gazelle. She shocked him by taking a handful between his legs. "You know how to use this?" she asked giving him a squeeze. He didn't have to say a word because Jennifer could feel him growing and throbbing in her hand.

"Yes, sweetness, I believe I do."

"Come with me," she said, pulling him by his tie for a few feet before moving out in front and taking the lead. She directed him out, down the street, and across to the lobby of an expensive hotel. As she approached the front desk, the man behind it saw her, smiled, and straightened his coat, "Good evening, Ms. Gladstone!"

"Good evening, Anthony."

"Will you want the same room this evening?"

"I believe I will, Anthony. Is 411 available?"

"Yes, it is," he said. Knowing what she meant, what had happened every time she had stayed there, he gave her the key for 541.

She took the 541 key, handed Anthony a folded bill, and then turned to her victim/companion. "They keep 411 for me when I'm in town."

"I'm impressed," he said while staring down her dress.

They walked to the elevator with brass doors, pushed their floor, and when another couple tried to sneak in the lift with them, Jennifer pushed the close door button, held out her hand to stop them, and said, "Sorry, we're full…at least he is." After the car had started to move, Jennifer pulled the stop button and slowly dropped the straps of her dress so that her breasts were totally uncovered, "Is this what you want?"

He was all over her with his hands and his mouth. When she heard him make a snarling moan, and saw his nostril flair, she pushed him away, lifted her dress, and released the stop button. "Be a good boy, or you won't get your dessert," she teased.

He laughed and couldn't believe his luck.

When the lift opened, she led him to an unmarked door just to the right of the elevator, "Here we are, 411," she said, sliding in the key for 541 and pushing open the door.

It was an expensive but small room and a bath. She led him to the expensive, solidly built wood bed then turned to face him. She cupped both hands around him between his legs, and he closed his eyes. "Oh, yeah."

"My turn," she said and had his suit coat and shirt off in a flash. He tried to reach for her but she pushed his hands to his sides. "Let me do the work," she said, unbuckling his pants, letting them fall to the floor, before she began running her hands over his chest and down his shorts.

"Oh, baby," he moaned. Her hands felt like fire. When she pulled down his shorts his member snapped out bouncing, fully erect.

He moaned again, and she laughed a wicked little laugh, "You are a big boy," she teased. "Take those shoes off, get on the bed, and make yourself comfortable while I wash up." He greedily complied and lay on the bed with his rock of a penis bouncing up and down against his stomach in throbs of excitement.

Jennifer began to walk to the bathroom dropping her dress and bra, and then she stopped and returned to the bed. From the nightstand she pulled out a preplaced item and turned to sit on the bed beside him. When he reached for her breast, she gave him a long feel and then grabbed his wrist, wrapping it in a scarf and nimbly tied it to the bedpost.

The Texan chuckled. "You're kinky, huh?"

She rubbed her swollen breasts back and forth over his face making sure her nipples slid between his lips each time. Then she took his other wrist and likewise tied it to the bed.

"Man oh man, you are one sexy bitch."

She smiled coyly and then turned to look at him confidently. "I know." Jennifer went to the foot of the bed and ran her fiery hands down his thighs to his ankles, making him pulsate and bounce on his stomach even higher. She tied his ankles and laughed.

Jennifer walked to the dresser and took out another pre-staged item, a bottle of scotch and a crystal tumbler. She poured a triple or quadruple shot amount into the tumbler and turned to him, taking a long drink while sliding her hand into her thong and played with her clit, giving him a good long show. The Texan greedily watched her and pulsated. Jennifer drank in the sight of how happy he was to be under her control. When she got back to the bed, she could see he was so excited that a white bead of semen had begun to come out. She laughed a wicked laugh and collected it with her tongue. He moaned loudly and began to shudder. Jennifer moved up the bed and put her finger over his mouth, "Not yet, big boy. I've got plans for you." She took another drink, put the tumbler to his mouth, and tipped it up. He drank from it and then tried to stop. Jennifer's free hand grabbed his balls and squeezed until he opened his mouth again and finished the glass. "Good boy," she said, as she got up and moved to the bathroom, turning off lights as she went, until the room was mostly shadows aside from the light entering from the bathroom. In that light, she stopped to let the Texan see her drop her thong to the floor before closing the door. She loved hearing the aching moan he made.

When she opened the door to return, Jennifer stood in the silhouette of light for a moment and then snapped off the light. As she moved toward him, now, she seemed different. Her legs seemed longer. She seemed taller. Her skin seemed to glow. At first the Texan thought she was in a beam of moonlight, because he could see her swaying breasts and the slit between her legs even in the darkness, but no moonlight entered the room through the drawn curtains. "Ride me, you sexy cowgirl," he invited. When she got on the bed and straddled him, suddenly the moonlight glow disappeared.

Carmine Camino too was having a late night. His plans to expand his empire were ready to be executed. He had rebuilt his organization, mended fences with the other bosses, and solidified his authority. He knew the B.I.B. still stood in his way but had not been idle developing a cure for that problem either.

He had been in contact with everyone one of Gambrelli's men, now in prison, who had taken part in the ill-fated attempt to liberate the Tool and finish off the B.I.B. To a man, none wanted to ever mess with the B.I.B. again. They all shook their heads when asked to confront her again; some immediately began to pace nervously at just the thought of it. They all talked about her speed, like a ghost, and her power, putting their lights out with one fist or back of her hand. Not one wanted a rematch. Not one could give Carmine a clue as to a weakness in the B.I.B. Not one except Dennis Mastrangelo.

Mastrangelo was a cocky young thug. Carmine had seen the type before and almost dismissed him. "Yeah, I'd love a rematch with the bitch...I cut her, ya know. I cut her good right here," he said, lifting his right arm and pointing to his ribs, "We'd have had her too, if I'd had some help. While she was putting out Benny, I sneaks in catlike and gave her a slash. If someone had been there to help, I'd have cut her like a pig. Instead, her arm comes down and puts me out, like that. Hit me like a fuckin' hammer, she did."

"You cut her?" asked Camino, "You saw blood?"

"Hell, yeah. On her clothes and on my knife before she whacked me."

"You're sure?" said Camino, deadly serious.

Mastrangelo leaned over the table and stared Carmine in the eye equally as seriously, "On my dead grandmother's grave."

Immediately, Carmine made a mental note to cut a deal and spring Mastrangelo.

Now in his dimly lit office, as he contemplated the course of future events, he recalled his conversation with Mastrangelo. *If it bleeds, I can kill it*, he thought. *If it bleeds, I can kill it.* He lifted a brochure for new Israeli-built assault rifles, reviewed their rate of fire, and checked the various types of ammunition available. *She can't outrun a bullet between the eyes. If it bleeds, I can kill it.*

CHAPTER TWENTY-THREE

The Trail Leads to the Eastern European Jungle

I finally had the clue that would lead me to the B.I.B. A young man at Flanagan's told me that he had seen her at Skelly's not more than ten minutes earlier. The only problem was that, in return for his information, I had agreed to play him two games of "quarters," the drinking game. Both games I promptly lost, requiring me to drink two tall beers. By the time I was done with that and on my way, staggering to Skelly's, my blood alcohol meter was hovering just under the Pennsylvania legal limit.

My Pub Crawler avatar, a true Grecian-God-looking fellow, was now staggering, then dropped to all fours, crawling toward Skelly's. It was no use. I watched in horror as his blood alcohol level tripped the limit and he rolled over into the gutter, with Skelly's a mere two minutes' stagger away.

I had been playing Pub Crawler for an hour now, in a concerted effort to keep from doing anything that might better my life. But now, the frustration of being so close to finding the B.I.B. in the video game and failing had turned me back to real work.

In an attempt to escape from my escape, if you know what I mean, I looked to recover my old notes on the names of the other 1976 Super-Bowl-born women from my intricate filing system and found them right where I had left them, beside a stack of unwashed jeans. Boy, I had better get to those soon. It was already getting late, but I convinced myself with a bottle of Miner's Lite that I did my best work late, drunk, and without the slightest clue how to proceed. I fumbled through the papers trying to remember where I had left off before the Web site and celebrity had made me drop them like a blind roofer. It slowly returned to me, the master list of all the names with notes on those that had left town or otherwise disappeared. Jennifer Lowe's name had an X beside it, which told me how hot on the trail and perceptive I had been. Rebecca Sans also had an X. Of the fourteen or so names, eight were either X'd or had moved away. So I began Internet searches, just as I had done on Jennifer Lowe, checking public records and simple Internet searches for them.

I chugged my Miner's and got down to business. The next two name searches opened even my blurry eyes. Both, including one that was the second-closest born to Dr. Jones' magical halftime, blinked up on my screen as deceased. When I began checking newspaper articles and obits, my eyes widened yet again. They had died accidental deaths within six days of one another; one died in a car crash and the other in a bizarre cycling accident. No statistics I could imagine would support coincidence as a possibility, two relatively young women out of a group of just fourteen dying within a few days of each other. I followed the leads as far as they would go, making notes, and bookmarking sites where I had found pictures and other relevant info. It was a long, time-consuming effort, including searches that turned up nothing.

Of the final four, three showed up married, one in Washington, another in California. A third showed up married and living in town, and the final Super Bowl born was not even trying to hide, showing an address and phone. By then, my mind was too unfocused to generate a plan for meeting them. As I decided the night was over and I needed some rest, I looked at the glowing image of my computer screen to see the time was 5:32. At first, that seemed weird to my blurred mind, but then the light coming in from the windows made it clear, 5:32 a…m. Shit, I was right. I did do my best work late and drunk. Who knew?

As I weaved my way to bed, thoughts from earlier in the night jumped out and said "boo." I slid under the "covers" hit by the stark realization that one of these two should be the blonde from the bar. The thought made my heart race, and I stared at an empty spot on the wall. An hour later, the spot hadn't moved, and I still felt my blood racing. No deep breathing or reasoning quieted the anxiety. All I had of her was the image of her at O'Malley's and the photo of her at Skelly's; both played over and over in my mind, minus the part where she had spoken to me and I was unable to respond, naturally. Then I thought of her frightful words on the Web site the night before, how I had almost exposed her. I could feel the veins in my neck pumping rapidly, uncontrollably.

Then a realization shot through me, making me sit up in bed. I had three things going for me. I knew how she looked, I knew she was a single mom, and I had the computer address from which she had contacted the B.I.B. site. I would check birth records for the B.I.B.'s child and have Rebecca Sans interpret the hits log to try to locate that computer. By then, it was 6:37 a.m. Hell, I should be up anyway.

An hour later, I was cleaned and java-ed up, ready to go. I was full of energy and anticipation, but, at the same time, half of my stomach was in knots while the rest was sending an acid-spraying party up my throat. And you wouldn't want to be standing behind me for any length of time, if you know what I mean. Call it anticipation and fear or whatever, but I had it, a bad case too.

When I asked Rebecca for the computer trace, she seemed to know what I wanted even before I asked for it. I had a detailed explanation of my request prepared, but didn't get halfway through it. She had not only the IP address but all the information tracked down to the subscriber's home address within a minute. Damn, she's good! I remembered thinking like a sap. Little did I know that she had already traced the hit for Jennifer Lowe an hour earlier. But when it came time to give me the information, I could sense a hesitation in her voice. Little did I know that she was consciously right there and then battling the ethical dilemma of whether or not she owed it me to give me the true information.

I thanked Rebecca wholeheartedly and even missed the hesitation before her guilty, "You're welcome." I hung up and stared at the address on the paper for a long moment, as if admiring a priceless prize, the Mona Lisa, a personal note from God on the meaning of life. Then I cleared my throat to drive down the acid from my nervous stomach and navigated a route to her house on the computer: trip time thirty-seven minutes. *Thirty-seven minutes*, I thought, feeling like Neil Armstrong after being given the OK to start his descent for the lunar landing, Thirty-seven friggin' minutes to the B.I.B.

Thirty-seven minutes, my ass! It was almost a belching, farting, nervous hour later before I coolly slid past her house, 007-like, and parked along the street a block or so down. I sat in the car watching the door for as long as the untrained could take it and then began nervously patrolling the sidewalk across the street from her house.

Frankly, the neighborhood was not what I had expected at all. It was an old rundown part of Scranton, I mean even older and more rundown than the rest of Scranton. As I slowly walked, I could see the people were made up of either the very young, who had no money, or the very old, who had no money. RFDs lived beside retirees. I walked past one RFD who wore his jacket on backward and, when he turned to say hello, he promptly ran into and did battle with a small tree. His friend, working on his car in the driveway, laughed at him for a moment before the hood of his car closed on him. His neighbor, a small retiree just looked at the trapped RFD and waved his hand in disgust. "I'm not getting you out of there again, Jimmy," he said as he went inside. "I told you there's a stick to hold that up, a stick, you moron!"

The fourth inconspicuous time I belched my way past her house, I finally had the courage to knock on the door, motivated by a firm desire to get the hell out of there. As I started across the street, I heard the roar and saw the flash of a beer truck that had suddenly appeared around the corner and accelerated in front of me. It made me step back. It made an RFD on a bicycle run straight into a parked car. "I'm OK," he said, holding up an arm from the other side of the car.

When I got to the door, the veins in my neck were pounding like bongos and I was glad I hadn't tried to have anything solid for breakfast, if you know what I mean. It was early on a Saturday morning, so I thought my chances were good that she would be home. No answer. I tried a second ring and then heard an unintelligible voice drawing nearer. As the door swung open, I swear my heart stopped and felt like a rock in my chest.

In the doorway stood, not the B.I.B., but a middle-aged, dark-haired woman dressed in a robe. I asked her if there was another woman living there, and she replied in an Eastern

European language with a smile growing on her face. I tried again to make it clear that I was looking for a blonde woman, but I doubted she understood half of what I said. But the "looking for" and "woman" part seemed to incite her. She grabbed my arm, pulled me in, and closed the door. She continued speaking in her language, but the tones became slower and she emphasized words that must have been significant to her. The fact that her words hadn't sent me packing implied I was in agreement, bringing a smile to her face. How did I know what the hell she was saying? She got close and kept talking while she ran her hands over my shoulders and began squeezing my arms, each squeeze making her hiss a little.

I looked around the house in the hope that someone else was there who spoke English and then turned to her to try English one more time. As I turned, she loosened the belt and her robe dropped off her shoulders revealing a very hairy, naked, Eastern European woman. Should I mention a very sexually-excited, naked, Eastern European woman?

I knew that was my cue to leave, I didn't wanna do this again! I gracefully tried to back away without insulting a woman whose cause, I had to admit, I supported wholeheartedly. If there were a "Horny Women Who Want to Ravage Me" committee," I would be certain to give…regularly. As I shook my head and began to apologize, the nimble old minx pulled my arm and swept my legs with her foot, leaving me to fall right on top of her to her delight, while she continued to speak and hiss in her language. She took hold of my hand and stuck it into the soaking wet hair jungle between her legs and tried to reach up to kiss me, when the cavalry arrived in the form of a potbellied old man in pajamas who came waddling into the room, quickly, but still waddling. He yelled at her. She yelled back, as I began my feverish escape, all the while trying to push my hand in deeper to the steamy, excited jungle. As he got close, she turned her attention to him, I pulled away, and then she got up. She and the man continued in loud tones and definitely negatively gestured toward one another while I backed away. The fact that Mr. Potbelly didn't give me the slightest concern told me that she "may" have done this before. By the time I closed the door behind me, their tones had already changed and I heard them begin to laugh amid a quieter vocal display. Apparently, someone else had entered the jungle, "L'Amour."

I was devastated as I walked to my car without finding the B.I.B., especially because I knew I didn't have any hand wipes in the glove compartment. How could that be the wrong address? I looked back one last time to make certain it was the house Rebecca had given me. I shook my head as I opened the car door, but then heard a laugh and saw something dark under my car. When I looked down, I heard another laugh and saw an RFD slide out from under the front of the car and run into a yard nearby. I shook my head thinking, *What the...* Then two more appeared from under the back of the car and ran away, one tripping over a raised section of the sidewalk, while the other howled with laughter as he continued to run.

"I could have killed you!" I screamed after them, shaking my fist. "Fuckin' RFD morons!"

I looked under the car and all around, not seeing any more RFDs except for the one across the street who had run his bicycle into the parked car. He remained on the ground behind the car. He was not holding his hand quite as high as before and his "I'm OK" didn't seem quite as believable anymore. After a minute, I watched his hand plummet, and he began to plea "water!"

I called Rebecca, and she insisted that the address was the house from which the online access to the site had occurred.

I accepted the information in defeat, knowing the Eastern European jungle was a dead end. But that was the first time I began to doubt anything Rebecca had done. She told me that she was at home but I could hear the cars passing her on a street. I put down the phone and headed home. This time, I looked left, right, left, and right again, before pulling out; you never knew when a fast-moving beer truck would appear in this neighborhood.

I started crashing from the lack of sleep and overdosing on adrenalin, even before I got home, in thirty-nine minutes, still not thirty-seven. I hit the couch and felt everything drain out of me.

I still knew what she looked like. I still had the Super Bowl Born information to research, but my "ace in the hole" computer trace had vanished. Could the B.I.B. know that woman or have actually been at that house in RFD/retiree land? I doubted it. I doubted Rebecca and I doubted myself…again; welcome home.

CHAPTER 24

Finally

I couldn't tell who the woman was, but every time I passed the kitchen window, I saw her sitting in her car seeming to look right at me. She spoke on her cell phone now and again but spent most of her time staring at my apartment. The first time I noticed her was an hour or so earlier.

So I crouched to see her and hoped she wouldn't see me. She seemed to yell at someone on the phone, and then took a last look, seeming to look into my eyes, before her car sped off with a squeal. It made my blood run cold. Had someone found me? I was glad that Paige was staying with my sister. It seemed the time had come.

When I blinked and found that it was already dark outside, I knew I had crashed badly. I didn't even feel rested, just… nasty. But then I found out what had broken my slumber in the first place. My cell phone was ringing merrily somewhere like a joyous bird, which I hated and wanted to kill. I dug around furiously and finally found it on the floor beside me. "Yeah," I said, pushing my hair back out of my eyes.

"She's 'ere!"

"What?" my bleary mind started. "Who's this?" Smooth, ain't I.

"It's me, you old sod, Martin from O'Malley's. You told me ta call when she was 'ere and I'm calling."

"Huh?" I stammered cleverly.

"Your blonde bird, remember, the big tipper? She's 'ere at her table as we speak!"

My body found a new supply of adrenalin and shot into a panic. I leapt to my feet and started turning left and right trying to decide what to do next.

"It's still $300, right? You said $300 if 'in she were ta show."

"Sure, sure, whatever." I knew he had inflated the reward, but I didn't care. What, money didn't matter anymore? Did I have a fever? "You hold her there. I'm on my way!"

"Sure, sure, I'll just sit on her till yous gets 'ere…If she leaves it's still $300!"

"Give her free drinks," I stammered as I fumbled for my shoes in the dark and found the hard table leg instead. "The drinks will be on me, whatever, free food, just keep her there!"

"It'll be my pleasure. I'm sure she'll love the lobster/steak flambé special we're havin' tonight."

I remembered the greasy chili fries O'Malley's served and knew the old man was just telling me that he was inflating the bill some more. "Just keep her there!" With that, I clicked the phone off and started through the door. I returned a few seconds later, remembering that a pair of pants would be a good idea….and a shirt.

When I walked into the bar and found her sitting at the same table as in all my wet dreams, my heart changed neighborhoods and began bouncing around my body. But I kept my cool and walked slowly toward her without a word in my head to say. Martin broke my cool when he came running over with an order pad trying to collect his money up front. But I pushed him on his shoulders with both arms and gave him a glare that put him in his place. He and I handled the quick negotiations and were done. I coolly slid into the booth across from her and feasted my eyes, waiting for the blue/green flash, giving her the greatest opening line ever.

When he walked into the bar and stood staring at me like a hungry puppy, I first thought that he was going to hurl. Then, when the old bartender nearly ran him over and spun him toward the bar, I had no idea what to think. He slipped something into the old man's hand, they exchanged some rough words, and then he zigzagged his way back toward me. For a minute, I thought he was going right back out the door, but then he zagged and stood over me.

"Mind if I sit?" he asked uncertainly, and was that a belch he muffled?

I gestured for him to sit. He sat, looked at the table for a minute, and then looked up and said, "You come here often?"

She was obviously impressed. She remembered me in an instant. Apparently, I had made the same kind of impression on her that she had made on me a few months back, with the possible exception that she hadn't made a Web site for me, been searching for me feverishly, or appeared to be under any sort of gaseous attack, as was I. Other than that, she felt the same as me. I was sure. Her eyes glowed and she smiled at me earnestly. "I remember you! You sat right over there," she said, turning and pointing, "with that Dr. Jones I've read so much about in the paper. I saw him on TV. He's the big B.I.B. expert, right?" she said, totally unruffled by the sound of an RFD firing in the back room during the antler game.

I nodded. "Dr. Jones and I have 'both' been…in the media a lot lately," I crowed. "I have a Web site…"

"I know. Pub Crawler and B.I.B. Rescue, love those games you have," she interrupted in a milder tone, her eyes dropping to the table, which was littered with empty Miner's Lite bottles and two barely touched orders of chili fries. She offered me a basket of untouched chili fries.

"No…thanks."

After an RFD slid past us on a chair pushed by two other RFDs, I felt the words regurgitating from my mouth without control; hey, at least it wasn't another burp. "Look, it's no accident that I ran into you tonight. I paid the bartender to call me if you showed up. Your feast here," I said, gesturing sarcastically to the table, "was to keep you here until I arrived."

"Why?" she asked bewildered and amused. "Most guys…"

"No, that's not it…I'm not most guys…You see…I just have to know…Are you the woman who complained the other night about a fish-face picture on my Web site?"

She waited a long minute and stared off at a distant speck before answering. "Are you the one who took the picture off?" she said, turning to stare right through me.

"Yes."

"I wanted to thank you. My friends and family know that face and they were sure…"

I held up my hand to stop her. "I know who you are."

"What do you mean? I'm just a single mom. I'm nobody."

"You were born January 18, 1976, during the Super Bowl, around halftime, I would wager. You have growing powers you can't understand and aren't sure you want. You're the B.I.B., and now it seems everyone is after you, me included."

Her amused look turned to concern. "Oh...So that's it. You think 'I' am the B.I.B.?"

My heart stopped flopping and I became deadly serious as I fixed my eyes on her. "I know who you are...Don't worry. I'm the one who took the picture off the site, remember. I won't tell anyone."

"Then what's this all about? You've got your story, don't you?" she grew angry thinking of my making money off the site and about the woman outside her window. "Are you the one who's got the dogs on me? Was that woman outside my apartment working for you?"

"What woman? No one knows but me, not even Dr. Jones knows about you." But then I began thinking.

"She was sitting outside my window for an hour. I haven't been able to go back home since. That's why I'm hiding here. Everyone knows only morons come here."

"Describe this woman."

"Well, about my age, well dressed, short dark hair, rose-colored glasses...Definitely not the mob or a cop. She could have been a reporter. She kept talking on her cell phone. She had a heated fight with someone on the other end. She was alone...little economy car."

I began to match the description to all the reporters with whom I'd worked, no match. Then I ran the description by Jennifer Lowe and realized that even a woman couldn't have missed noticing the peaks of Mt. Lowe. I began to draw a blank until I matched the rose-colored glasses to Rebecca Sans. How could it be mild, sweet, efficient Rebecca? Then the "ton of bricks" hit me. "Goddamn it!"

"What? What is it?" the B.I.B. wondered, concerned at my extreme agitation.

"God fuckin' damn it." I slammed my fist on the table. "I am such a friggin' sap!"

"You know her, I take it."

"Son of a bitch!" I cried.

"OK, you really do know her. Who is she?"

I continued in my self-pitying rage, shaking my head and staring at the ceiling.

"OK, now. Let's focus here."

"I don't believe that bitch set me up!" It all flashed through my mind and connected like an old black-and-white detective movie's last ten minutes. I thought I was hunting the Super Bowl born with my little survey and list of women born January 18, 1976, and all along they were playing me. It was too easy that I needed a graphic designer/computer nerd for the Web site, and up pops Rebecca, the perfect candidate. Then she put the site together well and quickly. I'll bet it was already planned and programmed. She took over full control of the site and all its information, because they knew I was a lazy asshole, just counting my money and TV appearances. I was the front that kept them out of sight. All along, they were monitoring it to try to locate the B.I.B. and, like the patsy I was, I handed her to them with the Goddamn fish-face picture. Rebecca traced that contact from the B.I.B. even before I asked her to do it. She fed me the wrong address to try to dead-end my lead and to try to give me finger herpes, I guessed, but Rebecca? What would she want with the B.I.B.? She seemed so sweet and… and what?

Then the mobile phone calls while Rebecca was watching the B.I.B.'s apartment hit me. Sure, one may have been the call I made to her after almost being forced to get lucky in the Eastern European jungle. I knew she wasn't in her house. I heard the cars go by. But we didn't argue and it was just the one call. She was working with/for someone else. It had to be Jennifer Lowe. My God, all the Super Bowl born were working together? Why? What did they want with the B.I.B.? How many of these "mothers" were there? Then I remembered the two Super Bowl born that had died mysteriously, and, with a face frozen in fright, I looked across the table at the B.I.B.'s soft features and shimmering eyes, afraid of what they might have planned for her.

"What?" she asked. "You have to tell me."

"I know who was at your house, and I know how she got your address…She is a Web designer that manages my Web site."

"So it was you," she glared.

"No, no, she only does the Web design for me. She is working with another woman behind my back, using me, using my site to gather information about you. I didn't realize it until just this second. They used me and the site to get to you, and I fell for it like a one-legged Irish dancer. That's why I'm so mad. I swear I didn't know what they were doing, until you told me about the car outside your apartment. But it all makes sense now."

"Who are they? What do they want with me?" she pleaded.

I sighed, realizing how big the answer was and trying to come up with a short version. "Dr. Jones' theory is that women born the same day as you have a very high chance of developing superpowers. The others I've met seemed normal to me at first. I thought you were the only one. But now I see that you probably all have superpowers but have just chosen different ways to use them. You stand up for the defenseless, the underdogs, for all American morals. One of them is using her powers to make money; she's a multimillionaire, at least, but acts like an everyday woman. The other is the one you saw outside your apartment, Rebecca Sans. She's somehow mixed up with the rich one, Jennifer Lowe. I didn't think Rebecca had any powers, but now I have to wonder. She acts like any chick I've ever known."

"This rich bitch, Jennifer, what powers does she have?" she asked, seriously concerned but apparently believing my spiel and worrying about her ability to defend herself.

"Well…I'm not a hundred percent certain…She melted my pen."

"Melted your pen?" she almost laughed. "What kind of power is that to have?"

I shook my head. "Tip of the iceberg…This woman owns real estate all over the world. Who knows where else she's connected. I just know she's not the kind of person you are."

"Kind of person I am? What does that mean? How would you know?"

I dropped my face to look at the table, wanting to tell her how she made my body rebel against my control, how much I admired the things she had done, and how I could think of little other than her since the flashes of blue then green had hit me from her eyes. I looked up at her face wanting to tell her how beautiful she was, how her scent was driving me wild, how I wanted my mouth on her lips that instant, and how I had done all this just for this opportunity to see her again. I wanted to tell her how important this meeting was to me, explain how

I had risked my life in the Eastern European jungle to find her. It all sounded too childish to believe. I fumbled for the words and could see her expectantly waiting for my answer without a clue of what I was going to say.

Luckily, I didn't have to answer. The barkeep came through the front door with a couple of plastic bags and plunked them down on our table without much regard for the items in the bags or the items below them on the table, "There ya go," he said putting out his hand.

I looked up at him as I handed him some cash. When he started to walk away, I had to grab him. "Hey, hey!"

He stopped, "What is it now, sire?"

I started taking containers of food out of the bags, real food. "You have any plates, spoons, forks in this dump?"

"Next I should guess you'll be wantin' a wee rose for the table, I suspect." I put out my hand and snapped my fingers as if to say give me back my cash. "Oh, bloody hell, I think I can find something."

"Good lad," I said jokingly, before he responded with a disgusted wave of his hand.

"What's this?" asked the B.I.B.

"I felt bad about the chili fries and asked him to pop around the corner for some real food from Michael's. Hope you like shrimp and chicken."

She looked taken aback at first but then started checking out the food as I unpacked it. "That smells great."

The barkeep shuffled to the table with some old unmatched plates and silverware and dropped them on the table as a small group of RFDs started gathering around the table, staring at the food, pointing at it and discussing it among themselves. I called to the barkeep and returned with some empty chili fry baskets and plastic forks. I made up four or five baskets with small amounts of the courses of our meal and handed them out to the RFDs, along with the cold chili fries. That seemed to satisfy them and they drifted away, chuckling, except one that dumped out the chicken and shrimp preferring the paper basket as a more valuable prize. When the barkeep returned again with a plastic red rose and a small candle, he held his hand out again, and I filled it before he would leave us alone. What a romantic he was at heart, I thought, as he walked away with a pocket full of my cash.

When I looked back to the table the B.I.B. was already into her meal. "I haven't eaten all day," she said, loading a forkful.

"And yet you could somehow resist those chili fries," I joked. "Well, they're an acquired taste."

She only nodded as she chewed.

It felt good to watch her doing something so normal and everyday as that. I smiled but couldn't escape the thoughts that the meal had interrupted. Hopefully she would forget what we were talking about. I fought with myself to keep from getting too melancholy and over thinking things. I decided to throw off my analytical defensiveness and just enjoy my time with her.

But then I realized, hell, she was eating everything! She was packing it away like a busload of tourists at an all-you-can-eat buffet! My first instinct was to start defensively loading my plate too, but then I stopped, took only a few bites, and watched her smile, enjoy her food, and begin light conversation with me. In an instant we were connected. My stomach calmed, and I smiled in the back of my mind. Fuck, was I doing something right for a change?

With the RFDs as a constant sideshow, we were soon laughing together as we ate and downed Miner Lites. She ate everything in sight, including a few forkfuls off my meager plate.

We bantered questions back and forth about ourselves and our lives, to date. I was tactful to avoid questions about her as the B.I.B. She told me about her daughter and of the rigors of being a teenage single mother. She talked about her job as if her superpowers didn't exist.

When the RFDs started a chair race, pushing one RFD one lap around the main room on a chair with other RFDs as engines, I quickly grabbed her hand, found a chair, and entered her in the chariot or should I say chair-idiot race. When the B.I.B. pushed over our nearest competition, we were home free for a win. Our prize? Miner Lite's presented to us with chili fry baskets as our crowns. We gave them both to the runner's up. What class!

Two Miner's Lites later found both of us wearing the antlers for the antler game in the back room. They missed us, of course, with the new law requiring blanks, but we dropped and rolled on the floor anyway as if hit by the same shot. We both laughed and rolled up on our sides facing each other. Even in an antler helmet, her gray eyes glistened and the shimmering smile on her lips was lovely to behold. I had to get out of there fast.

Back at the table, she suddenly seemed to sober up. "I've got to get to my sister's house. Thank you for the info on those two bitches, the food, and a fun night. I needed it."

I panicked. "You can't go."

"I'll be OK. I know who they are now. I just need to find a new place, make them start looking all over again. I'll find a way to get my stuff without them following...Paige will be pissed but what can you do?"

As she started to leave, I grabbed her arm. "You can't go. How am I gonna find you again?" Before she could answer, I felt how warm her arm seemed, but then the feeling changed. She noticed it too. I could tell by the surprised look on her face as she looked down at our entwined arms. The intensity grew and I soon learned why the cat in the news article had risked being run over by the beer truck just to be back in her arms. My entire arm began to feel like, well, like another part of my anatomy, let's say. The pulsating warmth made it easy to surrender to it. She dropped my arm, because I wasn't planning to drop hers anytime soon. She stepped back a step and let out a deep breath with a look of surprise. I pushed her back down into her seat with a hand on her shoulder. "It's just your sister. You can be a little late."

Two hours later found us sitting on the toxic floor beneath the nasty plastic tablecloth of our booth at O'Malley's with our backs to the wall. Several Miner Lites to the good, we had both become quieter and subdued. Despite the alcohol running through her veins, she kept space between us, avoiding a repeat of the arm incident. Somehow our conversation had become more and more full of expletives as the night wore on.

As she took a long sip from a Miner's bottle, I had to ask, "You know…why haven't you done that thing…that thing you do with your eyes tonight?"

"What fuckin' thing with my eyes?" she said, leering over at me.

"You know…that thing! Like you did the first night I saw you."

"No…no, I don't know. You wanna fuckin' enlighten me?"

"You know what a fuckin' lighthouse is?"

"Do you know what my fist is?" she said, putting up a low unthreatening fist.

"OK, you know a lighthouse has a light on top that rotates around? You know how the light turns away and you don't see it, then it gets brighter and brighter as it turns toward you, until it flashes right in your eyes? Then it spins around again?" She nodded. "When I first saw your beautiful gray eyes..."

"My eyes aren't fuckin' gray! They're hazel...everybody says they're hazel."

"Get the fuck out! Hazel, my ass! They're gray...gray with little specks of blue and sometimes green."

She shook her head. "No fuckin' way. They're hazel!" she said indignantly.

"OK, OK...when I first saw your <u>hazel</u> eyes, I looked at you and your eyes flashed blue then green like a light on a lighthouse. It was fuckin' amazing. Jones, he couldn't see it. But I did...Right in the old eyeballs," I said, pointing two fingers at my eyes.

She didn't say a word or react. "You know what the weird thing was? No one else can see it but me. That's how I knew that there was something special between us," I added, pointing a finger at both of us repeatedly. She drank from her beer and stared at her feet, totally ignoring my attempt to make a connection between us. "What's that shit all about? Why do you do that shit?"

She was silent for a long moment, and then tried to take a drink from a bottle that was already empty. "...I marked you."

"Marked me? What the fuck does that mean?" I asked, giving out a little sarcastic laugh.

She turned to me. "It means none of those other bitches can get to you. Jennifer fuckin' whoever can't have you...You're mine," she said in a low tone.

I laughed, "What?"

"Any woman," she said, arcing her bottle in a sweeping motion, "can't mark you. They can't have you 'cause I already have you marked. Even those super bitches…Have you met her yet?" I nodded before taking a long sip. "Well, did she put any moves on you? Did she try to get you to do something you didn't want to do? Did you tell her about me?" I shook my head. She pushed the bottle in her hand forward. "That's 'cause I marked you."

I laughed, "I didn't tell her about you, but she tried some moves."

"And?"

"And I walked the fuck out!"

"What'd I tell you," she said, again sucking on the empty bottle.

I thought it was funny until it dawned on me how nonexistent my sex life had been since being "marked." I stared at my bottle and then took my last sip, uncertain about this "marked" thing. I looked over at her for a moment surprised at how different and real she was now.

"What the fuck are you lookin' at?" she said after noticing me.

"You know…for a conservative, moral, superhero lady, you say 'fuck' a lot…fuck, fuckin…"

"Who said I was conservative, moral, or a fuckin' lady?" she said, apparently not sure which word bothered her most.

"You are…You're not out making money or beating people up with your powers like Jennifer Fuckin' Lowe or two-bitch-faced Rebecca. You're helping people. Fuck, you know how many people are alive today because of what you did to save that plane from crashing? And it's not just them. It's their kids and their kids' kids…" I paused, wondering if I had used too many "kids." "Hell, it's a Goddamn army of people when you think about it, generations! Shit, you're a fuckin' saint!" She didn't say anything. "You could really be out fuckin' things up but you don't."

She gestured with her finger over her mouth, seeming more subdued, "Shhh, you shouldn't say 'fuck.'"

"Shit, you say fuck all the time!" I protested.

She gave me another "shhh" with a finger over her lips and then dropped her empty bottle on the floor. "...I think I'm fuckin' wasted," she said, as I gave her a "shhh" this time. "Sorry," she said putting a finger over her own lips.

I looked over at her and found myself staring at her eyes. *Hazel, my ass*, I thought, while studying her gray, almost colorless, peepers. She looked over at me and held my gaze with a smile growing on her face that made me feel connected with her, drawn into her. Then her face distorted and she gave out a loud burp, covering her mouth with her hand. "Sorry...I'm not usually a pig...really."

Just then the tablecloth at the other end of the table lifted up and the face of the barkeep appeared. "So this is where you fuckin' assholes went!" We both gave him a "shhh" in unison. "Get your ass out of there. It's past closing time."

I stared blankly at him. "And why is your fine establishment closing so early this evening?" I asked, trying to sound sober and coherent.

"'Cause it's 3:00 a.m., numb nuts. Come on, let's have a go," he said, reaching for the B.I.B.'s hand to help her out. He pulled her up while I jealousy watched their arms interlocked, wondering if he was feeling what I had. As he pulled, she sat up and halfway out smacked her head on the bottom of the table, dropping to the filthy floor laughing. The barkeep dragged her out on her back while she still held her head and giggled. I followed on my hands and knees, but when I got to the end of the table, I stood up too soon and likewise cracked my head on the edge of the table, faking a fall to lie on the floor, cracking up beside her. The barkeep straightened up and shook his head. "You can go ahead and be assholes, just do it elsewhere. I've got an appointment with my bleedin' bed ta keep." With that he walked away.

We continued to crack up and hold our heads until we rolled over and inspected one another. Then the laughs faded and I helped her to her feet, again feeling the warmth of her skin beneath my hand. We tried to brush the floor grime off our clothes to little effect. There was paper in her hair, and I pulled it out, tugging gently, running my hand through her hair. She closed her eyes for a quick second. The pleasured look on her face sent iron to my shorts. To get away, I slid my hand slowly out of her hair, but even that felt great. It felt dangerously sensuous and sobered both of us quickly.

The barkeep came back with a coat on and shooed us out of the door. We stood on the sidewalk of a now quiet street facing each other in air that was surprisingly cool.

I looked at her. "I don't think you're in any condition to drive to your sister's."

"Who's gonna drive?" she asked, giving a little laugh. "I'm flyyying," she said spreading her arms and swaying side to side.

"Flying...Fuckin' flying?" I asked while she gave me a "shhh."

"You? You're in no condition to drive. Why don't I fly you home?"

I laughed. "I don't think so!"

"Afraid?" she asked, leaning into me.

"I'd like to leave with at least an ounce of male dignity left."

"Strong women who fly intimidate you?" she asked jokingly.

"It's more the drunken 'crash and burn' that worries me."

"Well, it's been nice knowing you and all the people that are gonna die when you crash into them on your way home tonight."

I laughed and paused. "Gee, I didn't think you knew those people I'm gonna hit...I think an hour or two in that coffee shop over there should do the trick. Just need some fuckin' caffeine."

She "shhhed" me and then slowly put her steamy finger over my lips and held it there while I melted. She looked deeply into my eyes making me swallow hard. Then came what I had been expecting all night, a repeated blue/green flash of those gray eyes. Hazel eyes....you know.

When she pulled away and said, "See ya," the trance broke and I reached for her.

"Wait! You can't go! How will I find you again? You'll have a new apartment, a new identity!"

She turned her head back to me and just kept walking away. She smiled, saying in a tone that was as solid as granite, "I'll find you." With that, the fog I had seen before materialized around her and then was gone with her. But a couple of seconds later I heard a clang and someone in the distance saying, "Shit!"

CHAPTER 24

Hung Over and Hung Out

I have become accustomed in the last few months, OK, years, to waking up in unusual places and positions, but this one had me baffled. I found myself lying on my side in a cramped space like a letter in an envelope. To my back, I felt the smooth firmness of a wall and, to my chest, I had a little room but not much. At the end of the envelope, I could see the dim predawn light. My eyes were a little blurry still from the previous night's Miner Lites, but I was certain I saw light and made the decision to move toward it. That was a mistake. My shoulders and neck were tight and sore, screaming as I moved. My back and hip were twisted from a night sleeping "on the edge," so to speak, and rebelling against any further attempts at movement. Being the trooper I am, I fought off the pain and wormed my way toward the light until my head was free of the envelope. There, I stopped to see if any further "surprises" were waiting for me in the general vicinity; I didn't wanna do that again. Assured that the coast was clear, I managed to lift my arms from my sides and grab the rim of the envelope then discovered that the rim was the leg of my couch. Confident, now, I pulled myself out and stood there in my boxers with my entire body tight, sore, and unhappy. I stared at the sofa trying to figure how the hell I got back there. I soon found a trail of my clothes leading to and then onto the couch. My socks were on top of the back of the couch. Apparently I had curled up there and then fallen down the crack between the couch and the wall. I shoved the couch against the wall to prevent further incidents then was hit by panic from my murky mind.

I tiptoed to the bedroom and peeked my head in the doorway to see if any unwelcomed, or welcomed, surprises were sleeping there. Relieved at the sight of my empty unmade bed, I sighed in relief and began to try to piece back together the events of the previous night.

The little article on page 3 of section C of the newspaper caught my eyes after the steaming mug of coffee had kicked in and opened them. A man had been found unconscious and injured in the ritzy Maxim Hotel. The man had been found naked, tied to a bed, with severe hip, back, and internal injuries. He claimed he'd been raped by a beautiful young woman; right, that'll get you a lot of sympathy, Charlie. Buried in the text was the description, "deformed genitals." *Oh, my God*, I thought, *that guy is lucky to be alive!* Somehow he had survived the spinderella move, unlike poor Demitri. But who had he been with? Jennifer, Rebecca, the B.I.B., or were there more of them? After a brief mental vacation imagining them all naked and in action with the guy in the article, I read the article again thinking that if things had gone further last night, but for the grace of God that could have been my fate this morning.

Then I had to face it again: what to do now? With her identity being changed as I sat, all the information I had was useless. I didn't even know her old address let alone her new one.

The birth record game was a loser. Did I really have to wait and hope she meant what she said about contacting me? Crap.

One thing I knew to do was log onto the Web site and change all the access codes. Monday, I would find a security company to set up a new firewall and check to see if Rebecca had installed a back door. I thought of calling her to officially terminate our relationship but chose my usual path of least resistance and did nothing but eat some toast.

I turned my thoughts to Dr. Jones. Could he help? Should I tell him everything? No, she was mine, Goddamn it. I couldn't tell him about the B.I.B., but I needed his brain again. Dr. Jones was my next call.

I had never seen Jones quite like this before. His hair was unkempt, his clothes dirty, and he hadn't shaved in days, showing a thin spotty beard. But he was glad to see me, turning down his sitar music and telling me to help myself to a drink from the fridge. I took a step toward it , then remembered the contents of it the last time I had been given that offer—books, a cat, and curry. "No, thanks, I'm good."

"What can I do for you, my friend?" he said, returning behind his desk and continuing the work I had interrupted, but I could see B.I.B. Rescue running on his laptop.

I wondered, "What are you working on there? Is it about the super born?"

"Ah, the super born! Is that what you're calling them now?" He seemed to get irritated. He pounded the desk. "Yes, it is about the super born, everything is about the Goddamn super born. I can't sleep. I don't eat. This mystery is ruining my life. I have been so close…"

"We are close," I volunteered.

He looked up with a snap, "We are? You have good news?"

I told him everything, well everything less a lot of things. I updated him about Jennifer Lowe, the connection to Rebecca Sans, and how Rebecca had used my site to search for the B.I.B. I told him about how she had directed me purposely to the wrong address. I made certain he understood that the B.I.B. would now have moved and assumed a new identity. I just forgot to mention my meeting with the B.I.B. or what it felt like to run my hands through her hair or look into her eyes... Anyway, I left out the good part.

I made certain he understood that the birth record search would be useless and that we needed a new plan to deal with them. The whole time, Jones remained calm and silent, nodding on occasion. "Well?" I asked him after he continued his silence.

"I am just thinking. As it happens, what I am researching right now is a theory that may explain things. You see, my friend, I have come across indications that the social structure of the super born will probably be similar to that of bees."

"Bees? You mean like buzz, buzz bees?"

Jones nodded, "It makes sense in my research and now is confirmed by the information you've supplied. There can be only one queen. These three or however many there are will naturally have to seek dominance. Only one will remain. We are all drones for them, my friend," said Jones, appearing sad.

I thought quickly back to the birth record search I had made and the unexplainable number of young women born during the Super Bowl who had died mysteriously. "Only one queen..." I muttered.

"So it seems. The battle is going on right now, and here we sit. I am telling you the picture is sad, very sad indeed."

"What can we do? I have to warn her." I slipped up.

"Warn who?"

Luckily I knew how to recover quickly. "Just kiddin'."

"Kidding about what?" Jones demanded.

"The B.I.B. I wish I could warn her about the others. But I can't 'cause I don't know where she is." Smooth, aren't I?

"How do you know which of these super born is good and which are the bad ones? The B.I.B. could be the one exterminating the others."

I opened my mouth in her defense but then realized not to slip up again. "Well, what do you think we should do? If you're right and we're the drones, we'll end up like Demitri . There is no way to approach any of them safely," I lied.

Jones shook his head. "Your guess would be as good as mine. Why do you think I look like shit! This whole thing has gotten out of control. How could I be so right and be so unable to prove it? It is a dilemma," he said, coming around the table and putting his hand on my shoulder.

Simultaneously, we both thought of the other, *He smells like shit.*

CHAPTER 25

Three Superwomen in One Night:
Not as Much Fun as It Sounds

On the way back to my palatial two-bedroom, I stopped at a drive-through for some gourmet takeout (and fries). I was just digging through the bag trying to figure out how the suckers had ripped me off, when my mobile phone vibrated on my belt. I answered with a fry or two, in my mouth, "Yeah?"

The voice on the other end was rushed and near panic. It was a woman's voice but with a terrible amount of banging and crashing in the background I couldn't identify her. "Don't talk to her! Whatever you do, don't tell her anything! Please be careful! I'm sorry!" With that the call dropped.

With a few more fries in my mouth I asked, "Hello? Hello, who is this?"

There was nothing. You know, you used to at least get a dial tone when a call was cut off, but now all you get is nothing. I realized then that I couldn't even have asked the B.I.B. if it was her. I didn't even know her friggin' name. Stupid.

It haunted me all the way home, a whole bag of fries worth, imagining her in danger, battling with Jennifer Lowe; those two beauties tearing at one another, clothes ripping, hair flying around their heads, rolling on the floor, breasts pressed against one another, legs grinding….I almost wrecked the damn car and ruined a good pair of pants "worrying" about it.

When the blood returned to my brain, I couldn't think of anything to do. I didn't know who had called, where she was, or where to even look. Jones didn't know where to look either. I was afraid to look for anyone except her. I was at a dead end.

I opened the door to my chateau wondering if I had any Miner Lites left to wash down my feast, when I saw her sitting with her arms stretched over the top of my lavish sofa. The bag containing my half-eaten burger slipped from my hands.

She laughed. "Drop something?"

I wasn't certain if she was referring to the bag or my jaw. Jennifer Lowe looked at me with the eyes of a butcher ready to chop meat. Luckily, I was cool and had a snappy recovery. "What are you doing here?" Smooth as silk….on sandpaper.

"That depends," she said uncrossing and spreading her legs until only the sides of her skirt stopped them.

There wasn't anything "cool" left in me after that. My heart decided it was a track star and tried to burst through my chest like a finish line tape. My brain was full of so many thoughts, possibilities, and worries that it went into overload. *Fuck, is this it? Am I about to buy the ranch right now, today? Dead as in D-E-A-D? Would she rip me in half or do the old Demitri spinderella move on me?* (I leaned toward the latter) Generally, what the fuck was going on? I wondered.

"What is it you want?" I asked finally, circling around to the kitchen. "Can I get you something?" Cool customer, eh?

She laughed.

"Can I get you something to drink?"

"All you have are those fucking Miner Lites."

I opened the door to the fridge, then found out she was right, "Well, I have two eggs in here as well," I suavely offered.

She smirked at me, left the sofa, and moved to the kitchen, apparently tired of games. She picked up my laptop and shoved it into my arms. "That's how you're supposed to do it. She's easy to find in the Pub Crawler game." On the screen was a picture of the B.I.B. at Flanagan's with a big text banner blinking, "You found the B.I.B. You Win!"

This is fucking it! I panicked in my head. *You're a dead man!*

She rubbed her hand over my shoulder and down my arm. "I need a man."

Holy shit! Demitri , here I come! I told myself.

"I need a man to help me find someone," she said, starting to rub my chest. "Are you that man?" Jennifer said, confidently reaching for my crotch. Then when she found nothing there, she looked down in amazed surprise for a second.

"How…how am I supposed to do that? Sounds like you… you need a private…"

"Dick?" she said, trying her luck again and beginning to dig around my pants in search of her illusive prey. "I've tried private detectives and they've just wasted my money. No, what I'm looking for has proven very hard to find," she said, with her second hand joining the search. "But I know you know where it is."

"What…what makes you think that?" I asked with my voice jumping on the last word.

She stopped her digging, realizing she couldn't overcome the B.I.B.'s mark. "You know where she is. Christ, you have a whole fucking Web site worshipping the bitch! I need to know where she is 'cause they're gonna kill her. You want that to happen, lover boy? They can do it. She's next. Only I can save her, and only you can get to her. Think it over and call me, before it's too late," she said, turning to leave.

I began to think I might actually survive. "How am I supposed to reach you?"

She stopped and turned at the door. "My number's burnt into that little excuse you have for a dick. Figured that's the only place I could put it where you wouldn't lose it," she said before slamming the door.

Those numbers are going to become gigantic, I feared. I sighed deeply and felt my heart returning to my chest. I went to the fridge for a Miner's Lite, thinking, *What the fuck?*

Then I became aware that my near-death encounter had given me a firm desire to go to the bathroom, deciding to check out her number while I did. It should have bothered me that I had to open the bathroom door, which I hadn't closed, but it didn't. So, waiting for me, cowering in the shower, I found Rebecca Sans staring at me through her rose-colored glasses.

"Is she gone?" she whispered in a near panic. When I just stood in disbelief and didn't respond, she said again more emphatically, "Is she gone?"

I nodded and she came running at me like a bill collector. "You didn't tell her anything, did you? Did you?"

I shook my head, my mind thinking, *I'm not gonna get killed again, am I?*

She stuck her head past the doorway and looked down the hall in both directions while I protected my crotch with my beer bottle. "You got my phone call, right? I tried to warn you she was coming." Then she began to pace. "I'm sorry I lied to you. I really am. But if I'd told you where the B.I.B. was, you'd have led Jennifer right there."

I had even less of an idea what was going on now than before. "Wait, wait, maybe you should start from the beginning. How do you and Jennifer even know each other?"

She paced for a moment then sat down on the edge of the tub, her elbows on her knees and her hands on her head. "You're not going to believe me, but I have these special powers. I'm not like other people…"

"You're a super born, just like the B.I.B. and Jennifer."

"You know?" she said, looking up at me in both disbelief and joy. "I met Jennifer about a year ago. It was a rough time in my life. I was just beginning to feel my powers and thought something was wrong with me. I put my high school sweetheart fiancée in the hospital; I don't even know how. He still won't take my calls. I started to be able to make things happen with my mind, communicate with machines…" she looked up at me, as if checking my credulity quotient. "I didn't program your Web site, I just thought it. Jennifer came to my house and said she had been looking for me. She knew I had new powers I didn't understand and she would help me. She said there were others and she needed my help to find them. It made me feel a lot better to know I wasn't alone…you know? So, of course I agreed and, right away, using the Internet, I found a woman named Alyson. She had just started being able to know things before they happened and it was driving her crazy. Her husband left. She started to get sick over it. When we found her, she was thin and almost gray."

"After a few days, she felt better too. She told Jennifer a number of things that were going to happen in the world financial markets: stocks, commodities. Jennifer made a lot of money. Even I invested a little money and it worked. Then, for some reason, Alyson started to get sick again, and her predictions turned sour."

"Around that time, Jennifer told me about the B.I.B. and asked me to find her. But I couldn't. She was like a ghost. That's when you met Jennifer for that fake survey at the coffee shop.

When she realized that you had been marked, she knew you would know where the B.I.B. was. When you called me for the survey, she already knew about your ugly Web site and knew you'd take the bait and hire me to run it if I let it slip that that's what I did for a living…cheap. That way, we could monitor your site, your communications, and your phone. She was sure you would lead us to her."

"That's when it all went wrong. Alyson disappeared. Jennifer started talking like she was glad to be rid of her. I started to suspect that Jennifer had her killed. Then she sent two men to my apartment with guns, guns like I had never seen before, to kill me…"

"Kill you? What happened?" I asked.

Rebecca stood up and turned away. "I don't know. I saw them point the guns, and the next thing I remember, they were gone. The room was empty. There were just black burn marks on the floor."

"That was right when you helped me find the B.I.B.'s home address. I didn't know what to do. I thought if I told her the address, then she'd kill the B.I.B. too. I couldn't let you lead her to the B.I.B. either. So I gave you the phony address and decided to go to the B.I.B. myself and warn her. But then I started to worry that Jennifer was having me followed. She called me and we had a fight. I've been running from her ever since."

"Quite a story," I said.

"It's true," she said, empathically, after turning to face me. "Do you really know where the B.I.B. is?"

It was then I started my suspicions. Was I being scammed…. again? "No, I have no idea where she is. She worked up a whole new identity after you closed in on her."

Rebecca looked at the ground. "Then we're lost…Without her help, I don't know what's going to happen…Jennifer will turn on you too! She'll kill us both! As soon as you are of no use to her! She has to believe you know how to find the B.I.B. or you're not safe."

"Listen, you're safe here. She's already been here, so she won't expect you to be here. Stay here for now, until we figure this out. Don't call or visit anyone you know, no friends no relatives. She'll have my place watched, so don't walk out in the open...Is your car here?"

"Still at my apartment. I knew she could trace it."

"Good, try to calm down. You can use the back bedroom... stay away from the windows."

She nodded in agreement and then gave me a hug. Her body felt like a furnace against mine. "She didn't unmark you, did she? You're not working for her?" she asked, feeling my crotch.

"What is it with you people?! " I exclaimed, pushing her away.

"Sorry, I just had to be sure...sorry about your little..."

I waved her by me out the door. "I know. So if you don't mind I have to pee!"

She walked by, then turned back. "Sorry."

"I know, I know! I can still pee with it, so get the hell out!" I slammed the door and hesitated before checking for Jennifer's phone number...not gigantic as I'd hoped.

When I came out of the bathroom, I found Rebecca in the living room appearing distressed. "What's wrong?" I asked as I neared.

She looked at me with a burning stare. "Have you seen your back bedroom?"

"What?"

"Have you seen those nasty sheets, the stained pillows? Do you even own a vacuum?"

"If it bugs you, take my bedroom."

"Eeuuu, Do you really sleep in there? What…do you keep wild animals? Do people actually have sex with you in there?"

"OK, I'll get you new sheets and pillows. The vacuum's…. around here somewhere," I said, circling my eyes over the room till I spied the vacuum in a distant corner, "Right there."

"And the blankets, whose horse did you take them from?"

"OK, blankets too."

She reluctantly got up and grabbed the vacuum with the tips of two fingers, "Eeeuu, gross."

"You said you got along with machines," I joked.

"Yeah, but it's the slime I'm worrying about."

"I'll be back. Don't show yourself or answer the door or phone, OK?"

"There will be someone watching you," she warned.

"I know," I said, picking up my keys and wallet.

"And food, I can't live on beer and two eggs," she added.

Did everyone know the contents of my fridge? I nodded. "Got it, chick food." I stopped as I passed her, trying to stare behind her glasses. I slid them off her face and checked her eyes.

"Something wrong with my eyes?"

"No, they're a pretty gray, very piercing," I BS'ed.

"Gray? I don't think so! Try hazel," she pouted confidently.

Hazel, my ass, I thought to myself.

Before she could speak again, I slipped out the door. *Didn't know I'd gotten married*, I thought. All of the super born had been at my apartment except the one I wanted to be there. Life is weird.

As I walked to my car, I looked around, trying to find someone in my peripheral vision who would tail me. I didn't see a candidate but knew someone had to be there. I got in the car, slammed the door shut, and reached to put the key in the ignition, when a forearm pinned my neck to the seat. *What now?* I thought.

"Do you want to tell me why the two people who are looking for me have both been at your apartment within minutes of one another?" asked the B.I.B. before tightening her grip further.

"Careful, I'm being watched, they'll see you," I said with great difficulty.

"The guy tailing you is over there," she said, gesturing with her head to a group of cars nearby, "Caught him too busy playing B.I.B. Rescue on his mobile phone to notice me. But I don't think he's in any condition to do much watching. Now, answer my question," she said making my throat even more uncomfortable.

"It's so weird, you won't even believe it."

"Try me."

"Take your arm off my throat, and I'll tell you. Remember? I'm on your team."

She lessened her grip then her arm disappeared into the backseat.

I turned my head to look at her. I could see the serious concern on her face unlike anything I had seen before. That explained her aggressive attitude. "Well, hello, nice to see you too!" I said, rubbing my neck. "Jennifer was in my apartment when I got home from visiting Jones; thought she was going to kill me. She wanted me to help her find you. She said "someone" was going to kill you. She said you were next on their list, but that she could stop it if I let her know where you were..."

"And?"

"And that's it."

"What did you tell her?"

"I told her the truth. I didn't know where you were and didn't have a way to reach you."

"And?"

"She left...after feeling me up pretty good."

"What about Rebecca? She was the one outside my old apartment."

I shook my head, not believing the words coming out of my mouth. "She was hiding from Jennifer in my bathroom. She is convinced Jennifer killed one of the other women like you and that she tried to kill her too. They had a fight. She wouldn't give Jennifer your old address. She was trying to reach you herself to get help against Jennifer but was afraid of leading her to you. She has nowhere else to go and thought I would understand. She's hiding out at my place for a while...This all just happened. I didn't ask for any of it."

The B.I.B. looked concerned, staring past me through the windshield, her mind racing. "Who do you believe?"

I don't know why but the question made me think of the image of Jennifer's cleavage for a second, and then Rebecca's panicked looks, but then her questions about the B.I.B. "I don't know. They could be still working together, you know, good cop/bad cop...Who besides them would be after you, anyway?"

"Who indeed?" She appeared satisfied with my answers.

"Jones thinks you're genetically like bees, queen bees. Only one of you can survive."

"Does he? Where were you off to anyway?"

"My new wife..." I gestured to the apartment, "...wants new sheets, pillow, blankets, and she has this notion about having more than Miner Lite in the fridge."

"Some people," she joked. "Sounds like she's building a little hive of her own."

I nodded.

She turned to leave.

"When will I see you again?" I asked.

"I'll find you, remember?"

"No, I mean...like a date...the night at O'Malley's, remember?"

"My life is flipped upside down and you're worried about a date?!"

"Yes." My answer was immediate and without question.

"O'Malley's? That was just an accident! One night!"

"No, it wasn't. I spent months trying to make that 'accident' happen...So explain then why you marked me."

Her face betrayed surprise, her mouth left open by my remarks. She couldn't fight the logic of it. "Well...we'll just have to play that one by ear."

She opened the door to leave, then came back, leaned over the seat, and grabbed my crotch, all to a very different effect. "Just checking to be sure," she explained.

"Anytime...twice on Sunday," I answered in a mellow tone, feeling the warmth of her touch and glow of the strong erection she gave me. He was alive! Little, my ass!

She turned to leave and then turned back again. "What's with the numbers?"

"Gift from Jennifer. That's how you can reach her," I said; then, after a moment of thought, I asked, "Those will wear off, right?"

The B.I.B. smirked and left.

"Right?" I yelled after her.

CHAPTER TWENTY-SIX

Calm before the Storm—We All Have a Good Night

With my "tail" out of commission, I saw no reason to rush while collecting all the items Rebecca could not live without. I even threw in some extras for her, some food, and a gourmet treat for dinner—pizza. When I returned, my "tail" was still in Lala land or was it Lalaistan. I tried not to enjoy his unfortunate state or the new asshole he would be given by his superiors, but I smiled anyway.

It proved difficult to carry all the bags into my building in one trip, but the macho challenge was too strong; dropping one or breaking something by slamming a bag into a door frame was of no consequence in comparison with the challenge, not that I did or have done such a thing.

When I finally got all the bags into the apartment, in one trip I must add, and on the kitchen table, I found myself encircled by activity. On the dining room table my laptop screen flashed frantically, the TV surfed channels, the dishwasher ran, and I heard the sound of my vacuum cleaner in my bedroom moving back and forth around the room. Amid it all, Rebecca sat reading one of my old magazines, no remote controls in sight. Knowing what the B.I.B. could do, it was not that hard to get over the initial surprise and just accept everything that was going on around me.

I curiously, slowly paced to my bedroom as if afraid I would step on something. I peeked around the door frame to watch my vacuum round the bed, redo a spot it had missed, then retire to the corner and shut itself off. I crept back to the living room to find Rebecca digging through the bags.

"Pizza? You got pizza for dinner?" she reprimanded.

I quickly dug through another bag and pulled out a small container and displayed it, "And a salad," I said in defense.

She rummaged through the food, "You really eat this stuff?"

"You really like to bitch?" I responded, grabbing the food in question from her hand.

Then she stopped, smiled, and turned to me holding some basic female toiletries in her hand. She thought for a moment, and turned to face me. "Someone either had a lot of sisters or…" Then she laughed. "Or someone had a live-in girlfriend."

When I didn't answer and began to blush, she knew she had hit a nerve and came in for the kill with a simple little song she made up:

"You had a girrrl friend
And you reallly liked her
But you're a jerrrk
So she leffft you
Even when you bought her presennnts
And you bought her flowerrrs
You gave her pizzza
So she leffft you
Cause you're a jerrrk."

"Very funny," I said, wounded, but not telling. "You want the pizza or not? And I'm not bringing you flowers, no matter how you beg, so forget it."

She turned toward the dishwasher, which stopped and opened its latch when she approached. She returned with plates, forks, and glasses for each of us.

As she handed them to me, I looked down at them as if they were alien devices, "So this is what goes in there?" I asked pointing to the dishwasher. "You really eat your pizza on a plate? I thought there was a law or something?"

Rebecca cut a small piece of pizza with her fork, made a show of shoving it in her mouth, and turned to walk away.

"That's just un-American," I said to her back. "In fact, I think it's French!"

She did her best to ignore me and walked off toward the living room with a piece of pizza and a glass of water. I held up my empty glass and asked, "Just what am I supposed to put in here?"

She responded by continuing to walk away and holding up her glass as if she was holding up "the finger."

A few minutes later, I joined her on the couch with four pieces of pizza stacked on my plate, no fork, no napkin, and placed a sweaty Miner's Lite bottle on the coffee table without a coaster, declaring my independence.

"Nice," she said without looking at me. "Really nice," she said sarcastically, but I knew deep inside it was killing her.

We chilled, watched TV, and she laughed while I struggled with B.I.B. Rescue and Pub Crawler. "Those are so easy," she gloated. "I can't believe you can't find her!" She stole two of my pieces of pizza encountering little resistance, ate what was left in the box, plus the "healthy" salad. For a skinny chick that girl could eat. And did I mention the two Miner's Lites she drank? When we had finished and the burping began, I was surprised when her petite hand drifted over and curled up in mine. We watched some shows and old movies, laughed, joked; it was nice.

Carmine Camino was having a late night as well. He sat alone in his office hunched over his black desk stripped down to his white T-shirt and suit pants. One hand encircled a half-empty bottle of beer, while the other held up a brochure on the Israeli assault rifles that had just arrived in crates marked "farm implements." He dropped the brochure, which disappeared into the clutter on his desk, picked up his pen, and reviewed the handwritten list of the men he wanted for the job. He checked them one by one, paused, and then added two more names to the bottom of the list. He reviewed the satellite photo of a certain apartment building on his computer screen and checked it against the sketch he had made on his pad. Satisfied, he leaned back in his chair and took a long pull from his beer bottle.

Carmine stared at the ceiling while he gently rocked in his chair. In his thoughts, he reviewed the report he had received from the man who had been watching the apartment. The man had reported seeing a blonde woman outside the apartment assaulting a man in a car nearby. He then reported the same woman slipping into a car with the journalist, just before he left, returning with arms full of bags. The man reported the arms full of bags as highly unusual. "Most of the time this guy comes home with a bag of takeout and a twelve-pack of beer. The bags from a linens store tell me he's got a guest."

Confident in the intelligence his men had obtained, Carmine finished his beer, played a sarcastic game of B.I.B.

Rescue, ending squashed by a beer truck, then typed in the address for his favorite porn site.

At 3:00 a.m. the droning of the TV can get annoying. I lay back in the corner of the sofa barely hearing the commercial that was trying to sell me something or other. My hand still held the beer bottle I had let turn horizontal, spilling most of it. Rebecca lay asleep on my lap, her body feeling like the Sahara…at noon…in August…the fifteenth. The super born all seemed to run a lot hotter than the rest of us. Without giving it any thought, as I often did, I began lightly running my hands through her hair. It made me feel connected to her, like I was truly linked to her in some way. Plus it was a great opportunity to check out her rack.

I had become convinced that she was not a killer, a schemer, or a liar. Rebecca seemed like a genuinely frightened girl, who just happened to be able to run machines with her thoughts and ate pizza with a fork. The more I was with her the more I believed her story.

If that were true, I had to face the fact that I could not protect her. She was relying on me in some sick way, but how could I help her if armed men suddenly found her, if Jennifer Lowe suddenly walked through the door? What could I do, throw a beer bottle at them, an empty one of course. No one who had ever counted on me had been rewarded for it.

I took the last sip I hadn't managed to spill from my beer and sighed. Looking down at Rebecca she seemed comfortable, contented. Yet, was she safe? Did she know the person in whom she had placed her confidence? That was another question that I pondered for a minute, and then just went on with my life.

Just then, Rebecca stirred but did not awaken. I felt a pulse of heat leave her body, the laptop and TV turned themselves off, while all the door and window latches in the apartment clicked shut.

Jennifer Lowe was having a late night as well. She sat at the bar nursing a pink martini while the net of her tight, low-cut dress trawled the waters of the lounge around her. It wasn't long before two small fish took notice. The two young executives combined their post-college habits with their newfound high incomes to desire "real women" and not the co-ed prey they had already outgrown.

The confident, blond-haired one stared at Jennifer with desire-filled eyes, as if he were plotting to test drive his first Ferrari. His dark-haired companion just whispered and giggled, not as far removed from his college antics. "So? Are you gonna talk with her?" he prodded.

The blond ignored his friend and continued his gaze, watching as one shoulder strap of Jennifer's dress began a slow, "accidental" slide down her shoulder. He finished his drink in one swallow then stood up. "Let's go."

"Go? What are you talking about, man?" the other said, suddenly filled with anxiety.

"You and me, numb nuts, bet she does both of us."

"Hey, man, I ain't no freak."

The blond thought for a moment before a disgusted sneer came to his lips. "Oh, no, not a threesome. You're disgusting! I'll do her then she'll do you. Tits like that, I'll bet she could do the entire Atlantic fleet."

The dark-haired one had no idea what that really meant, as it was devoid of any logic, but it contained the word tits and implied that he was about to get lucky, so he smiled. "OK," he said, rising and following his friend. But a few steps into Jennifer's net, he stopped his blond friend with an arm on the shoulder. "What if she's married, man? Then what?"

The blond smiled and slid his friend's hand off his shoulder. "Do I look like I give a fuck?" The blond smiled confidently then turned and marched up to his Ferrari, while his friend watched.

When Jennifer turned and reeled the blond in with her smile, the other man felt assured and joined him in the net.

Jennifer looked deeply into the eyes of her catch and flashed them both with the brilliant beam of red and then deep violet from her gray eyes. (Hazel eyes, my ass.)

CHAPTER TWENTY-SEVEN

We're Blown

When I woke up the next morning, I was still backed into the corner of the sofa, but Rebecca was gone, leaving only a warm pillow on my lap and a handwritten note on my chest. I widened then squinted my eyes to focus on the letters she had penned. It was too short to be a recipe for world peace, too long for my mother's lasagna. Finally, I put together that this was a shopping list for things Rebecca needed; seemed she was planning to move in.

I leapt to my feet like a panther, a panther taking a crap, to see my laptop on the dining room table flashing the B.I.B. Web site. The site appeared to be updating itself, but I knew it was Rebecca doing her thing, so much for changing the site's passwords. Through the closed bathroom door came the sounds of falling then gurgling water as it drained in the shower. Rebecca was the ideal of a multitasker: showering, updating the Web site, and probably fixing a communication satellite, while she brushed her teeth and e-mailed the president.

For a letch it was surprising that I had no desire to take a peek beyond the bathroom door. Rebecca and I had quickly developed a friend or brother/sister type of thing. It was comfortable, and I had no desire to change that; plus I had gotten the chance to feel her up pretty good the night before as she snoozed. (Just kidding.)…(OK, not kidding.)

I ran my hand through my hopeless hair and pretended that had put it all in place. As I grabbed my keys, I found the vision of a plate of eggs, bacon, and toast on my kitchen counter. There was another note; apparently, Rebecca was a "noter." It read, "For you, my hero. Coffee is in the pot."

I have a pot? I wondered while standing and devouring the eggs. "This chick thing's not all bad." By the time I walked to the "pot" the plate was empty save crumbs. I tossed it in the sink and found a cup, sugar bowl, and spoon awaiting me. Sweet. As I poured the cup and turned to leave, the garbage disposal came to life for a second as did the dishwasher. *Bitch*, I thought, realizing she wanted me to say good-bye.

I tapped on the bathroom door. "I'm gonna go get your stuff. Be back soon."

"OK," she yelled. "Thanks, I appreciate it….Be careful."

"Don't let anybody in."

"Duh!"

I paced to my car still enjoying the taste of breakfast in my mouth. It was a different morning experience for me compared to the hang-on taste of beer I normally had. When I began to pull out into the road, I checked my rearview mirror for my "tail." I smiled when I identified a dark-colored sedan pull out after me. That turned quickly to an open-mouthed frown when a second car with two men in it began following both of us. Who were these guys? Were they doubling up on me?

Rebecca's list was not long, so I made no attempt to hide from them and did my shopping, plus a donut—OK, two—but I bought one for Rebecca as well; it just didn't make it to Rebecca, that's all.

When I returned, for giggles I watched in the mirror as one, then two, cars parked down the road after me. When a black SUV took its turn parking behind the first two, I had my first suspicion that something was up and I hurried into the apartment. I put the bags on the kitchen counter and snuck a peek around the closed drapes in the living room. On the street on the other side of the apartment was another black SUV with tinted windows just like the first I had seen.

Rebecca came in and noticed my behavior. By now, her hair and makeup were done, so she distracted my eye from the window for a moment. "What's up?" she asked, moving up behind me. She smelled great and the petite but noticeable cushions of her breasts teased into my back, but that didn't distract a pro like me...that much...OK, maybe the brother/sister thing wasn't completely true, depending on what kind of sister she was, I guess.

"I'm not sure. It looks like there're three or four cars out there watching us."

"Think they know I'm here?" she said in a whisper.

"Could be that. But it could be they're after me to tell them where the B.I.B. is. Either way, something is going to happen. Is there anywhere else you can go?"

"I have a friend..."

"No friends, no relatives, no one they can trace."

Rebecca shook her head. "I don't want to leave you alone. They could kill you."

"Killing both of us appeals to you more? No, I'm gonna get you out of here. We'll wait till tonight, when it's dark. I'm gonna sneak you out through the basement."

"We both should go. You can't do any good here anymore."

She didn't convince me. "Pack your stuff. We'll leave when it's dark," I lied…"And to think I even bought new sheets."

CHAPTER TWENTY-EIGHT

She's Not the B.I.B.

I watched the comings and goings through the windows all day. When the sun was gone, I turned to thoughts of getting her to the basement and out of town. I gathered as much cash as I could find; one bit of helpful advice, don't hide cash when you're drunk. I dressed us both in the darkest clothes I could find and gathered her stuff in a bag I used when I went to the gym. That being the case, the bag was new and unused. The hall led to the basement, which had a door no one used. I wasn't even sure it would open. It was hidden by brush outside, so it should give us a good escape portal.

"Let's go," I said, as Rebecca pulled up and then clung to me.

I guess I should have kept my eyes looking out the window, because the instant I opened the door and stuck my head out, I was greeted by three men in black. Then three more appeared down the hall. Not one had a pleasant look on his face. Each slung a compact, but mean-looking, assault rifle over his shoulder, hanging down at his waist, and pointing at me.

"Going somewhere?" said Carmine Camino, the only one not to have his gun at the ready.

I backed into the apartment holding Rebecca behind me. The six of them followed me in. Carmine looked around at my place. "Nice shit hole you have here." When he saw me looking at the windows, he added, "Don't even think about it. There's four more of us outside waiting. You're not going anywhere… anywhere I don't want you to go." He moved toward Rebecca as the others surrounded her with their guns trained. "So this is her, huh?…The 'B' fucking 'I.B.'"

"What? What, you think she's the B.I.B.?" I said, astonished and a bit relieved. "Don't you look in the papers or at my Web site?" I turned to the laptop, which Rebecca turned on, and surfed to the picture of the B.I.B. on my Web site. "That look like her to you? If she was the B.I.B. you'd be splattered over the walls by now. This is my…girlfriend, Rebecca. Sorry to disappoint."

Carmine checked the laptop picture and several others on the site. From beside him, Dennis Mastrangelo, the thug who had cut the B.I.B. before, chimed in. "It ain't her, boss." When he was satisfied, he gave a mean look at one of his men, and the big thug shrugged apologetically.

Carmine thought for a moment as he paced. He stopped, nodded to the man nearest Rebecca, who then lowered his gun and took hold of her arms and pinned them behind her. Rebecca yelped, and I started to worry big time.

"You know," began Carmine thoughtfully, "If she's the B.I.B., I don't think she's gonna let me shoot her." He gestured to another of his men who put his gun in Rebecca's face. "And if she isn't, I don't think you're gonna want me to be killing her either. Care to test my theory?" he asked, getting in my face. "I'm gonna have them pull the trigger in a minute. If she's the B.I.B., let's see her outrun a bullet from an inch away."

"Don't do that. She's not the B.I.B.; she's totally innocent!" I begged.

"Well then, my friend, I'm not leaving empty-handed. If she's not the B.I.B., you, my friend, know where the B.I.B. is. Tell me or we pull the trigger and find out for sure."

In my mind, I hoped desperately that the B.I.B. was about to crash through the door and dispose of these mugs. I wanted anyone to be in charge of saving us, anyone but myself. "No, No wait!" I pleaded.

Carmine appeared disgusted. "What kind of man are you?" he asked while putting his gun to my head. "You're gonna let me kill her when you could save her? Tell me or we do you both, right now!" He gave me a minute to respond. When all I could do was stammer and plead, he nodded to his gunman. "Maybe watching her die will make you remember."

The gunman showed no hesitation and pulled the trigger, or should I say tried to pull the trigger. Carmine sneered and pulled his trigger in my face. It wouldn't budge either.

As Carmine took his shoulder strap off and prepared to hit me with his gun, and I prepared to ward off the blow with my crossed arms, Rebecca went limp in the thug's arms, her eyes turned black, and translucent vaporous clouds began to form around Carmine and the three nearest thugs. I could see an instant of surprise and awe on their faces before they faded and disappeared with the clouds, leaving only black stains on the floor and a stench in the air. No gunman left to hold her up, Rebecca fell to the ground as I caught Carmine's falling gun, drew back the bolt, and pointed it in the direction of the remaining henchmen. Despite my best, and only, James Bond move of the night, I found the front door open and heard the sounds of the henchmen's boots as they beat feet. As the escapees reached outside, I heard more voices, yelling, and the sounds of fighting.

I slammed and locked the door before running over to Rebecca, whose eyes began to clear as she started to make erratic movements with her arms and legs. She seemed drained of all energy. When her eyes were bright again, I sat her up. "You OK?"

She appeared dazed and uncertain of where she was. She looked around the room to the black marks and assault rifles that marked where men had been. "Where'd....What..." then a look of terror covered her face and she looked at me. "I killed them, didn't I? I killed them all!"

I wrapped her head in my arms. "No! You saved us! You saved me! They were going to kill us, whether you stopped their guns from working or not."

She began to sob.

"There's no time!" I tried to shake her. "There's no time for this! We have to go!" I dragged her to her feet. "Come on," I said, as I grabbed for her bag with one arm while cradling her in the other. She still sobbed as we went down the hall, down the stairs, and into the basement. Above us, I could hear the shuffling of feet running into my apartment. I quickly led her to the old door. I was right; it hadn't been opened for some time. But I was wrong in thinking I was going to open it. Three pushes and a shoulder butt later, I was convinced that it wasn't going to move. I looked Rebecca in her tear-filled eyes. "Rebecca, Rebecca, focus. Can you open this door?" I shook her by the shoulders. "Open this door or we're gonna die! There's more of them! They'll find us here!"

She shook her head, still sobbing. "What does it matter who kills me? I'm a killer myself! Who cares?"

I shook her again and looked deeply at her eyes until she looked up at me. "I care. I care about you, you pizza-eating pain in the ass. I've got to get you out of here. I need your help."

She sniffled and smiled remembering the better moments we'd had. She seemed to settle down. "It was sweet the way you stroked my hair."

I was stunned and suddenly felt guilty having thought she had been asleep, wondering what else she had remembered. Then came the other surprise. Me? Sweet?

Then she looked at the door. It shook and quivered before popping open with a screech. The stairwell outside the door was full of debris and surrounded by bushes, offering perfect cover for us. I watched as two more men dressed in black ran toward the front door. It was our chance, and we hunched over as we ran into the darkness.

CHAPTER TWENTY-NINE

The Flight to Nirvana

W hen I saw the mess of his apartment and his car still in the lot, I knew he'd be looking for a place where no one would find him. Either that or they already had taken him away. Their panicked and erratic behavior told me somehow he had escaped. But what of Rebecca? Who had made this move on him?

Well, in this town, if you wanted to go where no one would find you or even think of looking, there was just one place to go, O'Malley's. It's where I had gone to disappear. I bet that he was there too.

When I entered, I looked at the old barkeep, who was drying glasses behind the bar. With his towel, he gestured at the booth where we had had our dinner and drinks nights before. The booth appeared empty, but when I lifted the plastic table cloth, there he was sitting on the floor, surrounded by empty bottles. "You look like shit," I said, climbing under the table with him. The barkeep just shook his head, before shooing away an RFD who was climbing on the bar like a jungle gym.

"What happened?" I asked.

He mopped his brow and sighed. "It was the mob, the new guy, Camino. They thought Rebecca was you. When they realized the mistake, they tried to make me tell them where you were. They were going to kill us both."

I put my hands to my temples. "This is getting serious."

He nodded. "Oh, yeah, you can say that," he said, taking a drink from the bottom of a bottle.

"Where's Rebecca? How'd you get away?"

He looked up at the underside of the table for a long moment. "She's on her way up into the mountains. There's a little B&B I know about. Very private and untraceable…She'll be safe," he said, nodding in agreement with himself.

I put my hand on his shoulder. "What happened? Where's Camino?"

He laughed. "Gone! They're just gone."

"How? What do you mean?"

He finally noticed my hand on his shoulder. "Rebecca did it all. I was useless. She made their guns jam, then she vaporized them, poof, gone!"

I shook him. "What do you mean, gone?"

He gave me a serious look as if from the grave. "Her eyes went to black and I watched Camino dissolve into the air…He had this shocked look on his face. He couldn't believe what was happening to him. Then he and his men were gone. I'll never forget the look on his face…or that smell."

"Now, we know she's a killer," I said, lowering my head.

"No, it's not like that. She didn't want to kill anyone. She only did it when they were about to kill us. It almost drained the life out of her. She fucking cried!"

I put my finger over my lips as we had done nights before upon hearing expletives. He responded by nodding and putting his finger over his lips too, but it wasn't amusing now.

I thought for a moment. "So, if you don't think she's in on this, why aren't you up in the mountains with her? They're after you too."

He locked his eyes seriously on mine; then, in a flash, his chest was against me, and his lips were pressing mine. Even with his beer breath, it was a remarkable and intense kiss. If I had let him, it would have lasted all night long. Despite feeling the exciting warmth throughout my entire body that his contact had stirred, I pushed him back, glad I had worn underwear that night. I sat without speaking for a long time while his warmth slowly drained away. "Guess that answers that question," I said with certainty.

Then my mind returned to the night's events. "If Camino is gone, who else is after you? Jennifer Lowe?"

"At least," he answered, laughing. "There were three, four, five cars following me at the end. Everyone thinks I know how to find you. Camino's men were fighting with someone else as they ran away. It's like sharks with blood in the water now."

"Sorry I got you into this mess."

He laughed out loud. "No one to blame but myself. You didn't ask for any of this. It was me. That's right; it was me…I'm not proud of putting you at risk, but other than that, you know, I wouldn't change a thing, not a fucking thing!"

I put my fingers to my lips but it wasn't funny at the moment—again.

He took my hands in his, starting the electric warmth to spread all over again. "I wanted to find you, and now I have. I wouldn't change that for anything."

What a sweet…deluded, drunken man, I thought. Why was I giving him such a hard time, pushing him away every time he tried to get close? … He seemed sincere. After all I marked him in the first place…Oh, what was the use? Just another man to break…But his touch was different …electric…and that kiss…Was chasing after me his job or his passion…Hell, what am I thinking? He was after a Super Hero…me; I'm just a single mom.

Ultimately, with my bravado and razor-sharp reasoning that night, I convinced the B.I.B. that I knew someone who we could trust, someone who could help us. Although it was against her better judgment, I convinced her to fly me to Dr. Jones' apartment. With so many looking for me, flying through the sky at night, no one could possibly see or follow us.

I was beginning to sober up by the time we reached the tiny parking lot behind O'Malley's. Suddenly, the thought of being hundreds of feet in the air with no sense of control was overwhelming the sense of "coolness" I'd felt when I had the idea. It was either that or the revolt of the chili fries I'd eaten earlier that was making me queasy.

"You sure you're ready for this? You look sick," she commented after looking me over.

I nodded, beginning to taste the chili fries for a second time in the back of my throat. She circled her arm around me and under my shoulder, before launching us into the dark night sky. The initial jolt was a challenge, but after that, and some deep, deep breaths, I felt the sense of coolness take over. There was like a magnetic force holding us together so I had no fear of falling or being blown away by the air that rushed past us at high speed. After a hot and dangerous day, the air was cool, and the vision of lights for miles around amazing. Scranton had never looked this good to me before. Flying was such a free feeling. Then it dawned on me that I trusted her, as I felt no concerns at my lack of control. It was liberating and exhilarating.

I pointed for her and gave her rough directions to Jones' apartment, when the same thrilling warmth as in the bar earlier began to radiate from her touch, captivating my entire body in seconds. I remember looking at her, and her body seemed radiant like molten silver. For those of you who've never seen molten silver, its allure is hypnotizing. Then I realized the glow was on me as well. We were both bathed in the same moonlit glimmer.

The feeling continued to slowly grow unrestrained. I found myself thinking, *Oh yeah,* and felt my pants tighten in a hurry. I think she was feeling it too, as I swear I heard her moan, a surprised pleasurable moan. That and the fact that twice she set us down on top of buildings, making an excuse, and letting go of me to walk around shaking her arms for a minute.

By the third time, though, I was certain. The excited feeling of warmth engulfed us both as I circled my arms around to climb beneath and face her. We kissed long, wet, and hard, well worth the price of admission. As I ran my hands over her cheeks and then down along her sides, the molten silver glow intensified wherever my hands traveled. Her waist and hips became awash in it. When I moved my hands back up and over her breast, the glow followed. It was the most amazing thing I had ever experienced, and I couldn't get enough of it. Before she could land us, she had moaned several times in my mouth, ending with a long loud one, just as our feet hit the roof. Her knees seemed weak and she sat down, breathing deeply.

"You OK?" I asked, "'cause I'm feeling great," I said, strutting in a circle around her.

"How much farther?" she panted.

"Just over there, maybe half a mile."

Shortly, her breaths settled down, and she wrapped her arms around me tightly, pressing a sharp, short kiss. "Let's take the long way," she said in a low animal tone that I had never heard before.

"Yeha!" I shouted, as we took off and the feelings and glow returned, starting with the kiss but then surrounding us from head to toe. It was even stronger than it had felt before. Our glowing bodies were filled with feelings of excitement, strength, and the sexual ecstasy you feel just before orgasm, but we felt that for minutes not seconds. There was no need for actual genital entry and connection as in normal sex. It was all full body and mental contact. And then came the orgasms…they seemed to go on forever while the pleasure seemed to merge us warmly together with the heat from her body. They were exhausting but motivated us to quickly recover, craving them again. I don't think we were flying in a straight line…at all.

I don't want to say that she took the long way, but there were a lot of rooftops before we got to Jones' apartment, and one of them looked like the Empire State Building in New York City some 125 miles from Dr. Jones' place. I vaguely remember people on an observation deck commenting and pointing at the sexy luminous bubble of our bodies. Along the entire route, I had no idea how many people had heard our moans and screams as we were flying in the glowing light, nor did we give a shit. Just a tip, this is the only way to fly.

When we finally made a rough landing on Jones' rooftop, it was my turn to be weak in the knees. Time had condensed into pleasure. I couldn't tell you if it was minutes or hours later, and you guessed it, nor did I give a shit. We both sat panting, before I fell back and lay on the hard tar-covered pebbles of the roof. My pants were a mess, and I had lost all sense of purpose. She wasn't much better off. She sat puffing, trying to straighten out the tangled chaos of her hair, and re-zip her jumpsuit that I had managed to pull open in flight. Just the vision of the mounds of her cleavage had me determined to battle my exhaustion.

After regaining some strength, I looked over at her to find her looking back at me. That was enough motivation, and, depleted as I was, I began crawling toward her. She smiled but then dropped it and put out her hand, unconvincingly she puffed, "No, Jones, remember? We need to talk to Jones."

I reached for her, smiling. "Who the hell is this Jones fella? We have the stars," I said, waving an arm up to the sky. "We have each other. Let's go flying again," I said, as I crept closer on elbows.

She smiled, tempted, but then sighed. "Remember? Almost being killed? Rebecca? The whole city is after your ass?" she pushed away the hand I had put on her thigh. "There'll be time later," she said, and then in a lowered voice, she added, "believe me." I reached out again but she pushed away my hand and repeated, this time even lower, "Believe me."

"Fuck it," I said, "I've got everything I need right here. You can fly us anywhere. Let's just disappear. To hell with them all!" I said, waving broadly like a drunken man; no wait, I was a drunken man.

Her look changed to serious silence. It was that moment I realized the difference between her and me. She could make millions with her powers, like Jennifer Lowe, or just disappear if she wanted. Her life didn't need to have any risks or concerns. But, instead, she stayed rooted in her hometown, risking her life and family to make the world a better place. Meanwhile, I just wanted her for myself and was ready to selfishly forget everything, everybody, now that we had found one another. If you had been up there flying with her, you would understand.

I dropped my head to the hard rooftop, sighed, and took a deep breath or two. "OK, you win…but then we fly home."

"Deal."

When she began to follow me down the stairway off the rooftop, I stopped and held her back with my hand. "You're my little secret. Jones doesn't know about you yet. Let's just keep it that way."

She nodded. "OK, I'll wait here."

I started down the stairs, then stopped, and turned back toward her with the "look." Her face became stern and she pointed down the stairs.

CHAPTER THIRTY

The Crash...

Dr. Jones answered the door in Penn State pajamas and slippers. Obviously, I had awoken him, yet he appeared glad to see me. "Oh! Come in, my friend. So late, you must have news of the B.I.B." We must have been flying a lot longer than I thought.

I suggested that he had better sit for this one. We proceeded to his tiny living room, and, after clearing stacks of papers from them, sat on outdated chairs. My silent drama made him show concern on his face.

"Well, what is it that can't wait until tomorrow?" he asked.

I told him the story of Rebecca coming to my apartment, all the men and vehicles tailing me, and then the attack by the recently deceased Carmine Camino and his men. I filled him in on Rebecca's powers over machines and the ability to dissolve men. Then I explained that I had sent her into hiding, and how I was now laying low. The entire time, he listened attentively and nodded, as I watched his dark little eyes beginning to glow from thoughts swirling in his head.

"Where is Rebecca now? We must protect her from Jennifer...and the B.I.B.—do you know her whereabouts?"

"Rebecca's in a little B&B up in the mountains."

"What little B.I.B. in the mountains? What is the B.I.B. doing up in the mountains? I was asking you about Rebecca. They are together now!" said Jones, not understanding yet, oh so very excited in his delusion.

"No, Rebecca's at a B&B. The B&B is in the mountains."

"Yes, I understand. What are they doing there together?

I wanted to laugh but decided to be patient. "No, no. I sent Rebecca to a bed and breakfast."

"Yes, I understand. So how did the B.I.B. find her?"

"She didn't," I said, now becoming irritated.

"Let's start at the beginning," Jones said, sensing the lack of communication. "You sent Rebecca to a bed and breakfast to hide, yes?"

"Correct."

"This bed and breakfast is in the mountains?" he asked uncertainly.

"Yes."

"Was the B.I.B. already there?" asked Jones forking left.

"No, it was just Rebecca at the B&B!"

"Together?"

"No! I don't know where the B.I.B. is. Rebecca is alone at the bed and breakfast."

"They don't serve lunch or dinner?"

I lowered my head, took a breath, and explained, while I pointed my finger with each word. "It's a bed and breakfast, has nothing to do with the B.I.B., I don't know their menu, but Rebecca is there and safe."

"Alone! You sent her there alone?" he said full of emotion.

I lowered my eyes to the floor. "I'm useless, Doc. I proved I couldn't protect her already. That's why I came here. I hoped you could help."

He got up and started to pace. "Yes, and it is a good thing you did, my friend...I have contacts with the security people at the university...and I have contacts in the government. We will get protection for her. We cannot let Jennifer Lowe go around eliminating all her competition. We must protect Rebecca and the B.I.B. before we try to deal with that bitch!" He paced by the window then turned back to me and stared into my face. "What about the B.I.B.? Do you have any idea where in the mountains she is? We must protect her too."

I paused, first trying to decide if it was worth the effort to explain again that the B.I.B. wasn't in the mountains at all, then trying to look believable when I would answer, knowing full well the B.I.B. was on the roof. Despite all my practice at it, I wasn't a good liar, so I lowered by eyes. "No, I have no idea where she could be."

Jones closed in on me slowly. "Then what the hell are you doing here, my friend? Why aren't you hiding with Rebecca? Why aren't you safe, with everyone else up in the mountains?"

I shook my head. "Just thought I should be here, see this thing through."

"Very honorable...very honorable, indeed," he said, but I knew he saw I was lying. He grabbed a pad of paper. "Write down the name and address of the bed and breakfast and the phone number if you have it. I can have men there by morning. She will be safe."

I wrote down the address then pulled out my mobile phone and looked up the phone number to the B&B. When I was done, Jones grabbed my phone. "No more of this. They will trace your phone." He walked to the desk, put down my phone, and returned with another mobile phone and charger he had taken from a drawer. "This is your phone now. We can communicate safely. Jennifer will never be able to trace this."

I took the phone and nodded a thank-you.

"What about money? Are you OK there?" Jones asked.

"I gave Rebecca everything I could get to before they hit us."

Jones threw me two piles of banded bills. "Here you go. No credit cards, no touching your bank accounts, no checks, don't go near your apartment, nothing until we have her under control. Understand?"

I nodded sheepishly. "Getting her under control won't be easy."

Jones' eyes glowed. He held up a finger. "Oh, I have plans. I have plans, you can be believing this."

"I hope you're right," I said, getting up to leave.

Jones came up to me, put an arm around my shoulder, and escorted me to the door. "Don't you be worrying. This is all good news. We are nearing the end. I can be feeling this. I will call you when we have Rebecca safe and secure. Let us hope the B.I.B. is safe in the mountains as well. Perhaps the B.I.B. will find the same B&B. But, for now, my friend, you are the bait."

I thanked him, but the conversation had heavily dampened my beer buzz and B.I.B. high. I returned to the roof concerned about the situation with Rebecca and Jennifer, yet slowly regaining my excitement to be back with the B.I.B. and the flight home. But she wasn't in the stairway or on the roof anymore. I searched for her, then waited for her, then searched again. She was gone. I was alone again.

My trip down the stairway was incredibly slow as I paused constantly and took small steps, unable to believe she had left. I was not used to being used for a "one-night fly." How could she be gone? Then I worried something had happened to her. Then I got to worry about what was going to happen to me. Where would I go? The trip from such an incredible high to the messed-up feeling I was in was quick and devastating.

I pushed open the door to the apartment building and stepped out into the night. Compared to the image of lights from the sky, this vantage of Scranton, not so good. Jones didn't live in the best part of town. I didn't want to be in the streets for long, so I ambled across the street to a fleabag motel. No one would know me there, and I was sure cash payment would be eagerly accepted.

I didn't know it then, but my major question would have been answered if I had just looked up at Jones' apartment. On the ledge outside his window, the B.I.B. stood, or should I say hung or floated. She had listened to our entire conversation and remained still listening to Jones.

After getting my room key from a nearly toothless man, I bought a soda and went up a flight to my lavish room. The ice bucket looked nasty, so I unwrapped a glass and proceeded to the nearby mournfully humming ice machine, filling the glass. I returned to my room, locked the door, and crashed onto the board like bed, full of troubles and uncertainty.

My beer high was turning into a hangover. My balls felt like raisins, my fluids gone as if vacuumed away. My little man was exhausted. And I sincerely wished I had a change of underwear. Despite my worries, I quickly dropped off to sleep even before I had time to turn on the TV, while my icy soda bubbled and fizzed, dying a slow death beside the bed untouched.

CHAPTER THIRTY-ONE

... And the Burn

To say I slept late would be to minimize late. It was well into the afternoon when I awoke refreshed and totally oblivious to the events of the night before or my current predicament. I felt a smile on my face. My little man was refreshed too and greeted me with an eager, *How ya doing?*

I showered to groaning pipes and pissing water pressure, cut myself twice with the high-quality razor supplied free by the fleabag, decided my underwear was beyond salvation, and left in search of food.

I was freakin' starving for some reason. Luckily for me and for the diner, there was a small diner nearby. It may have been my hunger, but every morsel I received tasted just great. I ate like a starving man; no, wait, I was a starving man. I was attacking some burgers and fries after eating a breakfast plate of eggs, bacon, and toast when Jones' phone rang, and all my feeling of wellness came crashing down. "Hello?" I said, disguising my voice a bit.

"My friend, I have bad news, oh so bad," Jones said like a panicked boy.

I paused, not ready for bad news and grunted a response.

"When the security men reached the B&B they did not find Rebecca. Her room was disturbed, and she was gone. The operators of the B&B said she left with two men in a dark SUV."

I swallowed hard but was relieved that the news was not about the B.I.B. "Is that it?"

"No, there was a note. It is addressed to you, my friend, and reads: "If you want to ever see Rebecca again then you will meet me on top of the Bank Towers Building at ten o'clock tonight. Bring with you the B.I.B. and no one else. Bring anyone else and I cannot guarantee your safety." And she signs it, "Your Friend Jennifer," the sarcastic bitch!"

I sighed and suddenly the taste of all the food I'd had eaten, not so good.

"My friend, can you do this? Can you bring the B.I.B.? Should we risk her for Rebecca? This is puzzlement…I can contact the security people…"

"No!" I said defiantly. "No offense, but your security people suck. You didn't see those mobsters dissolve like I did. And that was Rebecca; who knows what Jennifer can do," I said, remembering the pen she had melted and imagining it being me melting slowly into the tabletop.

"Then what to do? What to do?" he asked excitedly.

"I'll call you back," I said, turning off the phone, tossing it on the table, and then brushing back my hair with both hands, ending with my elbows on the table.

The image of stroking Rebecca's hair as she lay on my lap comfortable and safe, sent a dagger sliding into me. A second dagger followed when I was confronted by the fact that she was depending on me to keep her safe. Having been the one who sent her to the B&B in the first place planted a third dagger directly in the heart.

"What to do, indeed."

It was my waitress' lucky day as I threw down twice the amount of my bill on the table and left. It was easy to throw around Jones' money. But then I went back and retrieved a five. It was more of a stagger than a walk. I looked like a man needing support as I left the restaurant with three daggers in my chest, the whole while seeing images of Rebecca's smiling face, hearing her laugh, and remembering the little song she had made up to torture me.

On the way back to my room, I spotted a place to buy some clothes and toiletries before returning to lick my wounds in my luxury room, feeling useless yet responsible.

When I opened the door, I dropped my bags with my eyes downcast, just like my thoughts. But then the rollercoaster took another turn.

I looked up to see the B.I.B. sitting on the bed, back to the headboard. "How's the room service here?" she joked.

My heart leapt to life and a smile high-jumped on my face. In a second, I was bouncing onto the bed and crawling toward her like a six-year-old. "Where did you go last night? I looked everywhere."

"Not everywhere. If you had just looked up, you'd have seen me on the ledge outside Jones' apartment. I watched you check into this dump."

"Then why didn't you join me later?" I asked a little hurt.

She shook her head, and said, "Even a woman with super-powers needs a little rest...have a daughter, you know." Then she stared at her feet and said in a quiet tone, "Flying with you wore me out...In a good way."

"Thought you were gone," I said, sneaking up and giving her a short kiss. Then I sat next to her against the headboard. My quiet gave me away.

"What is it? What happened? You look like someone punched you in the gut."

"It's just the room service food. Makes you feel that way."

She smiled briefly. "No, what is it?"

I stared at my feet for a second. "Rebecca...Jennifer's got Rebecca. Jones called and said she was taken away from the B&B I checked her into." The B.I.B. showed no surprise. "And there was a note addressed to me." Again her expression was plain. "It said if I wanted to see Rebecca again, I needed to meet her on top of the Bank Towers Building at ten o'clock tonight...and I had to bring you with me." The B.I.B. said nothing. "It is a trap," I said at last.

"Of Course it's a trap," she answered back.

"Can you handle her?"

She appeared agitated. "You tell me Rebecca can dissolve people and she's the weaker one. Who knows what the strong one can do?" She shook her head.

"Let's just go. We can be in Rio or on the Mediterranean, away from all this."

She was angry now. "They knew you would think something like that, but they knew I couldn't just leave once I heard about it. It's a challenge with the cards stacked in her favor."

"I won't risk you. It's not worth it."

She paused and stared at me. "If you thought that you never should have told me. The choice isn't yours anymore."

It was time for me to man up. "Well then, we have about seven hours to come up with Plan A."

She sighed. "It better be a good one."

I slowly slid my hand over and found hers as it was sliding toward mine. We locked them together, felt the warm feeling begin, and then simultaneously let go and put our hands on our stomachs.

❖ ❖ ❖

CHAPTER THIRTY-TWO

Plan A

By 9:00 p.m., Plan A was in action. We were in communication, each with a walkie-talkie and a mobile phone. I had debated getting some type of weapon, but remembering the fate of dozens of thugs and Carmine Camino's fancy assault rifles, I decided it wasn't worth the effort and definitely not my style; I might shoot myself in the foot...again. I was on the ground floor of the building checking the comings and goings, while the B.I.B. used the darkness from a post on a nearby radio tower to cover the top of the building and the surrounding streets. I checked out the elevators, stairways, and all the routes to and from the roof. As 10:00 p.m. approached, there was still no movement or sign of Jennifer or Rebecca.

At 9:55 p.m., we chatted for the final time. "I don't see anyone," I radioed to her.

"You had still better get up there," she answered back. "Good luck. Be careful."

"Right," I said sarcastically. "Easy for you to say," I added, knowing Plan A. I sighed and marched to the elevator, a man totally unable to believe what he was about to do. After the elevator came another stairway, and then unlatching a heavy door that led to the roof. It was dark, breezy, overcast, with the only light coming from a few emergency lights. No one was there. I walked around displaying myself to anyone who cared to see. Five after 10:00 p.m., then a quarter after, and still I was alone.

I was getting ready to ask the B.I.B. about Plan B, when a golden light appeared fifty feet away, illuminating the entire rooftop and quickly taking the shape of a fit, long-haired brunette dressed in camouflage military-type clothing. Her hair was pulled back and tied in a ponytail. Her face appeared to mean business as she approached. "Where's the B.I.B.? You were told to bring her!"

Plan A was to get Jennifer to show me everything she had to fight us with before the B.I.B. would become involved. If the battle looked hopeless, she was to run—plain and simple. Live to fight another day another way. And I would be on my own to get by as I usually did, by the skin of my teeth, wit, and charm. Actually, the skin of my teeth never has done me much good, come to think of it, ditto for the wit and charm. Of the many things the B.I.B. and I had imagined that might take place, a mean-looking woman appearing out of a beam of light was not topping the list, or actually on the list. I had to get Jennifer to show herself and reveal her plan. "Where's your boss? I was told I'd meet your boss...Who are you, anyway?"

The tough woman pulled back her hand to strike me, and then stopped as if instructed by a voice I did not hear. Another golden light appeared just like the first one. This time, the shape of another woman in combat fatigues appeared but remained glowing in a pulsating gold aura around her. Attached to her by an umbilical of waving golden light was another woman co-cooned in an auric glow with her arms, legs, and eyes bound by sparking bands of white energy. The light waves crackled like high-tension power lines. Right away, I knew it was Rebecca muted in the cocoon.

Then, another umbilical of light shot out, connecting the golden woman to the tough one. Toughy smiled and lifted her head joyously as if being fed ice cream. "There…there is Rebecca," Toughy said, pointing, "Now, your part of the bargain."

"I don't see your boss. Let Rebecca go," I insisted.

"You are not in a position to dictate terms," she said angrily, getting into my face. "Where is the B.I.B.?"

"Safe…Where's your boss?" I said, trying to bristle back at her.

"Wrong answer," Toughy said, bringing her arm down on my left arm, sending me flying against a large metal utility box.

I lay there for a moment trying to decide if my arm was broken or my shoulder separated or both. She was on me quickly, lifting me with enormous strength, her hand on my throat. "You have no choice, little man. Now tell us where she is!" she said striking my jaw sending my head back. It felt like I had been hit with a jackhammer…again, don't ask.

I stared at her defiantly and spit out some blood. "I do have a choice and I've already made it." After a pause, I swung my free forearm and pounded her up under the chin as hard as I could. She didn't seem to notice, merely smiled, but it sure hurt me. That sure made me feel more confident— not.

She was getting ready to swing again when her arm abruptly halted as another light appeared next to the stationary golden woman, Goldie. Out of the light emerged another figure that quickly walked right up to us. Jennifer, come to gloat or take charge, not liking the way the deal was progressing, I imagined. But then I was surprised to hear a familiar voice. "My friend, there is no need for this," began Dr. Jones. "I have no need to hurt you. Just tell us where she is. Somewhere close, I imagine," he said, scanning out into the night around us.

Jones? I couldn't have been more surprised if I had woken up hanging from a flag pole...again. It all started to make sense. I laughed as best I could with my sore jaw. "You?" I laughed again. "You played me like a fiddle!"

"I did, didn't I!" he said, prancing.

"And I played right into your hands. Told you right where to find Rebecca."

"And the B.I.B.," he said, shaking a finger at me. "I could tell you knew where she was but you never would tell me about her. And why was that exactly? You could have made this much easier, but you protected her. Want to tell me why?"

I didn't answer, just stood there in pain. I figured he needed me alive...at least until he had the B.I.B. Regardless, I preferred talking with him to being pummeled painfully by Toughy. It was time to change the subject. "Want to introduce me to your friends?"

"Ah, yes," said Jones, proudly looking at Toughy and Goldie. "Maybe you can guess who they are. Let's see if you can."

"There aren't three super born. I'm guessing there are five, and you've collected three for yourself so far."

"Oh, close, very close!" said Jones, excited by the conversation and pacing around me. "There are...were, eight. Three did not...work out, shall we say. These two, after some genetic modifications are totally loyal to me. Rebecca will be soon."

"Queen bee? You're the queen bee?"

"You could say that. This one," he said, tapping Toughy on the shoulder, "was my first find. The weakest of the super born, as you call them. She has strength but was a disappointment until I found the second," he said, pointing to Goldie. "She molds energy. She can move me from here to there, bend energy, shape it, and transmit it. She holds Rebecca prisoner in it. Thanks to your information, we knew to isolate Rebecca's eyes to neutralize the power that vaporized poor Mr. Camino. My second one can also feed power to the first, increasing her strength at least ten times. That's when I realized that one could build on the others' powers and, by getting them to work together, they could do anything. I could do anything."

"The next three didn't want to join either, I take it."

Jones lowered his head. "Yes, not a complete success; there were objections to the idea. The genetic modification took some perfecting...All very unfortunate."

I sat, pretending to be too weak to stand. "So, you're starting with the easiest and working your way up, hey?" I wanted to keep him talking, while I tried to remember the layout of the mobile phone in my pocket without looking at it, turning it on and dialing the number I'd seen so many times lately whenever I went to the bathroom.

"Yes, right again, my friend. I am not ready to take on Jennifer just yet. But with Rebecca and the B.I.B. on my team, we will be more than a match for her. Then I we'll have Jennifer's empire, all the money I need for starters to go and get more. There will be no one more powerful on the earth. And they said I wouldn't even complete my doctorate," Jones said proudly, spinning a metallic stick in his hand.

"What's your little toy there, Doc?" I said, gesturing with my head, dialing the mobile number in my pocket again, on the odd chance I had screwed it up the first time...Who me?

Jones stopped and stared at the stick as if it were his true love. He had been dying to tell his success story to someone, so now there was no stopping him as I was a truly "captive" audience. "This," he said, presenting the shined chromed rod and handle surrounded by tubes of different sizes, "this is my creation. This is what makes it all work...You see," he said, bending down to my level. "You should be asking yourself, how I ever captured the first one. Naturally, I don't expect this type of thought from you, so I will explain. An average-sized man..."

"Small man, you mean?"

"An averaged sized man, such as me, could certainly not capture the first one here," he said, rising and tapping Toughy on the shoulder, "without the aid of technology. You see, Demitri did not die in vain. His sacrifice made it clear to me that there was a need for an equalizer, a way to approach the super born safely, make them cooperative. I call this the Interrupter. It gives off epsilon radiation of reverse polarity to the type that made them years ago," he said, pointing the Interrupter at Toughy. "It temporarily interrupts their powers, makes them manageable." Then he turned and pointed it at me. "As an added plus, it proved totally lethal to normal people...The military is going to love this, modified of course."

"Naturally," I said. I could see he was ready to get back to the B.I.B., so I tweaked him a little. "So I hope you don't mind my spoiling your little plan tonight?"

"Spoiling?" he said with a laugh. "My friend, you are the plan, always have been from day one. I picked you. You are perfect for the job; without attachments, without ethics, trusting, naïve, greedy, lazy, corruptible...and best of all," he said, leaning down and looking in my face, "no one will miss you."

I stood up pretending to be weaker than I was, but acting frightened wasn't hard with the Interrupter in my face.

Jones paced around me. "There is just one thing that bothers me very dearly, my friend. You came to me with everything you ever learned, except things about the B.I.B. The great B.I.B. expert never mentioned her once. That was how I knew you were in contact with her, yes, but why didn't you tell me? You still were trusting me then. What made the perfect 'grasshopper' to my 'ant,' the perfect 'Bugs Bunny,' protect her so? I expected you to bound in excitedly one day and say you had found her. But no, you were her guardian right from the start."

I wasn't about to give him the satisfaction of an answer and just hung my head.

"Let's see then. What if I offer the grasshopper twenty million dollars, right now, Twenty million for you to tell me where I can find her. Would that interest you? Fifty? You could be a lazy grasshopper the rest of your life. We could work together again."

"Get fucked!"

"Oh, I plan to repeatedly…all day long," he said, doing a little pelvic dance. "So, my friend, there is nothing I can offer that will save you? No amount of money, no title or position, no pleasures, no comforts? Imagine the women and the beer, the pure freedom to do nothing of consequence, is that not heaven for you?"

"You're a lifetime too late with that offer," I said with my head down.

"Yes, I see now that my plans for you have only taken us so far."

"So, you set the whole thing up, right from the first night?" I said, disappointed with myself.

"It was all too easy."

"You do know that she was there that night. Why didn't you grab her then?"

Jones paused and looked a little bothered. "Who was there?"

"The B.I.B. She was twenty feet away from you the night we met at O'Malley's…You didn't know?"

Jones was silent but I could hear his mind cranking, think-ing, rewinding images.

"How else did you think I found her? You really didn't know, did you? Ha…Maybe you don't know as much as you think you do…You know about marking?"

"Marking?"

"I thought not; there are a few things I could teach you about super born!"

"This is ri-god-damn-diculous. I have done years of re-search! I'm a fucking PhD, Goddamn it!"

"Oh, but you don't know about marking, do you? But I do," I said as annoyingly as I could.

Jones was perplexed, his eye movements rapid. I figured any kind of confusion might help.

"How about their amazing advanced sexual powers? Know about them, big guy?" Now I was on the offensive, staggering after him as he circled away.

"They have nothing but sexual frustration! No man can satisfy them anymore! Ask Demitri! They are totally sexually dysfunctional. Believe me, that is a power I have researched at length and am in the process of researching."

I smiled broadly, knowingly, certain it was frustrating the hell out of him, "When you catch up with me, let me know, and we can discuss it then."

"Discuss what?" he yelled, throwing down his arms in annoyance.

I beamed like the proverbial cat. "Super born sex, it's fuck-ing amazing…It's beyond sex," then I sobered a little. "It's a connection beyond love."

"You are making no sense! What could be beyond sex, be-yond love? These are man's pinnacle states!"

I merely slowly lipped the words: "F-u-c-k-i-n-g A-m-a-z-i-n-g."

Rather than confusing him, I was just pissing him off. "One last time, where is she?" Jones said, more sinisterly than I thought possible. Toughy moved threateningly toward me.

"OK, OK, "I said, flinching from the expected blow, holding up the one hand I could. "I'll tell you." Then when Jones straightened and relaxed a bit, even though it wasn't quite cricket, I gave him a front kick in the 'nads, which made him double over and groan. Then I gave him the same forearm I had given Toughy, but on Jones it was a knockout, sending him flying on his back, out cold while the Interrupter flew across the rooftop.

I turned, my eyes, following the sliding Interrupter, when the boots and thick thighs of Toughy blocked my vision. I looked up only to see her hand bitch-slap me, sending me to the ground, a little foggy. When another blow didn't follow, I turned sheepishly and saw the B.I.B. side kick Toughy, and then follow through with a hammer fist to the face, sending Toughy down on her butt. The B.I.B. wore her black outfit and mask; I have to tell you, despite the pain in my arm, the sight of her in action was turning me on involuntarily. That skin-tight jumpsuit and windblown hair was waking up something south of the border, if you know what I mean, olé!

I crawled over to Jones who lay nearby unconscious with "tweety birds" circling his head. I tapped him on the shoulder. "OK, Doc, I'll take the fifty mill, now. She's right there," I said, pointing, amused at how dramatically events had shifted in seconds. Not so powerful now, eh, Doc?

Toughy used her left hand to push her right shoulder back into its socket and wiped some blood away that had begun dripping ferociously from her nose. Then she looked up at the B.I.B. with a sneer, rose, and was ready to continue.

The B.I.B. was taken aback. When she hit someone they went down and stayed down. This round-two thing was new to her.

Toughy swung an arm and fired out a leg, but the B.I.B. was as quick as me picking out beer, and none of Toughy's blows landed. Instead, the B.I.B. landed a roundhouse kick that put Toughy back on her butt again. "Stay down, bitch," she commanded. Did that menacing voice come out of my little B.I.B.? *Whoa, that was kind of cool*, I thought, as my pants tightened.

I was starting to feel hopeful for the first time since they had arrived. Jones was down. Toughy was outmatched. There was hope. I tried to get up, but immediately thought better of it.

Then the roller coaster turned again. Goldie sent out an umbilical of light that caught the B.I.B. as she was flashing in for the kill. It held her in place and defeated her speed advantage. Toughy smiled as she stood up, reenergized, and kicked the B.I.B. into a group of ventilation pipes. Every time the B.I.B. got ready to fight, she was held in place and ended up trading blows at best. The shining, crackling umbilical had reversed the advantage. Now the B.I.B. was a stationary target. It was wearing her down. But she kept battling Toughy, giving as good as she got. They stood determinedly, trading horrific blows that would have turned a T. rex into a vegetarian or left him laid out quietly, waiting to become oil.

I started to worry, dragging myself across the roof, looking for the Interrupter, when the lava-red light began leaving the stairway door, revealing a humming, sparking column of light surrounding Jennifer Lowe. She was casually dressed like she was on her way to see a movie or have a snack, but surrounded in dynamic red energy. No nifty costume for her. She moved right at Goldie, who suddenly had the look of panic on her face. Jennifer's column met Goldie's aura and began to slowly shrink it. The humming and crashing of their powerful shields grew louder and louder, like two medieval warriors slamming sword and shield. She was absorbing more and more space, growing closer and closer to Goldie, eventually taking Rebecca's cocoon into her red column.

Goldie realized that she was being pushed back and needed more power. By now, the B.I.B. was a struggling heap on hands and knees unable to rise, and Toughy didn't need help. So she cut the umbilical holding the B.I.B. and the one powering Toughy. With the extra power, Goldie was able to push Jennifer back for the first time. Jennifer was made to realize she was in a battle, not merely doing her nails or having tea. So she pushed back harder with anger entering her face. Just a tip, you don't want to see Jennifer angry. Goldie responded by cutting the umbilical to Rebecca, pushing Jennifer back once more. Now, Jennifer was pissed and put down her nail file for good.

Confident anger circled her face as the whining and crashing of their power shields grew. As she felt Goldie beginning to yield, a smirking smile grew at the corner of her mouth. But Goldie was not without skills herself. She drew energy from a large circle of buildings and homes nearby, sending them all into darkness, transferring their energy into a powerful golden jolt that almost put Jennifer on her back...big mistake. There was no toying or mercy left in Jennifer after that slap in the face.

My eyes were full of horror, watching the B.I.B. struggling to her knees, while I was useless, as usual. It pissed me off and I became determined to rise and fight. So I did. I began to walk, maybe stagger, after Toughy with determination.

Toughy was not in good shape herself. She was exhausted, injured, but mobile. She crept up to the Interrupter. With effort she reached and lifted it. She turned to the immobile B.I.B. and smiled. "Game over," she said wickedly.

That was when I leapt into the line of fire. OK, maybe not leapt, but it was a good saunter or maybe a shuffle. You get the idea.

It threw Toughy off for a minute. I was no challenge; she wanted the B.I.B. on her resume. "Get away, little man. She'll just be drained but, this fucker will 'kill' you," she said, extending her arm to point the Interrupter at my face.

"No," was all I said, spreading my arms…arm, I mean, and legs, jamming in on her so that she could not shoot around me. Having finally found the B.I.B. and experienced her, I wasn't ready to surrender her now. I felt that any instant of delay was better than giving up. Any way of prolonging what I still had of her was worthwhile, no matter how fleeting. I could not give her up; they would have to take her away over my defeated body…What a sappy asshole.

"Your choice. I guess it will just have to be a two-for," said Toughy, smiling, no longer trying to shoot around me but aiming squarely at me, as she pulled the trigger.

"Glad I could make your day," I said, partially closing my eyes, moving as much as I could, to try to delay her. I flailed my arm feebly at her, reaching for the Interrupter. She stopped and laughed at me, prompting me to try again as she continued her amusement. Every time I reached for it, she pulled it away and laughed. Guess she laughed a little too long.

I had seen the look before of total astonishment, the helpless disbelief on Toughy's face as the vapors formed around her and she slowly faded from life. The Interrupter dropped unmanned to the rooftop smoking, twisted, and never able to party again. The night breeze swirled the horrible smell till I could taste it in my throat. Toughy tasted as mean as she had looked. Across the rooftop, Rebecca fell to the ground, bathed in lava light, liberated from her energy bondage, having sent Toughy into oblivion.

Jennifer closed in relentlessly now on Goldie, whose light had now turned from gold to white. Goldie even raised her arms to ward off Jennifer as she neared. Then she tried to run in a desperate attempt to escape, only to be held in the oncoming energy of the lava-red light. The crashing sounds from the energy fields were gone, leaving only a powerful humming that surged in volume like the opening, oncoming jaws of a shark. Her aura turned to a cloudy blue, then she slumped over as her energy drained further. In her last seconds, her form crystallized into blue/white ice, then started melting into fluid that drained across the rooftop or flew away as vapors.

Jennifer continued her humming lava glow for a long victorious moment; then, in a flash, the red light was gone, leaving the rooftop in silent blackness. She turned to Rebecca and helped her stand. Rebecca looked a horrible shade of gray as if the effort to dissolve Toughy had made her lifeless.

I sauntered over to the B.I.B., reached out my good arm and helped her up; damn that made my good arm feel good. We leaned against each other and marveled at the now quiet rooftop that had been such a lethal, frightening war zone seconds earlier. At that point, the adrenaline was still working wonders, and I kept moving unchecked by the pain.

Jennifer and Rebecca approached, and the four of us stood facing one another.

"Maybe you'll believe me next time," Jennifer directed at me.

I nodded. "Maybe." *Bitch*.

Rebecca was first to join the apology club. "It was my fault. I was convinced you were trying to kill me," she said to Jennifer. "I'm sorry," she said, as color began to return to her skin.

Jennifer shrugged. "That's what they wanted you to believe. Divide and conquer. They had us targeted one by one…I was really afraid for you when you left," she said, turning to Rebecca and giving her a hug. Then she let her go and turned toward the B.I.B. "I couldn't let them get you either. I've never had so much fun as watching you play with them, the mayor, the Mob. It was hysterical." Then she turned to me. "And you, I couldn't give two craps about you."

I probably had it coming, I realized.

Then she added, "But thanks for calling me and helping us like you did. That took some guts…Where the hell did you get those from?"

I felt a "little" better…*Bitch*.

Rebecca eyed the B.I.B.'s tight-fitting costume and lifted the end of her cape. "I have got to get a costume for myself. This is really cool," she said honestly to the B.I.B.

The B.I.B. posed a bit. "Thanks, it just helps keep my identity safe."

"It really makes a statement," Rebecca added, looking at the B.I.B. from head to foot. "That mask is so mysterious… those boots are so cool. You made this yourself?"

The B.I.B. nodded. "I know it's not some high-tech suit like in the movies, but it works for me…I'm on a budget, you know," she said, falling back into single mom.

"And how'd you get that killer nickname? I wonder what color would be good for me?" Rebecca rambled. "I need to write myself a note," she added, feeling her empty pockets for something with which she could write and looking around the ground nearby…Damn "Noters."

The B.I.B. took off her mask and let Rebecca try it on. Soon the B.I.B.'s cape was around Rebecca's shoulders. The two began to chat and giggle, while Jennifer thought to herself, *Oh brother, what is wrong with you two?*

After reviewing her casual, uninteresting attire and tapping her funky running shoes on the ground, she had second thoughts, remembering how hot she looked in red. Suddenly, the image of a red leather bustier costume with red leather accents entered her mind. Add tight-fitting pants, and while wearing that she wouldn't even need her superpowers to get whatever she wanted. *Hitler, what an amateur*, she thought.

"I think green is your color," she said to Rebecca, joining the conversation, directing her toward anything but red.

"Don't you think red would be better for her? It would go with her hair so well," injected the B.I.B., while Rebecca's head turned back and forth as if she were watching a tennis match as they spoke.

Jennifer fingered Rebecca's hair. "No, I would think green would bring out her hazel eyes; dump those glasses; get some contacts. She'd be a fox."

That made Rebecca smile. *Me! A fox*, she thought.

The B.I.B. shrugged. "You might be right…"

Rebecca smiled like a little girl and spun in the B.I.B.'s cape. But foxes aren't green, she realized. They're reddish brown.

The B.I.B. seemed to be recovering quickly. With the golden light gone, her strength began to return. "Did you see the way those two worked together?" she said, leaving me totally out of the conversation. "One was no match for me, but when they combined powers, they beat the crap out of me… Maybe there is a lesson in that. If I had faced them alone, as they planned, Rebecca and I would be in Jones' lab right now."

Rebecca nodded. "She's right. Alone, we will still be in fear; together, who can hurt us?"

I tried to join the conversation but finally realized it was the B.I.B.'s moment and slithered into the quiet background, tucking my useless hand into my pocket to support it. I waited patiently for the "girls" to finish their mutual admiration gathering so I could go get some medical attention, some good pain drugs, and maybe a "flight" home.

The B.I.B. could see my discomfort. "Just give me a minute; we'll get you to the hospital. I promise," she assured me with a sweet smile that did the trick as I sulked slowly away.

Jennifer liked being in charge and partners were never her strong suit, but how near they had come to being under Jones' control made her see the attraction in the idea. She paced a little and said almost to herself, "Together, who can hurt us?"

Rebecca added, "And who knows how many more Joneses there are out there? It might not be over. We could be being stalked even now!"

Like an idiot, I thought I saw an opening to be useful. "Yeah, there were a lot of people following me. I saw three, four, five cars at my place; could be anybody after us."

The three women simultaneously turned to stare at me with who-asked-you looks on their faces. I held up my good arm and backed away from the "girls," leaving them to their bitch session, cosmetic party, whatever the hell it was.

They continued to chat and plan while I staggered away." Fine way to treat a hero wounded in action," I bitched and moaned to myself. "See if I bail your ass out again!" Looking back hurt-puppy-like at the B.I.B.'s glowing eyes, I knew I would bail her ass out again and again. And did I mention again, twice on Sundays? What an ass to bail out it was too... and those thighs in that skintight jumpsuit...maybe three times on Sundays, I thought, as I watched her talking, and the compass in my pants began pointing her way...What was I talking about...? Whatever.

But Jennifer, she couldn't give two craps about me; well, I couldn't even give one crap about her. She was officially off the give-a-crap scale. The bitch was just so freakin' jealous that the B.I.B. had hold of my heart and everything else. Yeah, Jennifer wanted a deep dish piece of this man-pie that she just wasn't ever gonna get. Hazel eyes, my ass!

Just when I was feeling the most bitter, the B.I.B. glanced up at me, smiled, and flashed those blue-then-greens for me. I didn't feel so bad anymore...Hey, did that mean she was horny?

Nearby, I saw the melting ice remains of Goldie. I sat next to "her," and without giving it much thought, as was my method, I broke off a chunk of the cloudy blue ice and pressed it against my aching arm and shoulder. The cold ice numbed my pain, but it also burned wherever it melted and hit my broken skin. Moments later, when it dawned on me what an irreverent thing I had done, I looked at what was left of her and said, "The arm, it's really starting to hurt...sorry...This must be terribly awkward and embarrassing for you, just sitting there melting. I mean, I'm sure you had your good side too before Jones made you evil; parents and relatives that will miss you, maybe a dog or cat or something...I had a turtle once, so I know how you feel. He was afraid of water—or was it a newt? No, I remember now it was a gerbil. That would explain why he didn't like the water! I have to say this blue ice thing you have going on looks great," I said, patting what remained of her arm. "Not many women can pull off a look like that, but it works for you," I said, nodding. "What you've done has melted inches off your waistline, fabulous…"

We continued our one-sided conversation for a while. Before long, we were good buds and I had my aching arm and shoulder wrapped around her pain-relieving form. It turned out that Goldie was a really good listener. I was able to talk to her about anything, without fear of being judged. However, the advice she gave me concerning the B.I.B.—not so good, just a gurgle and an occasional crackle.

Our talk had brought a tear to my eye, or maybe it was the adrenalin wearing off and pain from Toughy's blows. I think Goldie felt it too, as I saw droplets running down her cheeks. Regardless, we shared a moment together. I looked deeply into what was left of her face and thought, *hazel eyes, my ass*. "Well, it's been great talking with you. Mind if I just get one more chunk to go?" I said, breaking off another piece of her arm.

Later, I saw that the B.I.B. was the first to put her hand out, followed by Rebecca's on the B.I.B.'s, then came Jennifer's. "From now on, we work together, protect each other, learn from each other; together, we can accomplish anything," chimed the B.I.B.

"We are in charge!" added Rebecca.

"I like the sound of that," Jennifer stated firmly, smiling, in the back of her mind realizing she could benefit from a partnership.

That was when we heard Jones beginning to stir. All four of us moved over and stood in a circle around him. Just a tip, you do not want to confront the searing anger that burned on each of the women's faces. One woman with that look was challenge enough, but three? And these had superpowers and super hormones, I suspected. Good luck, Jonesy. Nice knowing ya.

For me it was "c'est la guerre." Jones and I had had our moments. I couldn't hate him. The only malice I felt toward him came from his threats to the B.I.B. and Rebecca. (Notice I didn't mention Jennifer.) His using and turning on me was something that, unfortunately, I had grown used to in life… Wait a minute, I forgot my broken arm…Maybe I'd give him a kick, just one kick in the ribs.

But tell me, Jonesy, who was still standing and who was lying on the ground about to become pummeled-vaporized-energy-less ice…kicked once in the ribs? When Jones' eyes opened and could focus on us, they widened to full-moon size, and he let out a horrifying, little-girl scream.

9854877R0015

Made in the USA
Charleston, SC
19 October 2011